2183

Also by Laurel McHargue

FICTION

Waterwight: Book 1 of the Waterwight Series

Waterwight Flux: Book 2 of the Waterwight Series

Waterwight Breathe: Book 3 of the Waterwight Series

The Hare, Raising Truth

Dark Ebb: Grim Tales, Volume 1

Dark Ebb: Grim Tales, Volume 2

"Miss?"

QUACK [children's picture book]

NONFICTION

Peace by Piece: 10 Lessons from a Jigsaw Puzzle
[with co-author Nadine Collier]

Hunt for Red Meat (love stories)

ESSAYS

[too many to list here!]

2183

Laurel McHargue

STRACK PRESS

STRACK PRESS LLC | COLORADO

This is a work of fiction. All characters, places, and events portrayed in this book are the product of the author's imagination. Any resemblance to actual persons, living or dead, events, or locales is entirely coincidental.

2183

Published by Strack Press LLC
Salida, CO

FIRST EDITION 2025

Library of Congress Control Number: 2025900661
McHargue, Laurel, Author

ISBN: 978-1-945837-12-8 (paperback)
ISBN: 978-1-945837-14-2 (hardcover)
ISBN: 978-1-945837-13-5 (ebook)

Original Cover Artwork and Design by Elize McKelvey

PRINTED IN THE UNITED STATES OF AMERICA

For

Mike K. McHargue

Who never stops believing in me.

I TRUDGE ACROSS a stretch of something gooey—don't look down—to see what possible treasure my sister found in the Heaps.

"Look, Ing!" Two years younger than me, Tulip takes her scavenging seriously. "This matches Mom's teacup." She turns her back to the wind and hands me a hairline-crack-riddled plate.

Not a perfect match, but our blind mother won't notice. She'll treat it like her cup. She'll place it on a small shelf and touch it each morning. She won't use it.

"She'll love it. Nice work." I hate how tired Tulip looks. How old. Only thirteen, she already has dark circles under her eyes.

We alternate between schoolwork, hunting and fishing for food, harvesting our struggling crops, shearing our sheep for new clothes, and working the Heaps. We'll never uncover everything in the miles of decaying junk, but occasionally, something useful surfaces. An axe head. A shovel. Any tool, really. We have two more months of the Daylight, the worst months for digging in the steaming, stinking piles. We're used to the smells. There's no getting used to the relentless winds, though.

When Earth stopped spinning a century ago, the atmosphere didn't stop. It blows. It howls. It constantly messes up our work.

Tulip pulls a tattered tarp from a crunchy pile and wrinkles her nose. "Well? Have you chosen your mate yet?"

"Shut up. You're as bad as Javier." I toss away a badly rusted can. Might've had soup in it or some other delicious food. Canned food. They had it so easy back then.

"Can you blame him? You know he's ready. He and about five other boys sniffing around." She drops the tarp and kicks another pile. "And anyway, you won't have a choice much longer."

"Maybe I will. Why do they get to decide that fifteen is when we have to start making babies? It's stupid."

Tulip snorts. "You're so stubborn. Why can't you just be like the rest of us?" A jagged pipe snags her pantleg. "Dammit!" She catches herself before falling into the pile.

"You know I can't *just be* anything, kiddo." I want more, but my time is running out. The village Council will enforce the first-daughter requirement to start pumping out babies soon. Any one of my suitors can claim me as their mate. The Council will have final approval.

Lots of girls my age are already mothers. Some have died giving birth, though. Fifteen is considered the safe, appropriate, and expected age for healthy females to breed. So stupid. Any day now, the Council will insist.

I don't want to be a mother. The thought of adding a child to our messed-up world scares me. Council members, all men, scare me even more. They're like the church leaders in the old times who told people what to do if they didn't want to burn for eternity in a place called Hell.

I want to be something girls aren't allowed to be—a Swimmer. Their purpose is clear. Noble.

Tulip sighs and wipes sweat from her forehead. "Oh, come on. Just pick someone already. You're lucky you're firstborn."

Tulip should've been firstborn. She's smarter than me. She can grow food by guilting a seed into sprouting. She has a way with our parents that makes me feel jealous of their closeness. She wants to raise children. But she's the next-born. She isn't allowed to breed until a firstborn girl's baby—my baby—proves to be strong enough to survive.

The Council makes decisions about survival. It's not just a matter of having *more* babies to repopulate, it's a matter of having strong babies. Any indication of weakness is cause for elimination.

"Maybe I'm not feeling lucky. Javier and the others just aren't—"

"What? They aren't what? Attentive enough? Cute enough?"

She isn't wrong. Among my many suitors, Javier is strong, healthy, and attractive. But I just don't want that kind of relationship with him. I don't want to mother his or anyone's children.

"They're just not . . . never mind! I don't have to justify my feelings to you."

Tulip's mouth hangs open. "Damn this wind!" She turns away from me, screaming at the wind instead of at me, hiding her hurt.

I'm such an ass. Why can't I be honest with her? Tulip's my best friend. We share everything.

"Sorry for being such a bitch. It's just, things are crazier than usual lately." I pretend to find something interesting in a pile next to me.

How do I tell her the idea of getting pregnant is the furthest thing from my mind?

I hold my breath when I hear the flapping wings from a pair of clackers—our name for the noisy birds who never sing but circle the Heaps all day. Lurking over us. Watching.

We never find their nests.

Tulip throws a stone at one, and it flies off toward other pickers. She turns back to me. "Things are always crazy here, so don't change the subject. Do any of these guys have a clue? Because from what I've seen, they've all been pretty patient with you." We duck when a gust hurls a bent sheet of metal toward us. "Dammit," she mumbles.

As much as I love her, she's pissing me off. "Don't tell me you never dream about doing more than waking up every day wondering how many more plants didn't make it, dreading the Drearies and the Darkness, wondering how much longer Mom and Dad will live."

Her glare scorches me before her eyes water. She doesn't like talking about death.

"We don't cry, Tulip." My tone is harsh, but I want to hug her. We don't cry. Our earliest lesson. Tears waste energy.

"No, I haven't wondered about those things. I don't go there." She wipes her nose, leaving a dirty smear on her sweaty cheek, and spits. "What good would it do? We can't change our lives," she puts her hands on her hips, "and until you realize that, you're never gonna be happy."

Maybe she's right, but I'll never admit it.

Drained from hours in the stink with little to show for it, we gather our items. A once-beautiful plate, several pieces of metal our village forger will use, three pots, some large chunks of colored glass, parts of broken statues—an arm, a chinless head, a foot—and a few usable fabric remnants. We'll take these to the collection center where workers will determine how they'll be used.

When I turn away from Tulip, my foot catches on something. The handle on a crushed case sticks up from the muck.

"OPEN IT."

I clasp my hands over me ears and glance around me. "What the flood?" A booming voice. A voice that rattles my brain. Not male, not female, not . . . human. A voice like every voice all together in one. And it just told me to open this case.

The wind and heat must be messing with me. Still, I pull on the handle, releasing the case, which pops open to reveal a little silver book with the letters USMA stamped on the cover. I flip through the surprisingly clean pages and see photos of people in uniforms, massive stone buildings, and other military-looking things. My heart races.

"Tulip, come here!"

She rolls her eyes and trudges toward me. Her sack hangs heavy on her back, making her look really, really old. My heart hurts for her.

"Didn't Dad used to talk about one of our relatives before the Halt who went to a famous academy called West Point?"

"Yeah, why?"

"Look. This must be it." I hand her the little book, and she flips through its pages.

"Looks horrible. Could you imagine having to go to a school like that?" She hands it back.

I can absolutely imagine it. How exciting it must have been to live in a time with armies and air forces and space forces and navies. We learned about those things in some of our oral history classes. If only I was born back then.

For all their power, though, the military forces couldn't stop the disaster.

"I'll take this to the library and then check it out to show Dad. Maybe he can tell us more about him. What was his name?"

Tulip presses her lips together in thought. "Thadeus or Thoreau or Thayer or something like that."

I'd love to keep it, but books—especially in good condition—are more valuable than anything. Found books go to the library. It's really just a room with an orderly arrangement of written material in varying conditions.

"Hey, let's get back. Looks like everyone's done." I wave at a few friends, happy to see the clackers have flown off, and put an arm around Tulip's shoulder. "How were Mom and Dad when you left?"

About two years earlier when our parents' physical deterioration started, Tulip and I fell into a routine. I help them up in the morning, encourage them to move their arms and legs for circulation, fix something easy to eat, and settle them into chairs where they spend the rest of the day doing who-knows-what before we head out for chores. Tulip gets them to bed when it's time to sleep.

"Worse, I think. Dad couldn't remember my name." She slips on something gross, and I catch her. "Fluke!" Tulip never says the curse word *flood*. If she could live without water, she would. She trembles whenever she's near the ocean.

"I'm sorry, kiddo. Hey, tomorrow will be better. I'll spend more time with them, okay?" I tug on one of the wild, dark curls sticking out from her hat.

All is quiet when we get home. We do our best to keep out the sun at night. Heavy tarps over windows help, but we need openings for circulation.

We often give thanks to the first survivors. They build these homes using handmade adobe bricks. Had to have been grueling work. For the most part, they keep the inside cooler during the Daylight and hold heat from our fires during too many months of the Drearies and the Darkness.

Nighttime is extra challenging during the Daylight months. Despite our fatigue, falling asleep is always hard with the temperature and the blasted wind.

I toss and turn a lot. When I do sleep for short periods, I often wake with bizarre images from dream snippets. Sparkling stars, slippery tunnels, rough seas, cold hallways, and creatures I've never seen.

Other things, too. Vague images of babies that don't look like babies. I hate those dreams. But in my dream last night, a frightening voice called my name. The same voice I just heard in the Heaps.

"Morning, Mom. Morning, Dad." I tiptoe into their bedroom—same setup as the one I share with Tulip except their bed pads sit on wooden platforms—and part the heavy canvas curtain just enough to convince them it's time to rise. The sun's months-long brilliance is too much for any of us to bear all at once.

"Looks like another beautiful day. Maybe the potatoes will be ready soon." They aren't even close for harvesting, but I have to think of something positive to begin the day. "And Tulip has a new recipe." This is true. Tulip constantly tries to entice our parents to eat.

"Tulip," my dad whispers as I pull him into a sitting position, one small movement at a time, and swing his feet toward me. His urine container holds little. Too dark. I'm glad he still uses it without my help, but he obviously isn't drinking enough. I hand him socks. When he doesn't reach for them, I stoop to put them on his feet. Despite the heat, his feet feel cold. I help him into a lightweight coverup.

"Yes, your adorable daughter Tulip is making something delicious."

"Something cold, I fear. Cold as snow."

I frown. It's an odd statement. In several months, after the Drearies, there'll be too much snow during the Darkness. Another season of skimping by on what we can harvest and store during months of constant sun. "I'll ask her to heat it up, Dad. Come on. Time to get up."

I turn to my mother. "Mom, I'll come back for you in just a minute. Do you think you might get up by yourself today?"

She turns toward me, her eyes wide, as if I'd begged her to start the planet spinning again. It's a joke that lost its humor long ago—who will be the one to find the "start" button in the Heaps? Thankfully, Mom's milky, sightless eyes still have a spark of light in them. Her blindness happened gradually, and no one knows why. Without trained doctors and hospitals with machines like they had before the Halt, we do the best we can with injuries and illness. Any medications the first survivors might have stored are long gone. We have no choice but to accept too many conditions that we just have to live—and die with.

Despite her apparent annoyance over my request, Mom forces her elbows outward, readying to push herself up. But she stops there.

"Keep trying, Mom. I know you can do it." I grasp my father's frail hands, brace my feet against his, and pull him, slowly, to a standing position. It's easier now that he's frailer and I'm stronger. Whenever I think of his age, I have to shake off my fear. Too young. He's way too young to be so ill, but he isn't alone.

With few exceptions in our village, previous generations are already gone. Tulip and I have no grandparents.

Many of them probably just gave up, exhausted from doing their best to pretend things would improve in time—but not really believing it.

Survivors in the years following the Halt found themselves in a very different world. They suffered from malnutrition, physical ailments, and emotional stress as they tried to make sense of their new reality and find ways to stay alive. They lost everything but what they were able to relocate to the primitive shelters they dug into mountainsides before the disaster.

And then they moved from their high shelters back into the open, creating the beginnings of homes like the ones they remembered before the disaster.

It's a wonder my generation exists at all.

How long will we survive? We have more to eat than they had in those early years. Harvesting and hygiene techniques are improving, but so, so slowly. Still, there's a good chance Tulip and I will live longer than our parents.

"Here we go." Dad and I shuffle together to the sitting room like strangers made to dance at a funeral. We don't have funerals like they had before the Halt. Our Farewells are much more sensible.

I ease Dad into his chair by the window and place his scuffed sunglasses on to protect what remains of his vision after too many years of brutal sunshine. He trembles in the hot room. I snuggle him with a wrap.

"We're going to do some stretching this morning, Dad. Let's keep up your strength."

"It's yours now, always has been. Take it. It's time," he mumbles. "It glows, you know. Powerful." He stares at me with a frightening intensity.

"Sure does. Almost every day." He's been saying some strange things these past few months, but I'm not totally sure he's talking about the sun right now. "Glad it still rains to keep the ponds filled, though. Be right back. Don't want to keep Mom waiting too long. You know how she gets." I tease—Mom's the most patient person I know—and kiss his forehead. Cold, like his feet.

His dark brow wrinkles. He turns toward the window, saying no more.

When I leave him there to repeat the same morning process with my mother, I find her sitting upright with her feet on the floor. "Wow!" I announce too forcefully. She flinches. "Well done, Mom," I say more softly. I don't mean to patronize her. I'm thrilled. "Dad's ready for first meal. How about you?"

She squinches her nose.

"Tulip's recipe has a few new herbs today. Maybe that'll help. And it's a really bright green, like new grass." As if a different shade of green—which she can't see—will make the creation taste any better. I hope she might remember the green of new grass.

"I just don't see the point some days," she says.

"The point is to keep up your strength and your attitude, just like you taught Tulip and me when we were little."

She stares at me, toward me, with an expression I can't understand. Seems she's thinking about what I said.

Finally, she says, "My brave girl. You're right." She turns toward the window, silent again.

I go through the motions of readying her for the day, handing her a wet washcloth for a quick cleaning, dry underwear, socks, a day smock, and a brush for her sparse hair. I'm grateful she's able to do these tasks on her own.

"And look what you've already done. When was the last time you sat up by yourself first thing in the morning?" *And why now*, I wonder. What if I'd challenged her about her physical decline earlier? But I never want to embarrass either of them. They've never been big on sharing.

A hint of a smile starts at her lips but stops in her eyes.

"Your father and I spoke last night. It won't be long now." She keeps her face turned toward the bright window, and I watch a tear slide down her soft, golden-brown cheek. She won't cry, but she can't stop the tiny drop. Not sure she even feels it.

Motionless and speechless, I wait for her to continue, glad she can't see me because she'd notice a flash of relief cross my face. I'll deal with the guilt from my immediate reaction later.

"It will be all right, you know. Less work for you and Tulip. I'd be happy to go too, but I believe I'm not done yet."

"Mom," I protest softly and sit next to her. She rests her head on my shoulder. It's been a long time since we've sat like this, the two of us with arms wrapped around each other. Is it the first time? It breaks my heart.

Finally, she releases me.

"It's funny, you know, when your life doesn't unfold in ways you expect it to." She takes my hand and strokes it. "I'm not entirely sure what I expected. Your grandparents died when your father and I were quite young. Those generations who lived through the Halt barely survived the harsh conditions. Who were we to expect anything different? But you're right, dear. When your father gave up and I lost my vision, well, I suppose I just decided there wasn't much more I could do for you girls anymore. But you, you and Tulip, don't give up."

She never talks to us about her youth. I never knew of her expectations. But in this brief moment, I experience not quite a wave but a splash of hope. Does she want more for herself now? More for me? I hope so.

"Would you tell us more sometime? When you're feeling stronger? Tulip would love to hear your stories too."

"Of course, new cadet Ing—"

"Mom?" I jump at the strange words, startled. "What did you just call me?"

"Oh, forgive me, dear. I don't know what came over me. I had the craziest dream."

I understand crazy dreams. I'm happy she can still see in hers.

I sit beside her again and take her hand. "Are you afraid?" I ask.

"Of what?" She tilts her head and raises her eyebrows. She looks like a child.

"Of losing him? Of being alone?" I'm not sure what answer I want.

"Of losing your father? Oh, he left me long ago. You know that. And I don't see how I'd ever be alone unless there's something you haven't told me. I suppose I'm really not ready to go yet, but you and Tulip will see to my Farewell in time."

I press her bony hand to my cheek.

"As far as anything else I might fear, well, a mother will always fear for the health and happiness of her daughters. Someday, you will know this."

I'm not about to tell her I have no interest in bringing another child into our struggling world, though I'll be forced to. And soon. I stand to help her into the sitting room.

"One more thing, dear." She reaches for me but makes no attempt to stand. "In the drawer by your father's chair, there's something he's been meaning to give you. It's folded into a small piece of cloth. Go and get it, would you?"

"Sure. I'll ask him for it. Are you coming out now?"

Mom turns toward the window again and says, softly, "A small piece of cloth. Light blue, I think."

I wait. Seeing she's not yet ready to move, I return to the sitting room to ask Dad about the thing he wants to give me. I hope he remembers what it is. It seems important to my mother. And I'm excited to tell him about the little book I found.

Like my mother, my father is turned toward the window. Before helping Mom, I partially rolled back the window tarp in the sitting room. Though neither of my parents have the energy to go outdoors, they seem to dream of times when they had. Maybe they imagine themselves helping in the garden, visiting with friends, walking hand in hand down the road to town. Walking.

"Hey, Dad," I place my hand lightly on his arm, not wanting to surprise him. He startles so easily lately. "Mom said there was something you wanted to give me."

Nothing.

"Dad?"

Nothing. I shake him gently. It's not unusual for him to doze off during the day, but he just got up.

"Dad." I say his name louder, waiting for him to respond. But no.

Nothing.

I remove his sunglasses. His shining ebony eyes, a dusty gray now, see nothing. I close his eyelids. He looks peaceful. Happy, almost. He wears an expression I haven't seen in years.

He's gone.

And Mom already knows.

2

I FIND TULIP in the covered garden where she gathers what little she finds in the beds.

I have to tell her.

"Tulip?"

"Yeah?"

I can't just blurt it out, and I won't cry. Honestly, I feel a burden has been lifted. *What a horrible thought.*

"Come here."

"In a minute." She's clueless. She's the baby. We keep things from her.

"Sure, okay." What's another minute? Dad isn't going anywhere, and Mom will wait in her bedroom. I pluck a few more greens.

"What's up?" Her cheeks glow from the humidity.

"It's Dad."

She raises one eyebrow and sets her basket on the ground. "Is he . . . he can't be, not yet." She avoids the word as if saying it would make it so. She speaks without emotion. It scares me.

Daddy's little girl.

"We'll have to take him to the place of Farewells." Am I too abrupt? Too clinical? Too . . . ready?

"But he was just—"

"I know, I know. Come here." I pull her to me and let her tears soak my shirt. I won't tell anyone she cried.

Finally, she pulls away and looks at me, her copper-brown eyes rimmed red, her arms hanging slack.

"What about Mom?"

"Mom's going to be okay. Hey, she sat up by herself this morning." This surprising news won't soothe her, but it's something.

"So, she knows? What did she say? We should be with her now. What are we doing here?" She grabs her gathering basket and rushes toward the house. I follow.

"She's okay, really. She's still in the bedroom." I'm right behind her when she pauses at the front door. She drops the basket and turns toward me.

"What do I say to her?"

"You don't have to say anything, kiddo." Kiddo. She's still a little girl to me. "Mom's stronger than we think. I don't know. It's like something changed in her as soon as I brought Dad to the sitting room." I remember the thing Dad was supposed to give me and wonder what it is.

"He's . . . in his chair?" She winces.

"Yes. I'll ask Javier to bring the Swimmers." I could summon them myself, but I've been working up the courage to approach them with my desire to join them. It's not the right time. "Let's sit with Mom for a bit first, until she's ready."

"Okay. Okay." Tulip nods as if to convince herself she'll be okay. She lifts her chin and stares at the door before entering.

Once inside, she glances at where our father sits. I hear her catch her breath before moving slowly toward Mom's bedroom. I follow, my hand on her shoulder. She trembles. I try to convince myself the subtle change in the house's atmosphere is just in my head. The slightly sour odor is always present first thing in the morning.

"We're going to be fine, Tulip."

It startles us both to find Mom standing at the small, uncovered window, her back toward us, the wind making a mess of her silver-streaked hair. We'll board up the openings when the Drearies pass into the Darkness.

"It's okay, Tulip." Mom speaks with authority. She lifts one hand from the sill and extends it toward my sister. Tulip rushes to hold it. "Let's go, dear. Ing says you have a new recipe this morning. I'm suddenly quite hungry. Craziest thing, isn't it?" She chuckles without joy.

Tulip shoots me a questioning glance, and I shrug.

When Tulip tries to help Mom to her comfortable chair in the space set aside for comfort—really just a small extension of where we cook and eat—Mom protests.

"No. I'll sit at the table, dear. Time to do things right again."

Is it that, or does she not want to sit in a chair next to her husband's lifeless body? No matter. It's as if her life turned an unexpected corner and found new purpose—and so soon after questioning the point of it all. She sits at the table.

Huh.

"I'll attend, of course, with help." Mom turns toward the body by the window. I'm glad, again, that she can't see. Can't see how his once lustrous, olive skin, pale though it has recently turned, is now a waxy shade of blue.

"I think Javier will help," I say. I know he will. We've talked about my father's recent rapid decline. I wish I felt attracted to him as a mate—it would make all of our lives easier—but he's always felt more like a brother to me. A friend.

"I'll go now and have him bring the Swimmers, unless you don't want me to leave." With Dad sitting there ready for transition, how long should I wait with Mom and Tulip? I can't bear to stay any longer, can't bear to share a morning first meal with him waiting there, waiting for what he used to call "the perfect, peaceful plunge." His Farewell.

Dad taught me how to swim as soon as I could waddle into the water, but I won't be allowed to help the Swimmers with the last part of the Farewell ritual. I'm a girl. Girls aren't allowed to be Swimmers. So stupid. I plan to change that.

"You go on now, dear. Tulip will help me prepare."

Tulip nods, and I leave.

A five-minute walk down the road, Javier's house is a little closer to the ocean than ours. We're lucky to live near a great body of water. Sometimes it worries me, though. Rumors of the next catastrophe linger like scenes from my nightmares.

When Earth's rotation slowed to a stop after something from space crashed into it, how any species—plant, animal, human—survived is a mystery.

If recent rumors are true and the planet somehow starts rotating again, no one knows what will happen to the oceans, how fast it'll happen, and what destruction might follow. Scary.

Javier opens the door almost immediately. I guess the expression on my face tells him all he needs to know.

"Oh, Ing, I'm so sorry." He sweeps me into his arms.

I hold my breath so I don't cry. We don't cry.

"I'm okay," I say. And I am. I don't even have to ask him.

"I'll bring the Swimmers to your place before mid-day," he says. "You'll have him ready?"

"Yes, we'll all be ready. Thank you."

Javier walks me to the door and hugs me again. I run home.

———— ❧ ————

Mom wears walking shoes and a worn, but clean, dress. Seeing her in something other than a smock startles me. Nothing fits quite right, of course, having been passed down from the previous generation or handcrafted by those of us who make our own clothes. She sits in Dad's chair, closer to the window than hers, and smooths her hands over her lap. Will we call it "Mom's chair" now?

I crinkle my nose at the unpleasant odor in the room. It's not overwhelming, but still.

Dad's on a litter on the floor—most homes have one under a bed or propped in a closet, a not-so-subtle reminder of our mortality. Tulip has him wrapped snugly in the burgundy blanket that once warmed him in *his* chair. Only his face and feet are uncovered. As expected, Tulip already removed his clothes. They're neatly folded on the floor. No need to waste cloth we could use for other things. We'll bring the blanket back with us after the Farewell, but for transport, it will hold him fast.

"Javier will bring the Swimmers here soon, Mom. You look beautiful."

She nods, turns toward the window, and continues smoothing her smock.

"What can I do to help?" I ask my sister. We stand on opposite sides of Dad's litter, on opposite sides of our father's dead body, and in a moment of awkward silence, we bump into one another as each of us steps over him to be with the other.

Fortunately, we keep our balance, holding onto the other's shoulders. Tulip's eyes open wide. She does her best not to giggle, but the muffled sound draws our mother's attention.

"It will be all right, Tulip." She misunderstands the sound.

"Let's go outside for a minute." I grab Tulip by an arm and yank her over to my side. "We'll be right back, Mom." We're outside in a flash, just as Tulip loses it. I continue to pull her away from the house as she laughs like I've never heard her laugh before—a deep, hysterical laugh. It's contagious.

"This is so wrong," she says when we stop running. "I don't know why I'm laughing. Why am I laughing? Why are you laughing? Stop it!" She punches my arm.

I let out what I think is a final chuckle and shake my head. "We almost landed on him!"

We look at each other again and just can't help ourselves. Maybe it's wrong to laugh at what almost happened. It might be inappropriate, even morbid, but it feels good. Laughter is rare in our world.

"All right, kiddo. Think we might be able to hold it together now? I bet Dad would've laughed with us. Let's not think about it too much."

Tulip's smile disappears and she cries again. Not as intensely as before. "I'm a mess. Why aren't you?"

"Because I left to tell Javier, and you did all the hard work. I should've stayed with you to finish the prep before leaving. I'm sorry. And Mom—she looks great. Dad would be proud." I throw an arm around her shoulder and coax her back toward home.

As we walk, I wonder how Mom will make it to the transition site. "Can you get Mom to the beach? I'll be helping with the litter."

Tulip stops and kicks a stone. "Yeah. I'll get her there."

I nod and watch Tulip trot ahead of me, down the road to home. Like all the roads around us, it used to be a smooth surface. Cars would drive people for miles and miles. I can't even imagine living in those easy days. Now the road's a rutted mess of earth and tar.

Somehow, our recent ancestors found ways to clear most of the trash left behind from the apocalypse—fallen buildings, broken furniture, uprooted trees, dead vehicles, dead animals, dead friends. All in the Heaps now.

Some things are improving. We finally have water piped from the ponds into our homes. There's more than enough old wood to keep fires burning during the Drearies and the Darkness. One good thing about the wind is the electricity it produces—the first survivors were the smart ones. But there's still so much to do. Still evidence of what used to be here.

Huge foundations from big buildings and fancy houses. Rusted pieces of metal. Bones.

I often wonder if the entire planet looks like our village.

When I get home, Mom is still turned toward the window. Tulip stands behind her with a brush in one hand, ready to groom the new widow. I leave the door open, hoping to circulate the air, and hear hushed voices in the distance. I recognize Javier's.

"I'm back, Mom. I'm going to help with Dad, okay?"

"Of course, Ing. As eldest, it is your responsibility."

"I should've stayed to help prepare him before going to Javier's. I feel awful about that."

"Feeling awful about what has passed will not help you with what is to come. Your sister is more capable than you think." She reaches back for Tulip's hand, patting it when she finds it.

I nod and then remember she can't see my small gestures. "I know she is." I glance at the drawer next to her chair—*her* chair now—and think about the gift. Would it be rude to ask about it? Or is this the perfect time with Dad, well, still here?

"You asked me to get something from the drawer, something of Dad's, before I left for Javier's. Should I wait until after? This might not be the right—"

"It's the right time." Mom reaches a hand to the top of the small drawer, handcrafted like those in each room from wood our ancestors salvaged, and I watch her hand inch its way toward the pull knob. She opens the drawer. "In the back. Wrapped in a small piece of cloth. Find it, please."

Tulip and I never discuss what our parents might keep in the small table with one drawer that sits between their chairs. It's theirs. We have no right to their meager possessions. I peek into the drawer. It looks empty. I reach toward the back. When I touch the soft cloth, my heart flutters . . . and the voice from my dreams and the Heaps, a booming voice, speaks.

"SAFEGUARD IT."

"What?" Flinching, I spin around.

"What do you mean, *what*? What are you looking for?" Tulip eyes me like I've lost my mind.

"Did you—" The stress of the day is seriously making me loopy. "Nothing. Never mind." I pull out the piece of cloth.

A surprise.

Inside the cloth, an emerald-green coin. It fits comfortably in the cup of my palm. On both sides, three rings intertwine. I don't know what I'm supposed to say. Don't know what I'm supposed to do with the thing, but I like the weight of it in my hand.

Coins aren't unusual. Many turned up after the Halt, but they were worthless. You can't eat a coin. You can't build anything useful with them. They don't keep you warm or cool. No one trades anything valuable for coins.

"IT'S YOURS NOW." The voice echoes my father's words. I spin around again, eyes searching.

"What is wrong with you?" Tulip whispers. I shake my head.

Doing my best to stay calm, to convince myself I'm not hearing things, I focus on my mother. "This is nice, Mom. Why did Dad want me to have it?"

Mom closes her eyes, and something like a sad smile softens her face. She doesn't answer me. Instead, she gestures for the coin. I give it to her, surprised when a brief ache grips my heart when it leaves my hand. She rubs its surface between her fingers as if trying to read it.

Tulip finally interrupts the silence. "What's so special about that?"

Mom opens her hand, palm up. For some reason, I expect to see the coin glow. When my sister takes it from her, I breathe in sharply, as if it's been snatched from my own hand.

"What?" she asks. "It's not like I'm going to break it." She studies it briefly before tossing it onto the little table. I grab it before it slips over the edge. "It's just a piece of metal. Things like that turn up all the time in the Heaps. I like the color, though."

My fingers tighten around the coin, and the hairs on my neck prickle. *Is someone, something, really talking to me?* "Where'd he get it, Mom?" My voice trembles.

"I suppose you both should hear this," she says. Tulip sits in what used to be Mom's chair. "Your father, well, he was meant to be a Swimmer."

"What? How? When? I mean . . . what?" The news strikes me like a slap. Tulip looks at me, wide-eyed.

"It's a story we planned to tell you both when you were younger, but things happen, you know, and the time was never quite right."

"But was he chosen? It's an honor to be chosen, so how could he—how could his family say no?" It makes no sense. "And this coin. Who gave it to him? I don't think it's just a piece of metal." I don't say anything about the voice I'm hearing or how the coin makes me feel. As if to comfort me, it grows cool in my hand, a refreshing sensation in this heat.

"I wish your father could have explained it to you because I'm afraid I might bungle some details, but I'll do the best I can. Your great, great grandfather on your father's side was the original Swimmer."

Tulip and I stare at each other again, mouths open.

"He emerged from the floodwaters after the Halt, you see, with this coin stuck to his chest. He was instrumental in establishing our community along with other survivors. A voice in the sea spoke to him—"

"A voice?" I interrupt. "What did it say? What did it sound like?"

"I can't remember the exact words or how they sounded, but it told him that in exchange for helping him find his way back to land, back to a place he could call home, he would be obligated to bring those who perished to their final resting place in the great waters.

"And he was to find two others to assist. They would become the first Swimmers. Your great, great grandfather would eventually pass his coin on to an heir who would continue the practice."

"Did the voice say a male heir? Because if it didn't specify a male heir, then—"

"Patience, Ing. Let me finish before I lose track." Mom reaches out a hand. I take it and sit at her feet.

"Eventually, he took a mate and bore one child, a daughter. It was his belief, however, that since the coin had been entrusted to him for this task, the voice must have intended the responsibility to fall on the shoulders of men."

He heard a voice from the sea. Am I imagining the voice that speaks to me? My heart races.

"And so," Mom continues, "he told his daughter to keep his coin safe and pass it on to a son he presumed she would someday bear. But she, too, bore only one girl child, your grandmother. By then, the practice of three male Swimmers was accepted as the way it should be."

"But why do our Swimmers live alone now? How are they supposed to pass their coin to sons?" Tulip asks. Her interest in the story surprises me. She's never shown any interest in stories about the sea, which still frightens her.

"I'm afraid I don't know that answer, dear, and I'm not even sure your father knew. You see, when your grandmother finally bore a son—your father—she knew she was expected to offer him to the Swimmers here. There were two Elder Swimmers at the time, and they lived in the same house where our Swimmers now live. I suppose it would be difficult for a woman to live with someone whose life's work is to dispatch the dead. Perhaps it became a choice meant to protect a potential mate."

I scoff. "So somewhere along the way, Swimmers stopped having heirs and had to pick replacements from the village. That doesn't explain why girls can't be Swimmers, though. Shouldn't we have that chance?" None of the girls I know has ever said they wished they could be a Swimmer. The sea is the cause of so much destruction. It's a place for the dead.

"Well, perhaps. But only women can bear children. With our struggling population, it is best for all able women to reproduce. Wouldn't you agree?"

I will not agree, so I sit there silently steaming. What's the purpose of raising children if their only goal in life will be to care for their dying parents? There has to be more. But I need to know how my father managed to avoid his responsibility.

Noting my stubborn silence, Tulip asks what's on my mind. "So how come Dad didn't get to be a Swimmer?"

"Well, I suppose we never shared this story because it's embarrassing, really. Your grandmother should have offered him up when he came of age, you see, but the truth is, she stopped believing the Swimmers' story."

Wow. I wish I'd known her. She was a rebel, like me.

"That's amazing!" My outburst startles Mom. I shush my voice. "Sorry, sorry, Mom. So she kept it hidden until it was too late, or until they found a third from the village?"

"Yes. Until it was too late." My mother smiles again, that same sad smile, and nods. "When I was pregnant with you, his mother gave him the coin and told him to keep it hidden. Told us both not to believe in everything we were told, especially from sources that isolate themselves. I was only too happy to keep my family together. Selfish, I suppose. I've always wondered why she even gave it to us."

Because she must have known it was special.

I remember wanting to make my father proud. I remember Tulip crying and running away when he tried to coax her into the water with us. I remember standing on tiptoes in water chin deep and how when a gentle swell lifted me from the sandy bottom, I floated. I remember Dad's hand supporting my back as he taught me how to relax and float in the salty sea.

"Is this right, Daddy?" I shouted with my head tilted back, ears filled with water, my little body floating over the waves.

I remember his laughter.

I stare at the coin in my hand, mine now, for me, the distant heir of an original Swimmer, and for a moment, I feel dizzy. The rings on the coin seem to swirl. I look away, glad I'm still sitting.

"You might've been selfish, but I think I know why Dad wanted me to have this. He taught me how to swim for a reason." I feel bold. "He made sure I could so when the time came, I'd be ready. And I'm ready now. I don't care what the rules are. I'm not going to do what everyone says I have to do. I'm going to be a Swimmer."

"No, Ing, you can't! Mom, tell her she can't." Tulip looks horrified.

My attitude softens when I see her tears. Our father just died, our mother is blind, and here I am talking about leaving the house—and her. How can I just walk away and leave her with all the responsibilities? Since I first mentioned it when we were kids, I never again talked to her about wanting to be a Swimmer. I knew how much she hated and feared the water. She wipes her eyes but doesn't look at me.

"I knew this day would come." Mom pats my hand. "Your father taught you how to swim so you could teach a son we hoped you would bear when your time was right. A son you could pass the coin to. A son who would fulfill a commitment he never could. Not so you could become a Swimmer."

What a gut-punch. "But—"

"I know what's in your heart, dear girl." She releases my hand. "Your desire does not surprise me. But consider why your grandmother rebelled."

Shaking her head, Tulip turns from me.

"Well," I challenge, "did you ever consider that maybe Dad really wanted to be a Swimmer? That maybe he gave up on life so soon because he never got to be what he was meant to be? That he was ashamed of his mother's decision and maybe even believed I *could* do what he was denied?"

"Stop it! Just stop it!" Tulip spins toward me, and I feel horrible. I've gone too far.

"I'm sorry, Mom. I didn't mean for it to come out like that."

"YOU WILL MAKE IT RIGHT."

That unearthly voice again. I'm really losing it. But I suddenly know how to make things right.

I rest my hand on my mother's knee. "Mom, I have to do this. And when I leave, when I become a Swimmer, Tulip can claim firstborn."

Tulip gasps. It's true. Since I'd no longer belong to my family, Tulip could lead the life she wants. She won't have to wait for me to produce a viable child first. The Council will approve of a mate when she comes of age. I know of several already interested in her. I'm in the way.

Mom rests a hand on my head. "My foolish, brave girl. I may not agree with your decision, but perhaps it's time to reconsider our ways. The Swimmers would be crazy to turn away the heir of an original."

Not to mention the very distant heir of a West Point soldier. I might not be a badass like my ancestors, but it's time to stand up for what I want to do.

All I have to do now is convince the Swimmers to change their beliefs and the way they've done things forever.

I'm a little scared.

3

ASIDE FROM MY grandmother's rebellious distrust of certain groups and my dad's warning against cults, people believe the Swimmers are the most virtuous members of our society. They have one job to do. Two grown men and one novice live apart from the rest of society, apart from people like my family—the common families—who help to support them. Every household, regardless of means, provides portions of food and ensures the Swimmers' home remains in good repair. It's the least we can do for the service they provide.

Our interactions are limited to when we might see them on their way to the sea each day or to when it's our turn to collect and deliver supplies to them. And, of course, when we call them to perform their grim mission.

I've always envied them. They have a purpose. When someone dies, they deliver the body to the sea, swimming it to a point far, far from shore and releasing it. The sea provides food for us every day. It makes sense that we give something back to it.

Life to death to life again.

What doesn't make sense are the superstitions that started soon after everyone accepted the custom of burial at sea.

"Why don't we plant people in the ground?" I asked my parents when I was little. I watched them bury dead fish in the soil where vegetables grew. They brought me and Tulip to the beach for the first Farewell we witnessed. All parents teach their children what the Swimmers do after people stop breathing.

"Because if we don't bring them to the sea, the water will be angry and rise again. It will come after us, the living, and take us before we're ready."

The explanation was enough to shut me up. It left me horrified and awestruck—and wonderfully excited. The sea was alive.

There were no Swimmers before the Halt. From the first time I learned about them, I wanted to be one.

Now, while I wait for them to appear at our door to take my father away, I place the coin in my pocket.

I told my father I wanted to be a Swimmer when I was about five. He was teaching me how to hold my breath to swim underwater. "Survival skills," he called my instruction, and I took to it like the fish I'd occasionally feel flicker around me when I submerged. "But you cannot be a Swimmer," he said. "Girls can't be Swimmers."

I was the right age to be chosen as a novice, and I pouted until I fell asleep that night. It wasn't fair. And they could have taken me. I was an excellent swimmer by the time I was three.

We had two children in our family, and Tulip refused to go into the water. She's never gotten over her fear of it. She believes there's something unnatural about it.

I've always been fascinated by its immensity, its mystery, its aliveness, but maybe our first Farewell scared her. Maybe she holds onto a fear that if people live too long, the sea will do what our father suggested. I don't mock her superstitions, though. The sea holds power and secrets no one fully understands.

"But how come the Swimmers can't have two novices, a boy and a girl?" I asked my parents when I was about six. We were at another Farewell, and the novice was a year older than me. I thought he was cute with his shaved head and bronze body. When called to perform their duty, the Swimmers are dressed in no more than robes, which they drop before heading into the water, even on the coldest days. I wouldn't have minded shaving off my hair. It's still a nuisance, especially in the wind.

My father scrunched his eyebrows together before answering me. "Because three is a special number. Four Swimmers would not be . . . right."

I could tell he believed his answer was truthful, but he didn't know why.

When the oldest Swimmer is near death, the other two are supposed to swim with him to where they deliver our dead. No one knows what happens in the far beyond, but only two return. Then they choose an apprentice.

The Swimmers should have taken me when I was a youngster and the oldest had taken his "perfect, peaceful plunge."

But no. Since the Swimmers lead a celibate life, the custom now calls for them to select a young male novice from among those offered by fertile couples when it's time for the eldest to take his final swim. At about five years old, the chosen child says goodbye to his family and moves in with the experienced ones. He probably cries when his new brothers take him by the hand from his parents and lead him to the water for first initiation before bringing him to his new home at the edge of the village. I wonder if the cute boy cried.

I wouldn't have.

———— ❧ ————

Mom turns toward the door when the distant sound of Javier's voice tells us the Swimmers are on their way. "I suppose it's time," she says. She smooths her lap one more time, and I help her stand. Before I release her, she draws me into a hug. "Your father would be proud of you," she whispers in my ear. "I am proud of you."

"Thanks, Mom." I believe her. "It's not far to the shore. Javier will help."

"Ready?" Tulip draws Mom's right arm into the crook of her left arm.

Mom stands tall, though she's shorter than Tulip by several inches. This takes me by surprise. In my mind, my mother is a giant. She had been, anyway, when I was a kid. These last couple of sedentary years have not been kind.

"I'm ready, dear. Shall we?"

Tulip and Mom shuffle through the door. Javier and the Swimmers stand aside to let them pass, and Javier looks at me with his head tilted. I motion for him to join me.

"Will you follow them?" I ask. "If Mom stumbles or if Tulip isn't strong enough—"

"Of course. If she's having trouble, I'll grab the cart at my house when we go by. I'll bring it anyway, for the return, since she hasn't been walking much."

So thoughtful. We can see the ocean from our home, but for someone who hasn't walked much for months, the trek on foot could be tough.

"Thank you. You always think of everything."

"Will you be okay? Your dad was a great guy. Wish he could've lived longer."

"Yeah, he was. I do too. And yeah, I'll be okay. He's not very heavy anymore, and it's not far."

We stand together and stare at my father. I already miss his dark eyes. I'm deeply aware of the Swimmers outside, waiting to be called.

"You sure you don't want me to do this part? You could go with your mother—"

"No!" He means well—he always means well—but helping to carry the litter is my duty. "Sorry, I didn't mean to snap. You're a good friend, Javier."

He's heard it before. I've never led him to believe we could be anything more, but his shoulders still droop. "Don't be sorry. I'll see you there." He rests a hand on my shoulder before leaving to follow my mother.

Soon, I'll call the two Elders and the youngest—the novice—to enter. I'll help them carry my father to the sea.

They swim every day, even when they have no body to deliver. And while they never seem to go to the sea at the same time of day, I always sense when they make their trek. I've watched as the novice has grown into a man. At sixteen, he's . . . wow.

When I'm not lost in chilling, gray nightmares, I dream of him. Even during the coldest months of the Darkness, I'll wake in a hot sweat from fantasies of his toned body pressed against mine.

And he's standing outside my door, dressed in a loose robe with the Elders, waiting to be called in. Waiting to help take my dead father to the shore and swim him out to sea. I've never been physically close to him, though. He's always somewhere else whenever it's our turn to deliver portions of food to their house. I sometimes wonder if his absence is purposeful, like they're keeping him away from me. Or me from him.

I flush in anticipation—and then shake it off, refocusing on my father. My dead father lying on the floor at my feet.

"Thanks for the coin, Dad," I whisper, wanting him to open his eyes and tell me its story. I pull it from my pocket and unwrap it. "I wish you'd stayed with us longer."

It might be odd talking to him like this, but I can't stop. "I wish I'd asked you more about your life and what it was like when you lost your parents and what Tulip and I should do to live longer and what I should do next—I don't know what I should do next, but I feel like I can't just stay here and—I wish for so many things, Dad. And I wish I could just live like everyone else and be happy like Tulip says I should, but I can't, I just can't, and I think that makes me a horrible person and a horrible daughter and I'm sorry. I'm so sorry I felt relieved when Mom told me you wouldn't be long."

With this confession, I fall to my knees by his side and continue. I acknowledge my selfishness. I express fear for my mother, though I can't know what the future holds for her, and for Tulip, who'll be left to care for everything when I leave. I tell him I don't want the future others have mapped out for me.

I lose track of time until a gentle hand on my shoulder startles me from my self-pity. I open my eyes.

"Oh!" When I look over my shoulder, I see him. The novice has kind, penetrating eyes, pale jade, made even more gorgeous against his ebony skin. He turns away quickly, and something shifts inside me. Celibacy would be a challenge living in a home with him, but I can still dream.

I wipe sweat from my forehead with the cloth holding my coin before returning it to my pocket. I'm not sure what to say or do next. I've never seen what happens with others in homes when someone dies. I've only heard stories. I'm not ready. I feel . . . stupid.

We all convince ourselves we have more time, as if we can own it. Manipulate it.

The eldest Swimmer must sense my uncertainty because he holds out his hand to me. I take it. He walks me around to where my father's right foot pokes from beneath his blanket. The novice stands by Dad's other foot, and the two Elders stand by his shoulders. They all face inward. And then, they begin a chant that gives me goosebumps.

"Ahhhveyyyahhh, ahhhveyyyahhh, ahhhveyyyahhh." They repeat this strange word until I finally joined them because if I don't, I might scream or cry—not cry—or evaporate into the swirling wind outside. Our voices blend into a sound so beautiful I'm overwhelmed by a feeling I've never really experienced before. Joy. I could stand here chanting this word forever.

And Dad waits.

Finally, with no warning, the three stop chanting. And I keep going. My eyes are closed. When I open them, the Swimmers smile.

"Sorry," I mumble, embarrassed. I don't know if it was okay for me to join in this chant, but they didn't stop me.

As if on cue, they bend their knees to grab their corner of the litter, and I do the same. We lift together, and the two Elders turn to face forward. We move through the door. I match my steps with theirs, steady and precise. They stand tall and direct their eyes forward, never wavering, never acknowledging the people we pass, who move aside and lower their heads in respect. I keep my eyes on my father's peaceful face.

He has a beautiful face. I will miss his face.

I expect we might overtake my mother and sister as we march to the water and am surprised when we find them already at the shoreline. Mom sits in Javier's cart. I don't know if she made the walk without it, but it doesn't matter. She and Tulip are here. Javier gives me a little wave. No one else is near the water.

Farewells aren't often attended by people outside the immediate family. Death is a natural and expected occurrence, as natural as sleeping and waking, and it's improper to make a fuss. And although the sea provides food for us, it's still a mystery. It ruined the planet, drowning entire populations when—as scientists told our predecessors it would—the Halt sent waters speeding to the poles. It's an early history lesson none of us can forget.

The Swimmers stop in front of my mother, and we lower the litter. I step back, not knowing what else to do, and watch as they gently remove the blanket from around my father's body. A ridiculous urge to protect him, to cover him, to warm his cold body, surprises me.

The novice folds the blanket neatly and hands it to me. When I reach for it, our hands touch. As if I need to feel more of it right now, heat floods my body. He looks into my eyes again. I think he might say something, but he turns away quickly, back to his task.

"Here, Mom." I place the blanket in her lap. "He'll be gone soon."

She strokes the blanket with her face turned toward the sky. "Yes, dear. Another day. And a beautiful one, I feel."

She's right. The rain clouds haven't gathered yet, and the sea is calm. The atmosphere feels eerily still. There's no wind here. I can't remember a day without its noise and annoyance.

Tulip stands behind Mom and stares back toward home, seemingly uninterested in what the Swimmers will do next. I return to the litter. I look down at the naked body of the man who tried so very hard to teach me how to be strong. All bones now, held together by dull flesh. It's not my father anymore.

It's time for his earthly transition. His perfect, peaceful plunge.

4

I DON'T KNOW what comes over me.

The Swimmers drop their robes in one neat pile beyond the litter. Tulip is suddenly interested in the proceedings, and I see why. All three men stand as naked as my father. Their skin, dark and hairless, glistens.

Their presence amazes me. There's no shame in their posture, no hiding, and I admire the beauty of their sculpted symmetry. Even the Elders appear muscled and fit. And the novice, well, what can I say? His eyes lock onto mine, and I have to look away. My heart skips a beat. Two beats.

When they return to the litter, I take my place with them. Without a word, without another chant—though *Ahveyah* still echoes in my mind—we lift the corners and walk with it into the waiting water. I don't care if my clothes get soaked.

When we're waist-deep, the two Elders float my father's body free, and the novice passes the empty platform to me. My signal to leave. To return home with my family while the Swimmers deliver their gift to the sea.

Not much of a meal, I think, and then cringe, hating the idea of sea life feeding on my father's skeletal body. At what point will an island of bones rise from the salty depths? And how far out will the Swimmers have to go to prevent grisly remains from washing up on shore? It doesn't matter much since it's rare for anyone but the fishers—and me—to visit the beach area, let alone to swim in the sea.

By the time I drop the litter on the shore, the Swimmers are already a distance away. Tulip opens her arms, and we hug. She whimpers softly. As I rock her, a delicious chill reminds me of the coin in my pocket and—

"FOLLOW THEM." The mighty voice I've been hearing since before receiving the coin startles me but confirms what I've already decided to do. I'm either losing my mind or about to do something important. Maybe both.

Releasing Tulip, I turn to Javier. "Please take my mom home. Thank you for helping." I feel like I'm about to burst.

"Sure. But you're coming back too—"

"I can't, not yet." I cut him off. "Please, go now." I place a hand on my mother's shoulder and kiss her cheek. "I have to go, Mom. And I don't know when I'll be back. I love you."

"I know, dear. Do what you must." She turns her milky eyes toward the sea. "Farewell, love." Those two words are all she needs to say to the man who's been her husband, her friend, her love through so many years of hardship. The last goodbye. The final Farewell.

I return to Tulip, hugging her until she protests. "You and Mom . . . it'll be okay," I stammer, not sure what else to say. "Go home now. I love you." I leave her looking stunned.

I strip off my wet clothes, all of them, and drop them in a heap by the Swimmers' robes, my heart pounding with excitement.

"Ing! What the fluke?" Tulip looks horrified.

I don't answer. I'm already one with the sea. My bare skin tingles as I slide through the salty water, my nipples responding to its cool caresses, my long hair rippling behind me, my legs thrusting me forward like a fluke would a porpoise. Mom and Dad told us stories of great whales and dolphins and other monsters of the sea, but I'm not afraid. My eyes, lips, and tongue quickly adjust to the salty sting.

Vaguely aware of Tulip's uproar, I forge farther into the great water, led by some instinctive awareness of my direction. I'll catch up with the Swimmers, whose pace is slowed by their burden. I'll see my father one more time before giving him over to the depths. I'm breaking some unwritten rule, but I don't care.

Sparkling swells ahead tell me I'm closing in on them when, suddenly, the steady rhythm of ripples erupts into wild splashing. An attack? Is one of the sea monsters greedily attacking before my father's release? I swim faster.

The novice and the middle-aged Swimmer don't seem surprised by my arrival. They do, however, appear stunned by the second body floating alongside my father's. The eldest Swimmer is quite dead.

The three of us tread water around the two bodies for several moments. The Swimmers' duty is to the one they're summoned to serve. I imagine it's difficult enough pulling a body far from shore in calm waters, and not every dead person is considerate enough to stop breathing on a rare, windless, waveless day.

"I'll take him." Without waiting for permission, I wrap my left arm over the Elder's chest and pull him away from the others. Maybe I should take my father? No. That's their job.

They're alongside me quickly, the novice towing my father's body, the other swimming easily between us. I expect him to protest and take the Elder's body from me, but he doesn't. I briefly wonder how much farther we have to go and for how long I'll be able to keep up with the experienced Swimmers.

My father's lessons suddenly make sense. He encouraged me to practice when I was younger. He never stopped me when, many times each week, I slipped out to the water to work on my stamina while the village slept. I think he knew I'd try to become a Swimmer one day.

We swim for an eternity, and I force myself to stay calm. I've never been so far out before. My brain messes with me, making me doubt my abilities, but my body rejects the message. I'm strong. Mom said I was brave. I convince myself I can swim to the other side of the sea if necessary.

It isn't necessary.

What happens next shocks me.

The novice and new eldest slow to a stop, and we tread water around the bodies for another long while when, farther beyond us, the sea churns and rises. I inhale too quickly and choke, spitting out the salty water. What enormous creature could create such an upheaval, and why aren't we swimming like hell back to shore? The novice must sense my fear. He swims to me and stays close. He makes me feel safe, if only for a heartbeat.

"What is it?" I ask. He and the eldest show no change in emotion, no fear.

"Shhh," the novice hushes me.

Then he and the Elder gently, ever so gently, push the bodies away from us and toward the turbulence beyond. I nearly follow my father's body, suddenly realizing this is the last time I'll see him, but I stop.

"Farewell, Dad." I watch the two lifeless figures float away. And then I ask again. "What is that? What's happening?"

They say nothing, but the novice tilts his head toward the turbulence as if to say, "Watch."

We wait and watch. I see something like a large silver funnel breach the surface of the sea. When it tips toward the dead, the water tugs at me alarmingly. It pulls the bodies—and me—toward the void it creates. Fear grips me. I hold my breath. Suddenly on my back with my feet heading toward the anomaly, I shout. I kick and backstroke as fast as I can, but I'm still heading toward the funnel. Panic.

A strong hand, and then a second, grasp my wrists and tug me away until the pull stops.

Breathe, I reminded myself.

"YES. BREATHE," it says, and I want to scream, "Who are you? Where are you?"

Instead, I watch the glimmer of silver submerge. With the danger over, the Elder releases my hand first. A second later, the novice squeezes my wrist gently before releasing me to swim between them back to shore.

What the hell is out there? Who, where, what is that voice no one else hears? And that gentle squeeze . . .

———— ❧ ————

A figure paces the shoreline, stopping only as the three of us wade inland. I'm surprised to find Tulip waiting for me. I can only imagine the stress she feels being so close to the thing that scares her most. She picks up my clothes from the sand and runs to me.

"Ing! Dammit! I've been half crazy worrying about you." She gives the Swimmers a sideways glance before continuing her rant. "What got into you?" She searches the sea. "Where's the other one? Here, put these on, you're . . . you're—"

"Naked? Crazy? Wet? I'm all those things." I take the clothes but stand bold in my nakedness. I'm filled with excitement and curiosity. My words come out fast. "The eldest Swimmer died at sea and we—"

A hand on my bare shoulder stops me from saying more. I tingle.

"Hey!" Tulip yanks me from the novice's hold and glares at me. The novice acts like nothing happened. Instead, he lifts a robe from the pile, shakes off sand, and drapes it around me before putting on his own.

"She has her own clothes, you know." Tulip continues to challenge him. "Here. Put them on and let's go home. It's late. Mom's probably worried sick."

It is late, though the passage of time is never clear in days and nights of constant sunshine. But I won't be going home. I'm just not sure how to explain my decision to her. I hold my breath, a habit I've been trying to break for years. Like my new coin, it comforts me.

"Tulip," I exhale and pull her close, "I'm not going home tonight. I—"

"What do you mean, you're not going home? Where do you think you're going?" She raises her palms upward in disbelief.

I glance at the Swimmers, and much to my surprise—so many surprises in one day—both nod at me and simultaneously tilt their heads in the direction they live.

"No, I don't think so." Tulip stamps her foot in the sand. "I don't care if you are Swimmers, you're not taking away my sister."

"Stop. Please. This is *my* decision. They're not taking me away. There's something I need to figure out, so please, please, don't make this any harder."

"But I don't understand. What happened out there? What aren't you telling me?" Tulip hangs her head, and I briefly question my sanity. What am I doing? I don't understand what happened to our dad and the Elder, but when the novice placed his hand on me, in addition to feeling . . . aroused, I somehow knew I wasn't supposed to say what I witnessed. I have to leave with the Swimmers. Not *have to* but need to. Want to.

"Don't worry about me, okay? I'll be back. I'll be safe. I'll explain it all when I can do it better, I promise. And Mom, well, she already knew I wouldn't be coming home right away, so don't worry about her either." I reach into the pocket where my coin remains hidden and transfer it to the pocket in my robe. I hand my damp clothes to Tulip, who hesitates before taking them.

"Thanks for waiting for me, kiddo." I hug her, kiss her on the cheek, and leave her standing alone with her sandy shadow.

"You better come home soon, or else!" Her threat makes me smile.

———— ≈ ————

I catch up with the Swimmers, positioning myself to the left of the former novice. I feel foolish. Neither acknowledges me.

Did I misunderstand their invitation? I drop back behind them and continue to follow. If they shut their door in my face, I'll return home and remain ignorant of what I witnessed far out at sea.

While we walk in silence, I think about my father, who just died. Died without saying goodbye. Died without a last embrace, except for our shuffling dance to his chair earlier.

The eldest Swimmer died with even less.

But were they gone? What was the thing that seemed ready to take their bodies? It sure wasn't any fish I've ever seen.

The coin in my pocket cools me down, and I allow its presence—its reminder my father wanted me to have it—to calm me.

The Swimmers' home, no better than any in the village, is just ahead. I hope I'll be welcomed inside. I pause and watch the Elder open the door. He and the new second *Elder*, the one who makes my heart skip beats, go inside. I hold my breath and wait. The door stays open.

Am I crazy? Yes, I'm definitely crazy.

I approach, expecting the door to close. But it doesn't. Standing in the doorway, I take a deep breath before stepping inside. The sweet aroma of pine needles reminds me of the ones on the forest floor beyond our village. I walk there often to escape the nastiness of the Heaps. My time in the trees always gives me hope and makes me feel alive.

We were lucky the trees grew back in the years after the Halt. Many are perfect for chopping down now, for building new structures, for nicer homes and furnishings, but none in our village will hear of it. They never say it, but I think they're afraid of a land without trees. How anything green still survives these extreme seasons makes no sense.

A lot of things make no sense lately.

Two more steps and I'm inside. I close the door behind me and wait for my eyes to adjust to the dim interior. A small flame on a rustic table at the far side of the room illuminates the two sitting at the table. The younger Swimmer motions me to the empty seat and places a piece of fruit and a handful of nuts in front of me. I'm so tired. And hungry.

"Thank you," I whisper. It feels right to speak quietly in this peaceful place, but even my soft voice sounds too loud.

He nods, and the three of us eat our meager meal in silence. They don't look at me or at each other while we eat, keeping their eyes cast downward.

There's so much I want to know, but this isn't the time to ask. What will happen after we eat?

When we finish, the one who's not a novice anymore—he must have a name—stands and motions me to follow him into a tiny adjoining room where he points to a sleeping pad on the floor. Before he leaves, he looks into my eyes for longer than a casual glance. The room is darkened by heavy tarps that thwart the relentless sun, but his cool jade eyes glow. I hope he doesn't notice the heat my body feels like it's giving off right now. Or maybe I want him to.

I definitely want him to.

What's wrong with me? I want to touch him, to open my robe and invite him to touch me, to hold me, to lie with me.

And I want to cry. Can't.

Too much has just happened, too much loss, too many hasty decisions, too many bizarre moments, and here I am, expected to sleep in a strange bed until another day will find me still in the dark. I reach out to touch him, but he backs away, shaking his head. Again, I'm acting the fool. His eyes are kind, though. He steps away and closes the door, leaving me with nothing to do but curl up and sleep on what was probably the dead man's bed.

If only.

Just as I'm about to doze off, voices in the adjoining room startle me. Other than the soul-stirring chant I participated in around my father's body, I've often wondered, as most of us do, what the Swimmers talk about. They certainly aren't known to be chatty.

I wrap the robe around me, feeling for the coin.

As much as I want to burst in on them, I wait with my ear to the wall straining to hear their conversation. It has to be about me. I've disturbed the natural order of their world.

I hear the new Elder say something about a possible novice, a boy about six years old. The younger Swimmer seems to protest. I hear my name.

He knows my name. I never liked it until just now, until he spoke it. Never knew a name could sound so beautiful. Is he arguing for me to be the next novice? But I'm a woman. And I'm . . . old. Talk about breaking tradition.

I don't feel right eavesdropping.

I open my door slowly and tiptoe to theirs. I knock softly, and their conversation stops.

I wait, it seems all I've done lately is wait. After what seems like too long to wait for an answer, I talk into the door crack.

"Um, hello? May I join you?" My heart pounds. I have no right to interfere with their conversation, but they're talking about me.

More waiting, and then the door opens. The Elder sits cross-legged on his bed, and the other's jade eyes greet mine with a hint of what looks like mischief. Or maybe curiosity. I'm glad to see they're both still robed, unless they threw them on when I knocked. The younger's robe hangs uneven, exposing his chest. I try, unsuccessfully, not to stare.

"I heard my name." No need to avoid the fact that I've been listening. "I'd like to be included in your conversation." I half expect they might show me to the door and ask me never to return, but then again, they had invited me to follow them from the shore. At least that's what I tell myself.

The younger turns toward the Elder, who nods, and I'm offered a chair in the corner of the bedroom they share.

"You present us with a quandary," says the Elder. "Before we discuss anything further, let me share our thanks for your assistance at sea today." He frowns. "Joshua's parting was unexpected."

Joshua. That was my father's name, too.

"Yes, thank you. You're a powerful swimmer," says the younger. His voice, deep and warm, resonates within me. *Hot.*

The Elder speaks again. He seems to weigh each word on his tongue before releasing it.

Patience, I tell myself. Flood. Is the mysterious voice I keep hearing really just my own thoughts? Am I fooling myself into thinking I'm somehow special, that I deserve the life I want?

"What happened during your father's Farewell was unprecedented, and had you not been there to assist, well, our obligation would have been more arduous." He turns to the younger as if uncertain of what to say. "There must be three. There have always been three. Three male Swimmers. We thought we'd have longer, much longer, to select our next novice."

Our constant quest. More time.

As I listen, I wonder how old he is. Older than my father was, I think, yet he's still strong. How? Maybe because he has no children. Maybe because the village helps support the Swimmers. I want to know, but I don't want to be rude. I'll wait before saying anything else.

"We invited you here," says the younger, "because you've seen things others haven't, and you participated beyond your obligation—quite naturally—in your father's Farewell. We've never had a family member join us in the chant as you did. You must have felt a connection—"

"What Aiden means to say is that we appear to be at a crossroads of sorts."

Finally, a name. Aiden. His name reminds me of the story of Adam from a book called the Bible.

Mom once told us a bedtime story from the book about a man and a woman who enjoyed a lovely life in a beautiful garden until something bad happened. She was always vague about what happened, something about a snake and an apple—it never made sense to me—and then God kicked the couple out of the garden. The man—his name was Adam—had to work hard and the woman had to suffer great pains during childbirth. It sucked for both of them.

I hated that story. Still do. Maybe that's why I don't want to have children.

People still believe in that Bible God, but I don't. Pretty sure Mom and Tulip still believe, but Dad never did. During my swimming lessons, he'd talk about the power we all have inside us. He believed we're all responsible for ourselves and our actions. Warning me against blindly joining anything that looked like an isolated pack—just like his mother warned—he told me stories of pre-Halt cults with leaders who massacred their followers. Horrifying stories.

So I figured that after the Halt, anyone who still believes in a God or gods who love people or have favorites among them is ridiculous. Magic and miracles are for morons.

And yet—the Swimmers' chant and my mysterious coin. What are they for? Who, or what, is listening? The Swimmers keep themselves isolated. Are they a cult?

No. If they were, they'd want us all to become Swimmers.

"Aiden's right," I say. "I do feel a connection with the Farewell ceremony. With you. Crossroads or not, I'm supposed to be a Swimmer."

"Perhaps we will continue this discussion upon the new day." The Elder stands and motions me to the door. He doesn't want Aiden to talk about my natural connection with them, that much is clear, but there's no way I'll forget the comment.

"Wait, please." I stop in the doorway. "You thanked me for my help, but I haven't thanked you for the care you showed my family. I know you do what you do because you're obligated to, but it can't be easy. So, thank you."

The two bow their heads at the same time, and I wonder if there's more to their connection than the job requirements. I suppress the urge to bow my head with them.

"But I have to ask." They keep their heads down. "What was that thing out there, and what did it do with the bodies?"

"We cannot say." The Elder appears troubled by my question.

"Can't or won't?" I'm too abrupt.

"Both," Aiden says. "Not until—"

With a sharp glance at Aiden, the Elder silences him again. They have secrets.

"Until when? I'm sorry. I don't mean to be rude. It's just that, well, can you imagine what I'm going through right now? All of this is . . ." I can't find the words to describe what "all of this" is.

Silence. I wait.

"You're right. It wasn't wise to talk about you when you were so close by." The Elder's words aren't an apology. "You should not have witnessed what you did."

"But I did. So now what?" Will they have me take a vow of secrecy? Will they give me something to erase my memory? There are stories about such potions. Or will they keep me captive? No. Tulip knows where I am. Mom knows, too. My mind races, but I keep my mouth shut. No need to give them any ideas.

"That's what we were discussing when you knocked," says Aiden, who ushers me out of the room.

"And we still have much to discuss," the Elder is quick to add. "Several families have offered a next novice. We thought we had more time."

Those words.

It strikes me again that their loss, like mine, happened without a final goodbye, a final embrace. And for Joshua, no *Ahveyah*. What might that mean for him, for his body? What did the chant mean for my father, if anything?

I recall past times when we all knew of a Farewell about to take place and how I experienced an unexplainable urge to hum or sing aloud at some point during the day, despite not knowing much at all about who died. There were times I didn't even know about a Farewell, and the urge to sing still haunted me.

The Swimmers might not be capable of accepting it, but my connection with them is real and more powerful than any connection I've ever felt.

"Accept me as your novice." There. It's out there, hanging in the air between us like the static electricity we learned about as children. Who will be the first to release its energy? Aiden's eyes grow wide.

And I wait.

"It would be most improper—"

"But you've seen what I can do. You feel it, too, I just know it. I'm supposed to do this." The coin cools my pocket, my whole body, really, and I remove it from its soft cloth. "Look," I hold it out to them. "Tell me what this means!" I wait with my palm open. To my amazement, just as I imagined it would when my mother held it, the token glows green in the darkness.

The Elder's wide eyes reflect the glow. "The coin!" He reaches out to touch it but stops abruptly when it rises from my palm and floats to a place over my heart, where it stays.

I gasp.

"Where did this come from? Who gave this to you?"

"It was a gift from my father. He's had it for a long time, but my mother just told me about it."

The two exchange glances. The Elder's brow creases, but Aiden smiles.

Shaking his head slowly, he frowns. "This goes beyond all reason. A girl cannot—"

"Hey, girls—and *women*—can do dangerous things too, you know." I place my hand over the coin on my chest. "What does this mean? Does it mean what I think it does? That I'm supposed to do this? To be a Swimmer? Because I'm pretty sure that's what it must mean, that I should be a Swimmer. Right? How could it mean anything else?" I can't help myself. I babble. My head spins. Exhaustion makes me giddy, and exhilaration thrills me to the bone.

"It, ah, well?" He shakes his head again and looks at Aiden.

"It must, Sebastian. This is unusual, for sure. How can we argue against it?"

The Elder has a name too, of course. Sebastian.

Sebastian remains perplexed. "But your father . . . he wasn't a Swimmer. Where did he get this?"

In a flood of words, I tell him the story my mother shared.

I feel more alive than ever before. Aiden's eyes seek mine. My coin's cooling presence can't compete with my body's sudden heat, and I don't know if I can contain the energy trembling inside me.

But Sebastian's expression troubles me. It looks like he's just seen a ghost.

"The coin has been missing for generations. We decided the original story must be wrong." He puts his hand to his heart, patting it rapidly. "It is said that—should the coin reappear, it will be time—" Frowning, he stops abruptly.

"Yes? When it reappears?" Aiden evidently hasn't heard this story either.

Sebastian glances at Aiden, and then at me, and then at Aiden again. He clears his throat.

I point to my coin. "And now it's here. Doesn't this mean it's time for me to become a Swimmer?"

"This is not a decision to be made lightly. The life of a Swimmer is not an easy one. But enough of this." He points to me with a shaky finger. "You have had quite an adventure today, and quite a loss. Get some sleep now." Sebastian turns abruptly and retreats to the bedroom he shares with Aiden.

Sleep? How the hell am I supposed to sleep after that? Sebastian knows something he isn't going to share, at least not now. I slip the coin from my chest into the robe's pocket and feel a tiny ache in my heart. There's nothing more to do now. My body is losing its battle against fatigue.

"After we break fast tomorrow," Aiden says, "you should let your family know you're okay." He follows me to the other room. "You'll find work clothes in the drawer. They'll be a bit large, but you won't have to leave in a robe." He looks at me again, and I sense his desire to stay with me. I sense his desire. "You should sleep." He turns to leave.

"Wait," I grasp his hand. He doesn't pull away. "Sebastian knows something about this coin he's not telling us. You heard him, right?" I slide my hand slowly from his, my fingertips tingling from the touch.

He hesitates, his eyes fixed on the place our hands have just been. "I'm sure he'll share what he knows. I just became an Elder. I didn't expect this. I'll be given knowledge denied me as a novice. I want to stay here with you and talk about all that happened today—especially about what *just* happened—but I think we need to rest up for whatever comes next." He turns to leave and stops. "Do you really want to be a Swimmer?"

"More than anything." I mean it.

He grins, nods, and backs out of the room, his gorgeous eyes never leaving mine. The door closes silently. I finally collapse on the bed. I don't know how long I have to wait until breakfast or if I'm even capable of sleeping after such a strange day.

I struggle to settle my body, but visions of Aiden—his eyes, his voice, his naked body glistening in the sun at the shore—make me feel all jittery inside. Flood, what a man. No one in the village has ever made me feel this way. It's hot enough in the room without the extra heat my body is throwing off.

I retrieve my softly glowing coin and hold it above me, studying it as if it will magically enlighten me. Instead, the swirling rings make me dizzy again. In my exhaustion, the rings appear to create a tunnel . . .

Glad I'm lying down.

"What are you, and what do you want from me?" I half expect to be shaken by another demand from the phantom voice. Instead, my coin briefly quivers in my hand. I place it on my forehead, hoping it will soothe me, ground me, quiet the noise in my head.

It does more than that.

5

THE COIN'S COOL weight on my forehead stops my restless limbs and gives me something to concentrate on other than my questions. As I focus on its presence, it feels heavier. In a comforting way, it seems to push my head down into the slender pillow.

I fall asleep quickly, and then that dream again, the one that's haunted me since I was little. The one where I'm swimming on a calm sea, alone and unafraid, free as the fish that accompany me, lead me, follow me, and tickle me as they pass below. I lose sight of land, and my feeling of freedom turns to dread as I realize I don't know how to get back home. I'm rising—it's an unsettling sensation—and then a dark wall of water approaches in slow motion. I don't understand why I'm afraid. I love the water, I live for my escapes to the sea, I'm as comfortable in the sea as on land. But I can't see its crest, and I don't know how long I'll be able to hold my breath.

A tiny tap on the bedroom door wakes me. I bolt upright in a cold sweat, and my coin falls into my lap. Without thinking, I place it over my heart, where it stays. It's a part of me now. I don't question why. Too many other questions nag me.

Morning? Where am I? It takes a while to remember where I am and what happened yesterday.

"I'm up," I say, my voice hoarse. I sense Aiden standing silently outside the door. "I'll be right out."

I use the robe's belt to cinch a pair of baggy pants around my waist and slip into a tunic-like top. I must look ridiculous. My hair feels like a matted mess. There are no combs or brushes in this hairless household. When I open the door, Aiden grins.

"I'm sorry. I mean no disrespect." He seems to force a serious expression then, which makes me giggle. He's dressed in similar simple garments and wears them well.

"Don't apologize. I'm sure I look like something you'd pull from the Heaps."

If my father had found the coin there, it would have made more sense to me than my mother's explanation.

"You look—" Aiden turns away from me as if he's acci-dentally invaded my privacy. "You should eat something." He walks to the table where bowls of berries and nuts and two cups of something hot wait. The fragrant candle gives the scene a sense of solemnity.

I glance around for Sebastian, and not seeing him, follow Aiden to the table. He gestures toward one of the cups. "This will keep the chills away. It's a special tea. Sometimes after a Farewell, the chills can set in." He notices me looking at the other bedroom door. "Sebastian won't be up for a while." He focuses on his beverage. I sense his hesitation to say any more.

"I know I've caused trouble," I whisper. "I never meant to, it's just that—"

"You don't have to explain. Something's changing. I can feel it, but I don't know what. Your coin—"

"I feel it too!" I place my hand over his on the table. He starts to pull it away but stops. What's making me so bold? Our eyes lock for a second, and I release him, reaching for my tea. A distraction from the sudden awkwardness. The first sip warms me to my toes. "Wow." I fan my face with my hand, happy to pretend the tea is the reason for my flushed cheeks.

We sit in silence, picking at the food and drinking our tea. The urge to grab his tunic collar and pull him across the table into a kiss makes my heart beat faster. I'm definitely not feeling the chills he warned about.

I take a deep breath and hold it. I release it slowly. "Can I ask you a question? A personal one?"

"Sure, but I might not know how to answer." Those intense eyes again.

"Are you happy here? I mean, is this the life you always wanted? I remember when they chose you. I was so mad because you were the lucky one. I wanted them to take me." I don't ask if he cried.

He's not smiling when he answers. "It's a great honor to be chosen." He turns his attention to his food.

Why did I ask something so personal? I don't know this man. Don't know what his life has been like since the day he was taken from his home as a little guy.

"Of course. I'm so sorry, I don't mean to pry, but can you blame me for wanting to know more about being a Swimmer? Am I being ridiculous? Am I making a mistake in thinking this is what I'm supposed to do?"

"I don't know. I can't answer that for you. I didn't have a choice. This is the only life I know. My parents disappeared after they offered me as novice—it's like they never existed."

"Oh! I didn't know." I suppress an urge to hug him. I was just a five-year-old child when he was chosen and believed—as most children do—the planet revolved around me. I never even wondered about his family.

"It's okay. There's no reason you should have known. And yes. I'm content with this life as a Swimmer. Sebastian and Joshua—" he hangs his head. "They were my family."

We sit in silence until I make a decision. "I guess I owe it to my family to tell them I'll be joining you. My mom won't be surprised, and my sister will hate me for a while, but I'll be back soon, even if it's just to return this stunning outfit."

He grins and walks me to the door, where I think he might kiss me. Think he *should* kiss me. I hesitate there, staring not so subtly at his full lips, feeling a pull in my abdomen. I lean toward him when the bedroom door opens.

"Spend some time with your family, Ing." Sebastian appears disheveled, his eyes mere slits. "There is no need to rush back. Consider carefully what you must do."

Aiden backs away from me slowly, his hands folded in front of him. Without responding—because what more can I say?—I leave.

I practically run home, happy not to see another person, and stop at our front door, breathless. It's nearly time for me to help my mother greet the day, but then I remember her transformation yesterday. Has it been only one night since I left her at the shore? I enter the house quietly and tiptoe to her room. Still asleep. Tulip's asleep too. I climb into my bed.

———— ❧ ————

I wake to wonder again where I am.

Tulip isn't in bed. Hushed voices from the kitchen tell me where she is.

"I'm awake," I call, and Tulip runs into the room and jumps onto me. "Ouch! Get off me, you big goof. I told you I'd be back."

"Well? Tell me everything! No, wait, come out and tell us both. What are you wearing? Never mind. Come on out. Lunch is ready." She flits from the room.

Her enthusiasm jars me. Our father just died, and although we're taught to carry on without grief after a Farewell, Daddy's little girl could express some degree of restraint. Maybe she's putting on an act for me. Probably more for Mom.

I stretch, feel for the coin on my chest—still there—scratch my head through a tangled mop, and pull out a strip of seaweed in the process. How Aiden managed not to laugh out loud is beyond me. I shuffle to the kitchen to see Mom and Tulip seated at the table. Mom appears to have put on weight overnight, and she greets me with a genuine smile.

"I didn't expect you back so soon." Her comment hurts. Am I suddenly a burden?

"Thanks, Tulip. This looks yummy." Tulip passes me veggies and a mash of grains. "And Mom, you look great. How are you feeling after—" I don't want to say "after Dad's death," so I stop.

"Oh, you know. We'll think of him often, and that's okay." She sips a warm broth—from her China teacup. She's never used it before.

"So?" Tulip raises both eyebrows and leans toward me.

"Let your sister eat first, Tulip. She must be exhausted from her participation yesterday."

I shovel in a heap of vegetables and enjoy their crunch. "So, I was honored to help with Dad's Farewell."

"But what did you do? What was it like? What happens out there? What happened to the Elder Swimmer? And where did you sleep last night?" Tulip doesn't touch her food. She eye's me mischievously.

I won't tell them everything I saw out at sea since I have no answers, but I have to tell them something. "Well, we did just like the stories say. I followed them out really far to a place close to where Dad would be returned to the cycle, and that's when something happened to the Elder. He just . . . died. So I helped swim him out too, and then we released them both. It was simple, really, but they were glad I was there. Swimming while keeping another afloat is really hard."

Tulip scrunches her nose. "And you spent the night where?" She smirks. Won't let it go.

"In the Elder's room. It's not much different from our room, really. But Mom?"

"Yes, dear?" She sets down her teacup.

"I need to show you both something." Mom won't see what I'm about to do, but I'll explain.

"You both know I've always wanted to be a Swimmer." I ignore Tulip's eye roll. "And when I got to the Swimmers' home, something happened."

"What happened?" Tulip asks.

I pluck the coin from my chest and release it in front of her. Instead of falling to the floor, it floats back to my chest and sticks there.

Tulip's mouth hangs open. "What the . . . How'd you do that?"

"I didn't *do* anything. The coin attaches itself to me, to a place on my chest. I'm supposed to be a Swimmer."

"It makes me feel really good, like it belongs to me, or like I belong to it. I know that sounds crazy, but Mom, do you know if this ever happened with Dad?"

Mom bows her head for a while, and I wait. Finally, she turns toward me. "After you were born, your father was polishing it, something he'd do on occasion, though I never noticed it tarnish. I sat with him, rocking you to sleep. When he finished, he put the coin on the table, but it didn't stay there long." She pauses, rocking forward and backward almost imperceptibly, as if reliving the moment she describes. Tulip looks at me quizzically, and I shrug. "It slid across the table and came to rest on you just where you say it rests now." She frowns. "It never reacted that way to your father." Tulip paces between the table and the sitting area.

"Why am I just hearing about this? Why didn't he give it to me sooner? They could have chosen me instead of Aiden."

Tulip stops. "Who's Aiden?"

"He's the novice. Well, he's not a novice anymore." I forgot no one calls the Swimmers by name. They're always just the Swimmers.

"Don't blame your father. It was me. I couldn't bear to lose you. I never dreamed we'd have another child, and by the time Tulip was born, well, I just felt like the luckiest gal in the world. Two beautiful daughters who'd grow and play together and someday bring new life to this dreary world. I made your father promise to keep the coin hidden in the back of that drawer. I wanted him to dispose of it, really, but he wouldn't."

"Then, it's true. I'm the one who's supposed to carry on the tradition." If any of my foremothers had experienced a connection with the coin, they made the decision to keep it quiet.

"Or not." Tulip throws her hands up before resting them on her hips. "How do you know you're the only one it does that to? Maybe it's just some weird reaction to your . . . I don't know, something in your blood or something you eat that no one else eats. What about me?" She grabs the coin from me and places it on her chest, but it falls. I pick it up and place it back on my chest.

Tulip is quiet. Her chin quivers.

"Oh, kiddo," I wrap my arms around her, "I won't be far away. You'll always know where I am, and when you come to the home, you'll see. You'll see I belong there."

"But you won't be *here*. Who's going to giggle at my nighttime toots and say 'gobbleyou' when I sneeze?" She forces a chuckle through her tears—she never bought the "we don't cry" warning—and I laugh with her, but I don't answer. I stop myself from suggesting Mom might fill that role. It's time for my little sister to grow up.

"Does it hurt?" She pushes me back a step, all in control again, and points to the coin.

"No. It's hard to explain, though. It feels like it's always been a part of me."

"Good thing it's pretty," she says. "I wonder what the design means. Or maybe it doesn't mean anything."

"I wonder about that too. When I look at it closely, the rings on it—" I jump when my coin delivers a little jolt of energy.

"What's wrong? What happened?" Tulip grabs my shoulders and looks at the coin. "It's glowing. Take it off! Can you take it off?" She reaches for it but draws her hand back quickly. "Hot! Is it burning you?"

"No, I'm fine, really." I'm not sure, but I get the message I'm not supposed to talking about how when I study it, the rings swirl and appear to create a whirling tunnel. It makes no sense. "Listen, I'm going back to them later today. I know I'm making the right decision to be a Swimmer. It's like something's calling me." It's time to change the subject. "And it's not like I'm about to disappear from the face of the earth."

Tulip shakes her head.

"You should stay." She states it as a fact. "And I've never said this to you before, but I think it's time you committed to a mate. I bet they'd let you be with Javier." She looks at the floor, avoiding my eyes.

"Oh, really? You think it's time?" I pull one of her curls, and not playfully.

"Ouch! Quit it! I mean it. Things can be better for us now, right, Mom?" One eyebrow up.

"Better with only three of us now?" I shouldn't have said it, but it's true. One less mouth to feed, body to clean, failing mind to worry about.

"Wow, Ing. Really?" Tulip tilts her head toward our mom, who's been silent through our spat.

"Sorry, Mom, that was awful of me. I didn't mean—"

"No need to explain, dear. But do at least consider what your sister is suggesting."

"Yeah, and why do you suddenly want to leave so badly? Is it because of that hot novice?"

My face flushes. "No. Well, not directly because of him, and it's not so sudden. He's not a novice anymore, which means they need someone to fill that role, and it's something *I'm* supposed to do, not some possible boy child I might have someday."

Mom closes her eyes with an expression that tells me she knows I've made up my mind. I hate that I've made her sad.

Tulip is relentless. "But you're a girl, and let's face it. You're old. Novices are always children."

"Just because that's the way it's always been here doesn't mean it always has to stay that way. There's no law about it, is there?" I know of no written laws. The floods destroyed most books, papers, and records.

"No, but maybe it doesn't always have to be three, then. With your logic, just because they've always had a novice doesn't mean it has to stay that way. They can continue just fine with two." Her snarkiness encourages me. She'll be okay.

"You're right. They won't have to call me a novice because I'm already trained, and I've already completed my first Farewell."

"What-ever," she says. "You know I love you, but don't expect me to be happy about this."

———— ⟡ ————

After we clean up, Tulip says, "I'm going to the garden. I guess I'll see you when I see you, brat."

"*You're* a brat," I say, pulling her into a hug. She resists only briefly before melting against me, holding on to me as if she might never again, and then she leaves me with our mother.

"Mom, what if I'm making a mistake?" I don't want to give her a chance to tell me I should stay, but I don't think she will.

"You'll figure it out, dear." Her gentle hands reach for mine.

"How can you be so sure?"

"Mothers have a way of knowing things." Her serene smile calms me. Her misty eyes focus on a place no one can see.

"I'm leaving soon," I say.

"I know."

"But am I being selfish?"

She doesn't respond immediately. I hold my breath for her response.

"We make decisions based on what we've learned and what we believe. This doesn't mean things will always turn out the way we expect. We learn things from the decisions we make. You will learn things from this decision. And no. You're not being selfish."

"I love you, Mom."

"I know, dear girl. I love you too." She pulls me close and kisses my forehead.

I don't know what to take from my meager possessions, finally deciding on one change of clothes. I work through my tangles one final time with the comb I share with Tulip, then I cut off as much as I can, as close to my scalp as possible with scissors my father kept sharpened over the years. Who will keep it sharp now?

I feel weird and wonderful, light and free and ready to commit to a new life I—and the coin on my chest—believe is my destiny.

"Can I do anything for you before I leave, Mom?"

"Yes, dear. Promise me you'll take care of your sister when I'm gone."

"Oh, but you're not going anywhere soon." I stroke her soft cheek. "As for Tulip, you said it yourself. She's probably more capable than me. I'm off now." I don't make the promise.

———— ❧ ————

I run to the Swimmers' home, my new home, anxious for whatever indoctrination they'll put me through, and excited to see Aiden again. My stomach flutters at the doorway. Should I knock or just walk in? There's so much I don't know about Swimmer rules. I knock while opening the door.

"It's me. I'm back." I step into the dimly lit interior and see Sebastian and Aiden at the table. Aiden jumps up and meets me at the door. He looks at my hair and smiles. *Ooo, that mouth.*

Sebastian stays seated. "You're back soon. You were supposed to take time to help your mother adjust, and to question your reasons for returning."

"I did. My mother is fine. She and Tulip know that this is the life I want. I thought it was obvious from what happened with my coin that this is my calling." I speak forcefully, looking at Aiden for support, but he doesn't meet my gaze.

"Nothing is obvious in our world, Ing." The Elder stands and approaches me, his eyes scrutinizing. "What have you done to your beautiful hair?"

Self-consciously, I raise my hand to my head and feel like a fool. "It's a burden. I've wanted it gone for a long time, and as a Swimmer—"

"Do not presume so much," he says. "We have been offered a novice, a child of appropriate age and—"

"No! I inherited this coin from an original Swimmer in my bloodline." I place a protective hand over the coin beneath my shirt. The atmosphere in the solemn room isn't so peaceful anymore.

Sebastian draws back as if I've threatened physical harm. If he sees me as a threat, he shouldn't. I have no intention of overriding his authority as the Elder. But he's seriously pushing all my wrong buttons right now.

I sense he's withholding information and trying to keep me from being a Swimmer, but why? Does something about my coin scare him?

The Elder shakes his head and frowns. "Oh, but you vex me, girl. You must excuse me now as I have business to attend to. Aiden? You know what is expected." With that curious statement, he leaves the house.

Something in Sebastian's tone chills me.

"What did he mean by that?"

Left alone in the living area with Aiden, my mind races, and my body screams for release. Nothing is happening the way I want. I'm not about to return home bald and rebuked. When Aiden approaches me, stopping close, so close, his soft words tickle the skin on my neck.

"I'm sorry. Sebastian convinced me you'd change your mind, and with the offer of a novice, I was supposed to tell you and—"

I can't help it. I stop his speech with my lips and pull my body against his. His response is more than I could have imagined, more than I've dreamt. He devours my lips as if starved and, lifting me off my feet, shuffles toward the door.

I stifle a moan and realize, as he probably has, we need to get out of the tiny house. Who knows when Sebastian will return?

He lets me go only long enough to escape into the sunlight—*is there no place to hide?*—and we race into the trees beyond the house.

"I've never—"

"Me neither," I say.

We stare into one another's eyes. I sense a question in his, but I'm ready to give this man everything.

He watches me undress, his face serious, his breathing rapid. I stand naked before him, a person different from the girl who did what none other has. I'm claiming my right to be a Swimmer. My coin glows between my breasts and sends tingles throughout my body. I don't remove it.

He tears off his loose garments. My breath catches. We rush toward one another, drawn together by an unseen force. My body, slick with desire, craves his.

He has me on the crumpled leaves before I can take another breath. "Yes?" he asks.

"Yes! Please, yes!"

As natural as my coin feels bound to me, my attraction to Aiden feels no less magical.

The release from our coupling leaves us breathless. There's no embarrassment, no apologies, no turning away from the other. Our need was immediate and explosive and so, damn, right.

He keeps his arms around me and trembles, and in this moment of perfect physical satisfaction, I know there's no turning back. We lie together, our limbs entwined, our lips a breath apart. We fall asleep like this.

I wake first. It's time. I kiss him once more and sit.

"Aiden—"

"Yes?" he sits too. "Are you okay? Did I—"

"No! I'm fine, more than fine. Hey, this is going to sound crazy, but there's something I need to do."

"Again? I'm ready if you are. I—"

"No, no, I mean, wow! I have to go out there." I point toward the sea. "I have to know what that thing is. Sebastian's hiding something. Do you know what that funnel thing is?"

He shakes his head. "He said he'll tell me when I'm ready to know."

"But you're not a novice anymore. You should know everything about what you're doing." My coin glows again, as if in agreement. "I'm supposed to know, too."

He touches my coin while gazing into my eyes, and I pull him on top of me again. If there's a heaven, it's here.

"Okay." His voice, deep and sexy, stirs something inside me. "I'll do whatever you ask." He stokes my ridiculous hair, pulls away from me, and stands. "Let's go."

6

AIDEN'S EYES SPARKLE. He hands me my clothes, and we dress. There's a strong chance we'll pass villagers on our way.

"Are you sure?" I'm suddenly not.

He takes my hand and leads me at a brisk pace toward the sea.

"Yes. I think you're right. Sebastian's been less communicative lately, and not just since Joshua died. They've both been nervous about something. I heard them whispering before we went to your home. It's not right they wouldn't tell me."

We break into a run. The glittering water invites us in. At the shoreline, we ditch our clothes.

I place a hand on his chiseled chest. "Maybe you shouldn't come with me. Maybe you should cover for me until I know more. This is something I have to do, but you—"

He shakes his head with raised brows and a scrumptious smile.

Then, an inexplicable ache seizes my heart along with a frantic feeling that if I don't run into the ocean right now, all might be lost. The irrational fear drives me to turn away from Aiden and launch into the buoyant surf.

"I'm with you." Aiden catches up to me in three strokes.

———— ❧ ————

I've never felt more alive. All doubts vanish in the brisk sea water as Aiden and I match stroke for stroke away from the shore. Something, someone, has to be down there controlling the funnel. We're going to get answers.

I turn when Aiden stops to tread water. "I've never been out this far without—"

"A body," I finish when he hesitates. An unusual stillness as far as I can see across the ocean raises hairs on the back of my neck. The wind that blew our discarded clothes down the beach is eerily absent, like it was during my father's Farewell. The extreme salinity of the water makes it easy to stay afloat.

But something feels wrong.

Aiden feels it, too. "What if it doesn't appear? I mean, we only come out this far after a Farewell chant, and with an offering."

An offering. As if a dead body would somehow appease the gods many still believe in. Aiden sounds uneasy. How will we make the funnel appear?

"The chant," I say. It took over my whole being when I joined the Swimmers in its repetition over my father's body. "Do you think it, or they, or whatever's down there can hear it somehow and be ready for when you show up?"

"I don't know, but that could explain it. We're always so far away, though."

"My dad used to tell me sound travels really far over water. Not sure how he knew, but if he's right, then—" Then what? The funnel rose from below the surface. Dad never said anything about sound waves underwater.

"Let's try it." Aiden reaches for me, and we hold hands. The glow from my coin illuminates the water between and far below us. We glance down to see enormous, slow-moving shadows undulating toward and away from us.

I don't know whether to panic-giggle or scream.

Aiden's eyes light up, and he starts, softly. "Ahhhveyy-yahhh, ahhhveyyyahhh . . ."

I join him, and we continue the chant, louder with each repetition. We do this for several minutes, waiting in anticipation. But nothing happens.

"Well," I say, "it takes you a while after a Farewell chant to deliver the offering, right?" The body. Swimmers deliver bodies to that thing.

"Yes. Maybe we just need to wait longer. Come closer." He draws my body to his, and the ache isn't in my heart anymore. We tremble, but not because either of us is cold.

"Aiden—"

And then it happens. The nightmare from my dream. I sense it before I see it, an enormous swell rising from far out at sea and rolling toward us quickly, gaining height as it approaches.

"No-no-no!" I push away from him and point toward the eerie stillness filling the dwindling space between us and the monstrous wave.

Aiden glances between the tidal wave and me, and his expression turns sorrowful. No way either of us can avoid the approaching danger.

"You're faster than me," I scream. The wind whips up in a fury and its roar deafens me. "Go! I'll be right behind you." He shakes his head and swims back to me. He holds me tight and kisses me as the wave pulls at us.

Maybe it will lift us up and over it, like the small swells did near shore when Dad taught me how to swim. Or maybe we'll duck beneath it until it passes over. I can hold my breath for a long time—I've practiced doing it unconsciously for years. I don't know about Aiden.

We watch it with squinted eyes as wind whips water into our faces. A wall of darkness wrenches me from Aiden's arms.

"Aiden!" I scream, but I can't see him in the sudden storm. Can't outswim it. In a matter of seconds, I'll live or die. A white streak glows across the top of the wave—its crest. No hope of floating over its top, either.

Before it crashes on top of me with a force too powerful for my small body, I hold my breath and swim downward, thinking, hoping there will be calm water below the monster wave. That I'll rise to find a calm sea with Aiden swimming toward me.

The water below the wave churns and buffets me. Things—dense things, big things—bump me. With my lungs screaming for air, I struggle to get to the surface, only to realize I have no sense of which direction is up. Panicking, frantic, out of options, out of oxygen, my head heavy and dizzy, I make myself relax, wanting to believe I'll naturally—eventually—float to the surface.

But something cold and hard slams into me, knocking the air from my lungs. My eyes open wide as a flash of dread fills me when I inhale the salty seawater—and then, all goes black.

———— ❧ ————

Cold. Strapped to something cold and hard. A muted rhythmic sound, *thrum, thrum, thrum*, like a sleeping monster. My muscles ache. When I open my eyes, the brightness makes me wince. I try to sit up but can't lift my head.

Aiden! I try shouting his name. Can't form the word. Something's sticking out of my mouth and nose. I struggle and gag.

This has to be a dream. A nightmare.

"Relax, new cadet, or I'll have to sedate you." A tall, thin, sickly-looking woman leans over me and places her hands on my blanketed shoulders, pressing them back against the hard surface. Her pale blue uniform, tight around her body, emphasizes her angular frame.

New cadet? Where the hell am I? Am I in Hell? I learned about that myth as a youngster, but never believed it was a real place.

I do my best to calm myself but can't stop gagging.

"Glad to see you're awake. I'm going to remove this now, so do your best to relax. Ready?"

Without waiting for my response, which she must know I can't give, she eases long tubes from my nose first. My eyes water, and I want to sneeze, but my stomach lurches as she withdraws the tube from my throat. I think I might pass out. *This must be Hell.*

Finally, she removes a rubbery block from between my teeth. My jaw throbs. My throat stings.

"Aiden," I croak. I don't recognize my voice. "Where is he?"

"I don't know who you're talking about, new cadet, and you will address me and every other officer you will encounter in Ironhold as *sir*. 'Where is he, sir.' Do you understand?"

I do not understand. The expression on my face must tell her so.

"Answer me, new cadet. Do you understand?" Her hand reaches for some sort of lever.

I glance around the stark room. Dull gray walls, they look metallic, and a row of machines with blinking lights and wires. Pretty sure some of those wires are attached to me. Something in the air stings my nose.

"Where am I? Why am I strapped down? Let me up. Please let me up." A jolt buzzes through my body, and searing pain makes me cry out. "What the—"

"They said you'd be a smart one, new cadet. The smart ones learn quickly. Will you prove them wrong?" My tormentor smiles at me. It doesn't show in her cold eyes. Her manic expression shocks me more than the jolt she must have delivered.

"Please, please let me up from this table, sir." If all I have to do for my freedom is add a *sir* to every sentence, that'll be easy enough.

"In time, new cadet. In time." She turns and leaves me alone in the claustrophobic room, unable to move, nauseous— yet hungry. Wondering where on earth I am.

And if Aiden survived the tsunami.

Thrum, thrum, thrum.

The skeletal sir must have done something to put me to sleep before she left because my head feels heavy and I can't open my eyes. Voices murmur nearby.

"What have you done?"

"You weren't supposed to hurt her."

"Oh, Helga, you've marked her already? What were you thinking? He's not going to be happy about that."

Slowly, I try to lift my hands. Still secured to the surface.

"Shhh! She's waking up."

I force myself to open my eyelids. Several people stare at me. My stomach growls loud enough for them all to hear. One of the uniforms, way older than me, speaks. I hold my breath.

"I am Armand, Level Tango. You are new cadet Ing, Level Alpha. Do you understand?"

Again with the "new cadet." My mother started to call me that the day my father died. She blamed it on a dream. I must be dreaming. I hope I'm dreaming.

A tiny letter T glows between Armand's eyebrows. Weird.

"I said, do you understand?"

How many times will they ask me that stupid question before they'll free me from these restraints? I want to scream. Demand they call me my regular old boring name. I remember the jolt and hold my tongue.

This is no dream. I still don't understand, but I know what they want to hear. I can play their little game.

"Yes—yes, sir." A flicker of a grin on Armand's face.

"Good. We're going to let you up now, slowly. You've been under for several days and—"

"What?" I blurt. Can't help it. "I mean, excuse me, sir, but where am I, and how did I get here, and do you know what happened to my friend Aiden, sir?" An extra one can't hurt.

He motions to one of the others, and pressure from the straps loosens. I bolt upright and immediately regret it.

Thrum, thrum, thrum. What is that head-aching noise?

"At ease, new cadet. Not so fast." The officer catches me before my head smacks the table. He eases me back down. "It'll take you a while to adjust. As for your other questions, we rescued you from the tidal surge. You're in Ironhold. As for this Aiden you mention," he glances away as if trying to come up with a story, "we know of no one by that name."

Ironhold means nothing to me. How could there be another undiscovered village that survived the Halt? Our explorers have returned from days of travel with no news of other survivors.

In a frantic moment of panic, I reach for the coin on my chest. Gone.

"My coin. Where's my coin?"

Searing pain.

The jolt must have knocked me out because I wake restrained and alone again. At least they kept me covered. I scan the room again. Walls, ceiling, door, one small cabinet, machines, dull gray metal all around. The bizarre sound of the place or some . . . *thing* thrumming. Breathing? I'm scared.

Where am I? How did I end up here?

The door opens, and a girl about my age peeks into the room. She looks strong. Chiseled shoulders and arms, muscular legs. She could probably throw me over her shoulder and carry me away. Her long-lashed brown eyes hint at mischief, which immediately puts me at eases. She reminds me of Tulip. She puts a finger to her lips. After glancing to either side, she slips into the room and eases the door shut behind her.

"Hi! I'm new cadet Dez, Level Alpha. Don't be afraid." She slides over to me, moving like ripples on water. "Cool eyes! Green and blue, like grass and the ocean." She stares at me like I'm a puzzle she needs to solve. I'm the only one in my village with two different colored eyes, but no one ever makes a big deal about it. "What happened to your hair? Someone trap you in barbed wire?"

My chuckle comes out as a snort. We both laugh. My throat still stings.

"Long story, new cadet Dez, Level Alpha. Can I just call you Dez?"

"Sure, but only when the uniforms aren't around. What's your name?"

"It's Ing. What's a new cadet, and can you get me out of here?"

"Oh, wow, you really did come from somewhere else. I can't stay long," she glances at the door, "but save your questions for later, okay?"

"How'd you find me? Are you in trouble too?"

"Listen, I just want to tell you not to be scared, and for the love of your crazy hair, stop asking questions and don't give them any other reason to keep you here. The shocks will get worse if you do. Trust me, I know."

So I'm not the only one who's been mistreated in this bizarre place. A jagged streak of discolored skin spans from her left temple to just below her ear. Her spiky ebony hair, cropped close but not as ragged as mine, makes it easy to see.

"Here, take this. You must be starving. Either that or you're hiding an angry sea monster in your gut."

I want to laugh again but my throat tightens. The last time I laughed was with Tulip. Dez reminds me how much I suddenly miss being with my snarky little sister, but I have no energy to dwell on the thought. Dez tears off the top of a shiny packet and puts the opening in my mouth.

"It's gooey and gross, but it'll quiet the monster." She squeezes the stuff into my mouth. It tastes vaguely fruity and suppresses the pain in my stomach.

"Thanks, Dez. You better go. I don't know when they'll come back, and I don't want you to get into trouble because of me."

"Don't you worry about me. Just do what they say, keep your mouth shut, and you'll be with the rest of us soon."

"The rest? How many people live here, and where, exactly, is here? How'd you get here? Did you have—"

"Girrrl? Wha'd I tell you about all those questions!"

I want to ask if she has a special coin, or if they all do. I have nothing but questions.

"Zip it until I see you again, hopefully without all those straps." She leaves as stealthily as she entered. Although my partially satisfied stomach tells me I should close my eyes and sleep, my mind races.

Tidal surge. They rescued me from a tidal surge. My heart skips a beat when I think of Aiden and our village. The wave broke directly over my head and forced me to dive below the surface. Maybe that reduced its intensity by the time it reached shore or maybe it created other monstrous waves. There's no way to know. Dez made it clear I shouldn't be asking questions.

I don't know how long I'll be strapped on the damn, hard table. I don't know if it's day or night. No windows in this space. A dull glow from a place I can't see casts a dreary light on the cold gray surrounding me.

Finally, the door opens again. It's the cruel nurse.

"Did you have a good little rest, new cadet?"

I hate her.

"Yes, sir." Just answer her. Just tell her what she wants to hear. Nothing more.

"Aren't you the good new cadet." She sneers, staring at me for too long.

It takes everything in my power not to break the silence. She's testing me, waiting for me to say something stupid or give her a reason to jolt me. I'm in no mood to play games, so I close my eyes.

"Don't you close your eyes when I'm talking to you, new cadet!" Spittle splatters on my face. I cringe. She sees it. "Scared? Do I scare you, new cadet?"

How to answer? If I say no, she might interpret it as defiance. If I say yes, she could take it as an insult. I can't win.

Think!

"I'm sorry, sir, I must be jumpy from the wave. That's what scared me, sir, my memory of being crushed by it." Did I say too much?

Her face softens, if that's possible. "Well. I'm to take you to your quarters. You'll be given a cot and a wash kit. You're not to make a sound. It's been lights out for quite some time now, and if you wake the other cadets, there will be consequences. Do you understand, new cadet?"

No. Not really. "Yes, sir." Exhaustion and another wave of hunger grip me, but I force a smile. I don't care where she takes me as long as I get out of here. Here. A cold place far more advanced than our village.

"Are you *happy* right now, new cadet?"

Another trick question. It has to be. My brain hurts. I need the right response, one that won't provoke another jolt and more time on the slab of metal.

"Tired, sir. I won't make a sound tonight."

She considers my answer with her hands folded primly in front of her chest before finally moving to loosen my restraints. I briefly consider leaping from the table and throttling her. Then I'll find Dez and the two of us will escape from this place, wherever this place is. But I don't know how many other people like the nurse roam around here.

And I'm so, damn, tired.

She tosses a robe at me, and I put it on before sliding off the table. The cold floor prickles my feet.

"Follow me, and not a sound." The wicked woman spins away from me and rushes out the door.

I follow her down a long hallway—everything dimly lit and gray—and around several corners before she stops in front of a door. She opens it slowly, then grabs my arm and leads me to a bed. "You're a lucky one, new cadet Ing."

Where the flood am I, and how does she know my name?

7

A DEAFENING SOUND jolts me from a dead sleep and continues, nonstop, over an aggressively loud voice.

"All new cadets form for physical training. Uniform, as for P.T. with headgear. All new cadets form for physical training. Uniform, as for P.T. with headgear. All new cadets form for physical training. Uniform, as for P.T. with headgear."

"Move it, newbie." A guy from the other side of the room runs over and kicks my bed's metal frame. "Gear's in that box. Hurry up or we'll all be in trouble."

Where am I? What's happening? Strangers all around me strip and dress and tuck blankets around their thin mattresses, all in the same bizarre way. I struggle to focus my eyes in the near darkness. And that noise. When will it stop?

"Reveille, Ing. Here, let me help you."

Dez. She pushes through the scrambling bodies and fixes up my bed while I pull on the same clothes as the others—shorts, a shirt, socks, boots, and a strange strappy contraption that fits snuggly around my head, cheeks, and chin—all gray.

Somehow, everything fits. Everyone rushes about like ants after someone kicks their hill. The infernal noise keeps blaring, three harsh notes over and over and over.

Whatever reveille is, I hate it.

"Way to suck up to the newbie, Dez. Wouldn't get too attached if I was you. Stray dogs don't last long here." The bed kicker snickers. Several others around him join in.

"Ignore him," Dez whispers. "Lou's an asshole, but he's Armand's son, so be careful."

The Level Tango officer didn't seem so bad, but what do I know? I don't even know where I am.

A door at the end of the long room opens and someone announces, "Inspection!" Everyone runs to the foot of their cots. They stand rigidly, facing inward, like statues. I do the same. The obnoxious noise finally stops. My ears ring in the sudden silence.

Not a peep. Not a shuffle. Nothing happens. I almost giggle at how silly we must look. And then, another voice shouts, "The mission of the United Survivors Military Academy." I flinch when a chorus of voices chant these words:

> The mission of the United Survivors Military Academy is to educate, motivate, and activate the Corps of Cadets so that each successful recruit shall have the intellectual aptitude, the personal incentive, and the soldierly qualities necessary for a lifelong career dedicated to the protection of planet Earth against all enemies, alien or native.

I stand mute and confused. It finally hits me. I've been abducted and enrolled into a military academy. Could this be the same academy my distant forefather attended? And if so, what the flood am I doing here?

Just breathe. Don't panic, just breathe. You'll figure this out later. It'll all be fine. And then you can go home. The words I tell myself sound lame. Sweat rolls from my pits and down my back.

Militaries are things of the past. What use are they on a planet where the few people who've survived have nothing? But these people, these uniformed individuals who somehow rescued me from drowning, they're living in a place with things I didn't think existed anymore. Metal enclosures. Eerie lighting. Food in tubes. Clean clothes. Whatever the hell that thrumming noise is. And except for the evil nurse, generally healthy people.

My head spins and I fall backward. Thankfully, the bed breaks my fall. If only I blacked out completely.

"What is the meaning of this commotion?" A voice, male, booms from the doorway.

"It's the new cadet, sir." Lou glares at me as I push myself up at the end of my cot. Then he smirks.

"Permission to speak, sir." Dez. My hero.

"Granted."

By the time the inspecting officer gets to me, I can stand again with wobbly knees. Dez stands a few beds down from me.

"New cadet Ing just showed up this morning, sir. Must've been processed after lights out. This is her day one, sir."

The officer's face is barely a fist's distance from mine. I don't know whether to look him in the eye or not. I have a feeling he'd win a staring contest, so I lower my eyes.

"Chin up, new cadet. Shoulders down, neck back. And look at me when I'm talking to you. Do you understand, new cadet?"

Wow. Again with the understanding.

"Yes, sir." I try to obey, but dizziness sweeps over me again and my knees buckle. I sway, willing myself not to tumble over. The officer's brow furrows. He studies me up and down, and then he sniffs me.

What the flood?

"New cadet Dez, take new cadet Ing to sick call."

"Yes, sir."

As Dez walks toward me, the bully across from me says, "Permission to speak, sir."

"What is it, new cadet Lou?"

Dez stops next to the officer and glances at me with a glimmer in her eyes. I stifle a smile. Wouldn't go over well with the officer, who's still in front of me. I will my knees to keep me standing.

"Sir, new cadet Dez made up the new cadet's cot at reveille." Lou's accusatory tone makes my nostrils flare. They call these beds cots.

So this is how it's going to be with the asshole across the aisle. *It's okay*, I tell myself. I'll be gone soon. Maybe Dez will come with me. My village can't be that far away. The idea still makes me wonder how we've never found this place.

"Take her now, new cadet Dez." The officer does a slick thing with his feet that spins him away from me. He approaches Lou. "New cadet Lou, what is the definition of slicken?"

"The definition of slicken, sir." Lou's voice sounds strained as Dez escorts me from the room. "Sir, when the crushed shells of a bird, cleaned and separated from all—"

I can't hear the rest once we leave the room, which we do quickly. I can barely keep up with Dez. Her walking pace is nearly a run.

"What was all that about? And hey, could you slow down, please? I just—"

"Zip it," she scolds, talking through her teeth. "Stay behind me, keep up, and don't say another thing."

I do what I'm told. When we pass a uniformed woman, Dez nods briskly and says, "Morning, sir." I do the same. We're just beyond the woman when she stops us.

"New cadets, halt. Shouldn't you be going to P.T. right now?" Her voice sounds like sunshine, something I suddenly miss.

Dez stops short, does a neat turnaround like the inspecting officer had done, and I nearly run her over. She puts her hands out to stop me, then turns me so I face the woman too.

"Sir, may I make a statement?"

Such a strange way of communicating.

"Yes, new cadet."

"Sir, I've been instructed to take this new cadet to sick call. She's not well, sir."

"All right, then. Be off with you. No dallying, and no detours. Understand?"

"Yes, sir." Dez spins around again, and I try to mimic the movement but trip myself in the process, landing hard on the floor.

"Shi—"

"Permission to assist the new cadet, sir." Dez covers my outburst. As she helps me to my feet, the woman smiles—a real smile—before quickly schooling her expression.

"You might want to give the new cadet some lessons on the about-face maneuver, Dez."

The woman knows my new buddy's name. Doesn't even call her new cadet. I wonder how she knows Dez. She seems like a decent person. I have a feeling there aren't too many like her in this bizarre place.

"I will, sir. Thank you, sir."

Off we go again, racing toward sick call. Happily, we don't run across—or into—anyone else along the twisting, turning hallways leading to a place that looks like the shock table room.

"I don't want to go in there," I whisper.

"Don't worry, kiddo. These are good people. They'll help you."

Kiddo. Another reminder of Tulip. I press a hand to my chest to ease a sudden pang.

"Hey! Hey, it's okay. We'll have time to talk later, all right? Let's get you checked out."

I skulk into the room behind her. A petit woman in a white coat greets us. She reminds me of my mother as a young woman. Over her right breast, a nameplate reads: Dr. Vesper.

"Thank you, Dez. You may return to P.T." She motions toward the door.

"No!" I blurt before I can think. "I mean, no, please, sir." Even though the doctor doesn't come across as a disciplinarian, I can't bear to be left again in another cold room.

"You may address me as *Doctor*, new cadet." She looks at Dez and nods for her to take a seat. She asks me to sit at the end of a padded table. No straps on this one. I take a deep breath. "So you're the one they resuscitated the other day."

"Yes, sir—ah—doctor."

"Let's take a peek. What brings you here?" She shines a light in my eyes and in my ears and thumps places on my elbows and knees. I almost kick her.

"I fainted, Doctor. And I just fell on the floor on my way here." I don't say it was because I tripped over my own feet, but Dez snickers.

"Fainted, eh? When was the last time you had anything to eat?"

I panic. *Don't get Dez in trouble. Don't tell her about the packet Dez snuck in for me when I was strapped to the table.* "I can't remember, doctor. They told me I was unconscious for days." *Play it safe.*

Her brows crease. "Why didn't they . . ." She doesn't finish. "I'm going to do some bloodwork. That will tell me where you might be deficient. You will spend tonight in the ward, and when I'm satisfied with your health, you will return to training."

Bloodwork, whatever that is. I trust her.

"Are you ready to release Dez back to training?" she asks me. She seems nice.

I look at Dez, and she nods.

"Yes, Doctor," I say.

"But before you come back, new cadet Ing," Dez says, "memorize the heritage pages in the back of this book. This is yours now. I'll get a replacement." From a back pocket, she pulls out a small book with a silver cover and the letters USMA stamped on it. She hands it to me.

USMA. It looks identical to the one I found in the Heaps with *Bugle Notes* stamped on the cover.

Dez must notice a look of amazement on my face because she asks, "What's up? Don't tell me no one's ever given you a book before."

I shrug. Don't say too much yet. I really don't know these people.

"All new cadets get these. It's part of our training. You already heard our mission. Memorize the definition of slicken next. See you soon, new cadet. Thank you, Doctor."

The door closes behind her and, for the first time since I swam away from my village, I believe I'm in a safe space.

———— ❧ ————

"Let's get your headgear off, shall we? Unless you think it might protect you from another fall." Doctor Vesper smirks, but not in a mean way.

I put the book next to me and yank the strappy thing off my head. The doctor looks amused. I've never seen myself other than in random pieces of shattered reflective debris we might salvage from the Heaps. How people dress and groom isn't that important at home. It seems to matter here.

Where is *here*?

"Doctor, permission to ask a question?" I assume that's how I'm supposed to talk here too. So many rules. Maybe the answers are in my little book. *My* book.

"You may speak freely here, Ing."

Kind of like when I confessed to my dead father, once I start talking, I can't stop. I have to know what's happening to me.

"I was with one of the Swimmers from my village. I knew there was something out in the ocean—the thing took my dead father and the Elder Swimmer—and it was my right to take my place as a Swimmer. I was born for it, I inherited it, and the coin showed me so." I note a flash of recognition in her eyes when I said the word coin. I should probably stop, but I can't. "And right before . . . right before the tidal wave, I don't know what happened to him. What happened to him? Where's Aiden? Where's my coin, and where, am, I?"

I tremble.

Doctor Vesper reaches out as if to comfort me but pulls her hand back fast. She stares at my chest with raised eyebrows, points, and takes a step back. I look down to see something shining from under my shirt.

She remains speechless as I pull the material away. It doesn't surprise me to see a glow where my coin should be. *How do I explain this?* She seems to know something about the coin. Maybe she knows where it is.

"May I?" She points again, and I pull the gray fabric down far enough for her to inspect. She's a doctor. We're supposed to trust doctors.

We have someone in our village we call Doctor, but her main function is to deliver the occasional baby and tend to the mother's recovery. Mothers don't always recover. Neither do the babies. Those have to be the most difficult Farewells.

"How long have you had this—" She doesn't know what to call it.

"It's where my coin should be. Do you know where it is?" I suddenly feel bold. "And would you please, please tell me where I am?"

She steps back again. I can tell she struggles to look away from the glow. With her hands on her hips, she says, "This is most unusual—"

"Doctor," a voice from an adjacent room startles us both. "Please, I need help."

"I'll be right back, Ing. Put on this robe. No need for a uniform in the clinic. Please stay here." She hurries to the other room.

I use the opportunity to see what I might find in the little book and in the room's drawers. I'm not leaving the clinic without answers.

My little book.

The original survivors built shelters in high places and carried what they could from their personal libraries. Our village holds a collection of different *Holy Bibles. The Complete Works of Shakespeare.* Darwin's *Origin of the Species. The Interpretation of Dreams* by Sigmund Freud. I've read that one a lot. George Orwell's *1984.* Lots of science and survival books.

Fun books, too, like Tolkien's *The Lord of the Rings* and one of my favorites, Stephen King's *Fairy Tale.* Maybe I'm in King's kind of alternate world. Sure feels like it. But I have no dog to save.

I suddenly miss my mother, my little sister . . . Aiden. I ache for his touch again, his skin against mine, his hungry lips—

Stop it. Are they searching for me?

Feeling antsy, caged, I pace the small room. I'm excited to explore my little book's pages, but I have to find anything useful in the room first. The persistent *thrum, thrum, thrum* gets on my nerves. Where are there doors to the outside? I crave the sound, the feel, the salty ocean scent in the eternally blasted wind. I hear no wind. It's unsettling.

What I find in drawers and cabinets doesn't help. More books and stuff only a doctor would know how to use. I hold up the robe but don't put it on.

When will Doctor Vesper return? The windowless walls feel like they're moving in on me. My head aches in the dim light, my heart pounds, my armpits reek.

And then, the voice makes me jump. **"CALM YOUR-SELF. YOU ARE STRONGER THAN YOU KNOW. YOU MUST BELIEVE THIS."**

"Where, who are you?" I whisper, but there's no answer. My eyes dart around the room, but I see no one. Just like at home. I'm losing it.

Close your eyes, I tell myself. *Breathe in. Hold it. Exhale slowly.* "Ahhhveyyyahh." The mantra calms me. I think about Aiden chanting with me. Since no one here seems to know who he is, I have to believe he survived the wave. I just have to. He'll find me.

And what then? We gave ourselves to one another in a moment of uninhibited desire, but I'm not about to give up on my goal of becoming a Swimmer. A Swimmer with sexy benefits, maybe.

I try not to think about Aiden, the brain-jarring voice, and my sanity. Time to focus on something else.

Plopping onto a stool, I open my book. *My* book.

On page one, *The Mission of the United Survivors Military Academy (USMA).* Apparently, I'm in a place that has a military academy. But that doesn't tell me where this place is.

I pinch myself again. Ouch. Not dreaming. Flooding shite.

Dez told me to find the definition of *slicken* near the end of the book. Turning the pages carefully, I'm excited by the people and places pictured. I can hardly imagine that world existed. Then I find the paragraph I'm supposed to memorize and repeat without error.

> *The Definition of Slicken:* When the crushed shells of bird eggs, cleaned and separated from all feathers, fat, and other extraneous material, are submersed in a concentrated solution of eel oil, a chemical combination ensues. The fragile husks of the shells bind with the membranous materials and are converted into a durable substance, impervious to liquids, flexible under pressure, and virtually impenetrable. This, sir, is slicken.

This might be one of my most challenging reading and memorizing tasks. It makes no sense. What the hell is it, and why would any of us have to repeat it? *Slicken* must be important.

"Ah, yes. Your new cadet Bible." The doctor enters the room while my back is turned, and I almost drop the book. Her sarcastic pronunciation of the word Bible makes me question its contents.

"Bible?" *Oh, no.* Is this a religious cult like Dad warned me about? Stories of cult leaders and their followers gave us nightmares as children. People in cults never seemed able to escape.

"Well, not really, but that's what they call it. It contains all the information you need to know to make it through your first phase successfully. Let's get that bloodwork, and then we're going to get some food into you. You'll spend the night here." We're done talking about my book. She glances again at my glow. "Does it hurt?"

"No, Doctor, but you haven't answered my questions yet. I know I'm not supposed to ask, but please."

She takes my arm, and after rubbing it with something cold, sticks a needle into it and pulls blood into a small tube. I watch, fascinated.

"What happened to Aiden? Where are your coin? Where are you? These are the answers you want."

"Yes. Please, yes." My heart races.

"I know nothing about this Aiden person. I can't tell you where your coin is—"

"Can't or won't?" My temper flares.

"Cannot. I don't know where it is. I only heard mention of it, but I would certainly like to know more, especially if I'm to help you get better."

"Then, will you tell me where we are and how I got here?"

"You're in Ironhold, a safe fortress under the sea. The method of your arrival here was most unusual. And that, Ing, is all I can say right now."

"Wait a minute." Dizziness and nausea compete to un-balance me. "A safe fortress under the sea? This place is . . . *under* . . . the sea? How did I . . . why am I . . ."

The doctor puts an arm around my shoulder and leads me toward a door.

"Come. There's a bed made up for you in the other room. You're exhausted. Things will make more sense to you once you get adjusted." She opens a door to a dark room and whis-pers, "Please don't provoke the other patients as one is in delicate condition. I should have your results in the morning, and we'll go from there. You can wash beyond that door."

On a small, dimly lit table next to a bed, a plate of food awaits. I don't care what's on it. I devour it all.

The doctor is right. I'm exhausted, and sweaty, and more than a little scared. This place is . . . underwater?

Don't panic.

I shuffle to the place she said I could wash. It's a bathroom like I've never seen before. Fancy metal levers and tubs and sinks attached to pipes in the walls and on the floor. Nothing like our primitive piping at home. I wash in water hot enough to burn. It doesn't seem possible.

I dry myself and climb into the most comfortable bed ever. But I'm afraid to fall asleep. Is this a trick? *Careful*, I tell myself. *Remember the stories about cults and how they lure you in.* The idea of an undersea village intrigues me, but it makes no sense. It also freaks me out. Will I wake up on the cold metal table again?

"You can leave, you know," someone to my right speaks. And then he chuckles.

8

THE OTHER PATIENTS aren't asleep. They laugh, but I don't think the joke is funny. It doesn't sound like a joke.

"Don't worry, newbie, it's not that bad here." The guy.

"Yeah. We're still alive." A girl. More laughter.

I'm not supposed to "provoke" them, but they seem excited to talk. "Why are you here?" I ask. I can barely make them out in the dimness. Are there windows somewhere down here with views of the sea? I long to feel sunshine again. I suppress a wave of anxiety.

"You mean here at USMA or here in the ward?" The boy.

"Both, I guess."

"You first," says the girl.

I understand the idea of giving before receiving. "The people here rescued me from a tidal surge. I was swimming too far out, and it caught me by surprise. I'd be dead right now if they didn't find me." My words surprise me. Why did they rescue me, and in a way so harshly? I don't know whether to feel grateful or angry.

"You were swimming? Why?" The boy has a deep voice.

"Yeah, why? Don't you know how dangerous the sea is?" The girl sounds uncomfortable.

The boy asks, "So you're here by accident?"

Huh. Am I here by accident? Are they? I want light in the room to see their expressions. "Well, kind of. I wanted to find out what was happening with the bodies, and I—"

"Bodies? What bodies?" the girl asks, sounding alarmed.

Oops. I figure Ironhold must be somewhere at the end of the funnel that rose to take my father and the Elder, but maybe I'm wrong. There could be lots of undersea communities, and I somehow tumbled into this one. She doesn't know about the dead bodies. Maybe I shouldn't be talking about dead bodies.

"The bodies of water. There are different ones, you know." They don't know. I'm making this shite up. "And I've been studying them." Maybe they know nothing about my home on land.

"Oh. I wonder if they'll let you go," says the girl.

"Shut up, Shayla."

Silence. Interesting. Would they let me go? Am I a prisoner?

My turn to ask. "So you're here because you want to be here? Not in this ward, I mean, but here at USMA?" I pronounced the letters like others do. *YoussMay.*

"Well, yeah." Shayla's soft voice. "It's this or cleaning out fish guts for the rest of my life."

"Or going deaf in the mechanical rooms or mucking out the barns every day. Gross." The boy.

"But how did you get here?" I ask.

"Wow, you really don't know anything about Ironhold." Mr. Snarky.

I wait. I know a lot about waiting.

"This is our home." Shayla won't be shushed. "We're all born here."

Whoa. Not sure why it surprises me.

"What's it like up there?" The boy sounds genuinely curious. No more snark.

"Up there? You mean on land?" Have they never been on land before? Have they never seen the sun or felt its heat? Have they never been blown over by a gust of wind or felt the gentle give of a footfall on a forest floor after a rain? Have they never felt rain?

"Yes," Shayla answers. "They tell us land is a horrible, dangerous place. Is it?"

Don't provoke the other patients. The combination of fear, food, a hot shower, and a soft bed sucks every bit of energy from me. If I start to answer their questions, I'll be up all night. If they've never experienced life on land, they'll be as curious as I am about their lives. I'm not sure I should tell them anything.

"I guess every place has its dangers," I dodge. "You said the sea was dangerous. But hey, thanks for talking to me. I'm exhausted, and the doctor said I need to sleep. Maybe we can talk more in the morning?"

"If we're still here." The boy.

I wonder what his deal is. Maybe he's just an asshole like Lou. As much as I want more answers about this place, I'm struggling to keep my eyes open.

"Good night, Ing. I hope you're feeling better in the morning."

"Thanks, Shayla." I collapse under the covers and notice the glow is gone. Maybe it's worn out too. But the loud one has to have the final word.

"Can't trust everything the doctor says. Not like she's a god." He lets out a long sigh and thrashes about before settling.

A god? Does this clearly advanced civilization believe in gods? My head spins.

———— ❧ ————

Reveille wakes me before I realize I've even been asleep. I jump from the bed, searching wildly for my exercise clothes. Isn't that what I'm supposed to do? And then, laughter. This time more genuine.

"Chill out, newbie. No P.T. for us sickies."

I glance at the bed with the loud voice and catch my breath when I see the boy has only one full leg, the other one heavily bandaged at the knee.

"No biggie. They're making me a prosthetic." When he sees the question in my eyes, he explains what that is. "It'll take a while, but I'll be faster than you once I figure it out."

I scold myself for thinking poorly of him. In the dim light—I have to find bright light somewhere in this gray steel world—I see why Shayla's here. She appears ready to welcome a future new cadet to Ironhold. Based on the roundness of her belly, her baby will be large and healthy. Pregnant girls on land never look so fit.

Before I can ask what I should do, Doctor Vesper whisks into the room and asks me to follow her to the exam room. I look at my flimsy robe and back at her as if to say, "Should I dress?" She motions me to follow. I hope I'll get to stay another night with the others again after our visit. I already miss the cozy bed.

"Good news," she says. "Your bloodwork shows you have several nutritional deficiencies, all easily remedied. You're going to take one of these chews every day until I see you again in a few days. Eat all your meals, and no staying up past taps. As for . . ." she looks for the glow, but it hasn't woken up yet. "Well, I see a good night's sleep remedied that as well."

Really? Really, Doctor? You're going to pretend something like this happens all the time when your patients are tired? Pretty sure my mouth hangs open at her words, but maybe the lame boy is right. Doctors don't know everything. Maybe this one doesn't want to know any more about me, an outsider. A stranger from the land. Maybe the first of my kind to arrive alive in this bizarre fortress.

Chews. Some kind of medicine, I guess. None left by the time my generation was born.

"What are the chews for?" I have a right to know.

"Nothing to worry about," she says. "Everyone in Iron-hold takes one daily for maximum health benefits. Yours are a combination of antibiotic, anti-inflammatory, pain relief, and multivitamin. You're in a very different environment from the one you're used to. These will minimize any potential unpleasant physical reactions." She runs her hands down the sides of her white coat, smoothing out invisible wrinkles.

My question made her uncomfortable.

"Will I spend another night here, doctor?" *Please-oh-please say yes.*

"No need. You'll be escorted back to the barracks shortly. I've put you on a modified physical training program until next week. That should help you adjust to your new situation."

I never signed up for my new situation. Never volunteered to attend USMA. Wasn't born to live in a place—as my father would say—where the sun don't shine.

"Doctor, if I may ask, do I have options?"

She looks at me quizzically.

"I heard someone talking about mechanical rooms and food preparation and—"

"No. It has been determined that you're to be—you are—a new cadet at the Academy."

"But—"

"Good day, new cadet. I will see you in a few days."

She leaves me alone in the room. I notice a clean outfit, dull green, folded on the exam table with my little book resting on top of the pile. I dress quickly, not knowing when Dez will show up to take me back to the long, stark, cot-filled room, or wherever else she might take me.

I like my new friend. She doesn't seem like the other cadets.

I smile when the door opens, ready to greet her, but instead, Lou stands in the doorway.

"Let's go, newb. You get to do P.T. with the other weaklings." He does that thing, an about-face, in the doorway and walks away at a pace much like the one Dez set when she brought me to sick call. Why is everyone in such a hurry?

Halfway down a long corridor, an older looking cadet stops us.

"New cadets, halt!"

Here we go again. At least I don't slam into Lou when he stops.

"New cadet. What's your name?" He's looking at me.

"Ing." Should I add *Level Alpha*? I don't know.

"Ing what, new cadet?" His nostrils flare.

"Ing Level Alpha . . . sir?"

"Are you asking me a question, new cadet?" He pokes a finger at my forehead and backs me against a wall. I notice the letter B on his forehead, same place where he pokes mine. Lou just stands there with a smirk on his stupid face.

"No, sir. My name is new cadet Ing, Level Alpha, sir."

"New cadet Lou, why is this new cadet spazzing around in my hallway?"

Spazzing? So many weird words. I wish I could understand what people in this place are saying without someone having to explain.

The angry cadet's question about me makes Lou stand taller. His smirk disappears. I don't move from the wall.

"I'm escorting the new cadet back from sick call, sir. She is expected at rehab, sir. Permission to continue with my orders from Doctor Vesper, sir."

The older cadet hesitates for a moment before saying, "Dismissed, new cadets. And don't let me catch you spazzing around in my hallway again. Do you understand?"

Nope. I understand almost nothing other than we need to get away from that cadet fast. We do.

"I knew you'd be nothin' but trouble," Lou mumbles as we speed away.

He knows nothing about me.

9

LOU STOPS BY a door with a sign above: REHAB. More new words to learn in this submerged prison.

"Have fun in there, newb. Be careful you don't strain any muscles." He scoffs and leaves me standing there.

The windowless door leaves me no choice but to open it. It's not like I can run away. Where would I go? I fight off another wave of claustrophobia—and what I see inside tells me I don't belong here.

"Enter, new cadet Ing." A matronly officer in a uniform too small for her waves me inside. She leaves a muscular cadet balanced on one foot halfway up a short set of stairs between metal crutches. The cadet rolls his eyes. He looks at me, shakes his head, and grabs the handrails.

"Practice your balance, new cadet," the officer tells him before taking a piece of paper—so much paper—from a stack on her littered desk. "I'm Portia, Level Kilo, and you will call me sir." She doesn't look at me. Doesn't need to tell me her Level, either, as the letter K—short for Kilo, I guess—glows between her bushy eyebrows. "Let's take a look at your fitness for duty profile."

More jargon. She reads aloud from the topmost sheet. "Profile, new cadet Ing. Have patient work on altitude and strength adjustment. Birthplace: Land. Monitor daily chew intake." She holds out a hand and I give her the bottle of medicine. "Report anomalies in physique. Well, this doesn't tell me much." She finally looks me up and down. "I see no anomalies in physique. Why are you really here, new cadet?"

"Doctor Vesper ordered me, sir. I fainted and she said the chews will help, sir." I glance around at the splints, casts, and sickly patients—one soaking in a vat of steaming water—and the idea of returning to the mission-chanting cadets suddenly doesn't seem so bad. "Permission to return to full duty, sir."

She smirks. "Oh, my, new cadet. That is not how things work around here. Clearly, you're at a disadvantage." She reads from my profile sheet again. "Land. First generation. Nutrient deficiency. Altitude . . . and perhaps *attitude* adjustment?" She chuckles, probably thinking she's being clever. "And so, I'll ask you again. Why are you here, new cadet?"

I give her the short version of my water rescue and unexplained assignment to the USMA section of Ironhold. I leave out the shock treatment, the Swimmers, and my goal of finding out where the bodies and my coin ended up. I hope the glow doesn't come back. It'll draw unwanted attention. Something tells me I should work on blending in here.

I've never felt comfortable doing what's expected of me.

The officer listens while continuing to look me over, looking for the anomalies in physique Doctor Vesper mentioned. So I stand straighter and keep my shoulders down and my neck back, just as everyone keeps telling me to do. It's a horribly uncomfortable way to stand.

I wish Dez would show up and rescue me again. What's her story? I like her, but can I trust her? I want to. The well-fed officer is right, though. I'm at a disadvantage. I need to be more careful with initial impressions of people and situations in this foreign environment.

"Let's get on with it, then." At least she doesn't ask me if I understand. The woman tosses my paper back onto a pile.

"You will walk on this treadmill until you feel you cannot anymore, at which time you will push this button." She escorts me to a rolling surface on the floor next to a wall in a corner. The button glows red on the wall at about waist height. "I will adjust the speed. These will monitor your vitals." She grabs several small, round pads and sticks one on the right side of my neck.

I flinch.

"Shirt up," she orders. When I hesitate, she pulls up my shirt and slaps two more pads under my left breast. I hold my breath, wondering what might happen if she puts one where my coin should be. "On you go, new cadet. Start walking." With a firm grasp on my arm, she presses me onto the rolling surface. After stumbling, I find my balance quickly. "Good. I'm going to let go now. Enjoy your walk."

"Yes, sir," I say.

It doesn't take long to adjust to walking in place, but as soon as I fall into a comfortable stride, Portia increases the rolling speed. I never need to push the button, but suddenly my stomach growls loud enough to make the boy on crutches shake his head again. And then I catch him smiling. I smile back.

Just as I'm about to ask for food, wondering if deprivation is part of my adjustment, a loud announcement makes me jump. I nearly lose my balance on the spinning surface. "The uniform for dinner formation is white over gray." So much gray.

"You will dine and repose with your peers tonight, and I will see you after reveille formation tomorrow morning, new cadet Ing. You did well today. Take this now." She hands me a chew. "Get a good night's sleep. Tomorrow's training will be more intense."

"Yes, sir." The other cadets line up at the door, and I join them. The door opens and an older cadet in long gray pants and a white form-fitting shirt announces, "Rehab, fall in. Forward, march." I guess his uniform is the "white over gray" from the announcement.

How embarrassing. As much as I try to blend in, I attract even more attention as I trudge with the injured cadets alongside rows of neatly dressed cadets all marching in step toward where I guess we're going to eat. It's impossible to ignore the snarky comments.

I might as well have "Freak" written across my forehead.

Flooding shite.

I fall farther back from those in my sorry-looking group, wanting to distance myself from them, but that only draws more attention.

"What's wrong, new cadet? Can't keep up with the lame-o's?" An upperclass cadet's comment encourages others to harass me too.

"Think you're better than them?"

"Way to support your buddies, newb."

The comments come from older cadets, though no one stops me as we approach two large open doors with the words MESS HALL over the top. And then, a friendly whisper.

"Chin up, Ing."

I glance to my left to see Dez marching tall in a row of new cadets that quickly sweeps past me. Her few kind words numb the harsh ones. I hope I get to talk with her tonight.

Our escort leads us to a table away from the others. There are about 50 tables in the enormous room, each surrounded by eight cadets. When I start to sit down, the boy on crutches shakes his head at me. I look around to see everyone in the room silently standing behind a chair. I nod my thanks to him for the warning. He almost smiles.

From somewhere near the middle of the room comes a booming command.

"Take . . . SEATS!"

In the flurry of activity that follows, I'm the only one left standing at my table. Crutches nods at me to sit, and as soon as I do, people in white coats deliver platters of food on rolling carts. They plop something called chicken a la king over rice at one end of the table and Martha Washington sheet cake at the other. It all looks delicious. My stomach rumbles again.

I've never seen people eat so fast. All around me, bizarre behavior. It looks like every table has three new cadets at one end and older cadets in the other chairs. The new cadets—all sitting at the edge of their seats and looking like they have metal rods shoved up their butts—serve the older ones, who sit like normal humans.

An older cadet at the table nearest ours shouts, "New cadet Biz, how's the cow?"

"Sir! She walks, she talks, she's full of chalk. The lacteal fluid extracted from the female of the bovine species is highly prolific to the . . . 3rd degree, sir!"

"Well? What are you waiting for? Send one up!"

Biz passes one of three remaining beverage boxes to the older cadet. I want to ask my table mates what's the deal, but no one else is talking. In no time at all, I realize why everyone seems in a race to finish their meals. I barely gulp down my second bite of chicken and a sip of "the lacteal fluid" in a box—it's just milk—when a bell clangs. A signal, evidently, for everyone to jump from their seats and speed to the doors.

I take my cues from my table mates, who wait for our escort to stand. So much food will be left on these tables.

"Fall in behind me, rehab." As soon as the dining hall clears, he leads us back to the sleeping rooms. Mine is eerily empty. "Study your *USMA* pages until lights out. Be in line at the door after reveille tomorrow. I'll be your escort to rehab this week. You're dismissed."

He stares at me for longer than I think appropriate, does an about-face, and leaves. The others shuffle away.

Embarrassed that I can't remember which bed is mine, and not wanting to keep calling my classmate Crutches, I touch him on the shoulder before he turns away.

"Hi. I'm Ing. I'm new here, and I have no clue what I'm doing."

He smiles at me. "I'm Dash, and I can tell. Heard them bring you in the other night. Guess you slept at the clinic last night. Your bed's seven down on the left. They'll all be back from study hall soon." He hobbles off to a bed at the end of the room. The sound of running water in a room beyond catches my attention.

"Hey, Dash?"

He turns.

"Is that where we can clean up?" The dried sweat on my body makes me feel sticky and cold.

He nods yes and plunks onto his cot.

Alone in a large, open washroom with multiple shower-heads, I anticipate a much-needed rinsing under hot water like last night, only to be disappointed when the stream runs cold. So much for a cure for the shivers.

The shivers. Aiden made tea for me to ward off the shivers after my father's Farewell. He has to find me. He must know about the funnel now. I want to see him, hold him, kiss him, press my goosebumped body against his perfect bronze skin. The thought sends a flush of warmth through me.

Even when he's away from me, he makes me hot. *Where are you, Aiden?*

By the time I jump into my cot with my little book, I make a decision.

In fewer than two short days—the days seem way shorter here than on land—I've already earned a bad reputation. If I want to have any control over my life again, if I'm going to find out if my father's body is somewhere in this place, if I'm going to find my coin and figure out what I should do with it, I have to be smarter.

There's no way I'm returning to rehab tomorrow.

Thrum, thrum, thrum.

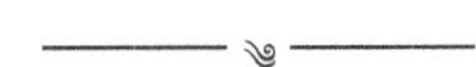

As orderly and quiet as everyone was the first morning I woke in this room, they're the complete opposite now. Cadets in these barracks—boys on one side, girls on the other—undress and change into nightshirts while teasing and shoving each other, laughing, and using the washroom. I counted 40 beds in the room while I waited for them to return. It's so damn noisy in here that I'm afraid we're all going to be in trouble soon.

Finally able to glance around, I'm stricken by the total lack of personality in the space. Nothing on the walls, which are white rather than gray. Not sure it's much of an improvement. Tulip and I practically covered our bedroom's adobe walls in fabric remnants and other pieces of colorful items. When Mom could see, she helped decorate the rest of our small home with whatever we could keep from the Heaps.

I have yet to find a window. Where windows could be in this room, bookcases hang over desks between the cots. I watched everyone stack their books with precision as soon as they returned from study hall.

I wonder what study hall is like. After all my oral history lessons and the most basic elements of math, the idea of school with books and learning scares and excites me. At least when I hear something, I can memorize it fast—my sister calls it my superpower—so I hope that will help me.

Is Tulip trying to find me too? Maybe she'll go to the Swimmers' home and guilt the Elder into searching the sea. There's no way she'll step foot into it, even to rescue me.

Tulip never accepted my wanting more. I have to believe she's still alive and the village was spared from the wave that tore me from Aiden. I want so badly to talk with her, to share secrets at bedtime like we used to. If she could see me now, she'd see this is the kind of life I've dreamt of—a life of challenge and learning and more unknowns than I can imagine. Everything I've wanted except feeling like I'm a prisoner.

Focus, dumbass. I have to find my coin and a way to contact my family and friends. Mom knew I left to become a

Swimmer, but she couldn't have known where I ended up. Could she? Could she somehow know I'm alive? And Aiden. He feels so far away. Like a dream. I question if what I shared with him was real, but then my skin tingles again at the thought of his hands on my body. It was real, all right.

The growing commotion in the barracks makes me nervous.

"Relax, girrrl!" Dez must see the wrinkles on my forehead. She sits on a bed next to mine, and another girl plops down next to her. "How'd torture—I mean rehab—go today?"

"It was okay. Dash did his best to keep me out of trouble." I glance over at him and can tell he heard my compliment. He has a great smile. He nods and pulls his covers over his head, evidently not interested in participating in the general end-of-day shenanigans.

"He's one of the good ones," says Dez's friend. "I'm Mette."

"Cool name," I say.

"No two people have the same here. The founding fathers of Ironhold believed it would give us a sense of being one big family. No confusion over who's who, and no last names like there used to be before the planet paused."

Huh. They call the Halt a pause. Sounds temporary. Not sure I like the "one big family" idea, though. Dad's warnings about cults—

"Your eyes. Wow." Mette's comment about my eyes interrupts my moment of concern.

"Hey, wha'd I tell you about comments like that? Ain't no one here prettier than me, but you got your points." Dez gently pokes one of Mette's breasts before shoving her playfully, and the two laugh.

Mette's appearance stuns me. She's beautiful in a strange way. Based on the people in my village and everyone I've already seen in Ironhold, I figured everyone had brown skin and dark hair in various shades. Mette's skin is almost see-through, her hair is straight and white, and her eyes are a soft pinkish gray, which matches many of the uniforms at USMA. She's scrawny compared to most of the others, but in a wiry, tough way. I can't help staring.

She frowns. "What? Do I have a booger hanging from my nose? Chicken in my teeth? What?"

"Sorry. I'm sorry," I say. "It's just that I've never—"

"Never seen anyone as beautiful as me?" She smiles with teeth whiter than her skin, and shoves Dez.

"Well, yes."

"It's called albinism, and it makes me extra special. At least that's what the Singers told me from the time I was little."

"Who are the Singers? Did they raise you?" I ask.

"No, but they made sure my parents brought me to the chapel all the time, and they taught me how to sing. They sing at chapel services and help with special occasions. They said I have a gift." She and Dez exchange a look that tells me they share a secret.

Not wanting to be totally nosy, I scan the room again. "It's really loud. Won't we get in trouble?"

"Only if there's a peep after taps," says Dez, "which'll happen really soon. Someone in the chain of command has at least half a brain. We get time every night between study hall and taps to let loose. It's not much, but I think we'd all just explode if we didn't, and nobody wants to clean up that mess."

"Body parts everywhere," Mette continues, "blood staining these freshly scrubbed floors, guts all oozing down the walls—"

"Holy hell, girrrl! You'll give me nightmares tonight. Hey, Ing, hope you don't mind, but I switched cots with Dalia so I could help you out. Not gonna make up your cot again for you," Dez sticks out her tongue at Lou, not that he notices, "but you're a couple weeks behind us, and it's tough enough even for people like me who volunteered to be soldiers."

Soldiers. These cadets are training to become soldiers. My parents told us horrifying stories of past wars. People brutally murdering other people, sometimes even people they knew. Why?

I'm in a military academy, and militaries are made for war. What did these cadets chant about a mission this morning? I close my eyes and concentrate.

> The mission of the United Survivors Military Academy is to educate, motivate, and activate the Corps of Cadets so that each successful recruit shall have the intellectual aptitude, the personal incentive, and the soldierly qualities necessary for a lifelong career dedicated to the protection of planet Earth against all enemies, alien and native.

But who are the enemies? Who, and where are the aliens? This isn't my birthplace. Am I an alien? I shake off a feeling of danger.

"Thanks, Dez. Hey, how much trouble will I be in if I don't go back to rehab tomorrow? I feel fine, really, and as you said, I'm already behind."

"Disobeying doctor's orders? Disobeying any orders? I thought I was the crazy one here. Don't do it." Dez absent-mindedly scratches at her scar.

"But—" Another blaring announcement interrupts my objection. Why are they all so loud?

"Lights out, lights out, lights out . . ."

"Get in bed, fast," Dez says, and I do. "And no more talking. Don't do anything stupid tomorrow."

The entire room shuts up and shuts down in a heartbeat. By the seventh or eighth or millionth *lights out*, the lights go out. Total darkness. Then, a sound so sad it chokes me echoes in the room and throughout the hallways.

"What the—"

"Shut up. Taps," Dez says. I'll eventually have time to ask what a tap is. The music moves me almost as strongly as the chanting of *Ahveyah* had when I was with the Swimmers. Why does this sound remind me of a meditation over a dead loved one?

La-la-la . . . the three tones fit the three-note pattern of a chant still lingering in my mind. As I focus on them, a sense of calm washes over me. I decide that instead of holding my breath, I'll comfort myself by repeating my chant. *Ahveyah.*

While I do my best to settle into sleep, a symphony of other sounds break the silence—snoring, farting, sighing, restless tossing and turning—but no talking. I can't sleep until I make up my mind about what to do after reveille tomorrow.

Dez's warning, and scar, make me question my decision to disobey my orders. But I'm in a different situation from all the other cadets. They all chose to be at the Academy, even Dez, evidently. I didn't. I'll plead ignorance, or forgetfulness, or just-dropped-in-from-landfulness. They'll have to cut me some slack.

There. Decision made. I'll dress like the rest at reveille, join them in spouting off the mission of the United Survivors Military Academy and the definition of slicken, whatever the hell that is, and get on with blending in. It's the only way I'll be able to succeed in this place that never seems to sleep.

Thrum, thrum, thrum . . .

When the time is right, I'll figure out a way to contact my family. There's still so much to discover down here. Maybe Doctor Vesper could cure Mom's blindness. Tulip would have countless opportunities to find a mate.

Maybe this really is where I'm supposed to be.

10

THE DEFINITION OF slicken must have been stuck in my mind as I fell asleep last night because the dream I woke from when reveille blared was a real *doozy*, a word my father was determined to keep alive from "the olden days." He always laughed after saying it. *Doozy*. It made me laugh too.

I miss my father. He's dead, he had his Farewell, and it shouldn't matter to me where his body is, but it does. He believed his remains would return to the sea. If someone in Ironhold is using his body for—who knows what—then I feel an obligation to find out what and why. I just do.

It's my second morning of waking in a room filled with noisy teens, the morning I'm going to disobey a doctor's orders.

In my dream, I woke in a very different place. A warm, confined, sticky place. My mother was there, and she spoke to me, but I couldn't hear her words. Her eyes were green and clear and bright. I felt more curious than frightened about my situation, excited and energetic, like everything about me was new and wonderful.

It felt like I was being reborn.

This reality, though, is totally different. I jump from my cot like the others, follow the neat way of tucking in the covers on each side of the cot, dress in my "as for P.T. without head-gear" uniform as announced over and over and over on the blasted speaker system. I notice how everyone pops a chew into their mouths as they dress and remember I left mine at rehab. Like the others, I stand tall at the end of my cot, no dizziness at all.

"Your rehab escort should be here soon," Dez reminds me. "Go line up. Don't be a damn fool."

I watch Dash and the others from yesterday's rehab group amble toward the door. I ignore Dez.

"Seriously. Go get in line." She stands at attention like me, just a few feet away. I keep my eyes straight ahead.

"Newbie's gonna burn today." Lou grins like an idiot, staring at me from across the aisle separating our cots. I ignore him too.

Same as yesterday, someone at the end of the room an-nounces, "The Mission of the United Survivors Military Academy," and we all spout off the words. A brief flash of surprise animates Lou's face when he sees I don't miss a word.

What might I do to avoid staring at his ugly face at every morning formation? He's handsome, really, but his attitude ruins it.

My attitude will mask my disobedience. I count on it.

"Rehab, fall in!" a cadet in the doorway announces. I know they're already in line, all but me, and there's an uncomfortable silence in the stark room.

"REhab . . . FALL IN!"

A trickle of sweat starts at the small of my back, but I don't flinch. There's mumbling, and then a "yes, sir." The shuffling of feet and the clicking of Dash's crutches fade away, and then Lou raises both eyebrows. Amused?

Measured footsteps from more than one person make their way toward me. Keeping my head facing forward, my eyes strain to watch as an officer and an upper-class cadet, a pair on each side of the room, stop in front of each new cadet to inspect uniforms and cots. My trickle of sweat continues down to my butt crack, and I shiver. Lou looks at me and sneers. He might try to get me in trouble again, even though his last attempt failed. I don't know how much influence he might hold in a place like Ironhold.

"New cadet, what's the definition of slicken?"

"New cadet, what are your three rallying points?"

"New cadet, what's the mission . . . how's the cow . . . describe the Academy Crest . . . how many lights are there in Study Hall . . . recite the Cadet Prayer . . ."

Cadet prayer?

I know the USMA mission and the definition of slicken, but stress over what they might ask when they get to me, and what my punishment will be if I don't know the answer. I never want to see that metal table again, that's for sure. So much sweat, and no breeze to dry it from my body. Never expected I'd miss the winds on land.

When the officer and upperclass cadet stand in front of Dez, I notice the cadet is giving me the same sideways glance

I'm giving him. I readjust my gaze to straight ahead, and Lou winks at me.

What the flood, dude?

"New cadet, describe the Academy Crest."

I listen carefully as Dez spouts off the description. "Sir, the crest comprises an octopus with three eyes holding a trident and a scroll bearing the motto, "Duty, Survival, Planet," and the words "North Sea, MMLXXXIII, U.S.M.A.""

"And what does the MMLXXXIII stand for, new cadet?"

"It stands for the year 2083, the year our Academy was established, sir."

USMA is 100 years old. People back then must have known what was about to happen to our planet. They had to have planned and built this place way before then, maybe even during the pandemic decades of the 21st Century. Our history classes covered the military academies on land back then. Army. Air Force. Navy. Merchant Marine. Coast Guard. Space Force. It makes sense that with all their knowledge, those in the upper ranks would have seen the need to prepare for an altered future. A windy planet wiped clean of just about everything.

My turn.

"New cadet Ing, it has come to my attention that you have not yet been adequately in-processed." The officer looks me up and down. It might be my imagination, but her eyes seem to stop near my nonexistent glow for several seconds.

Not sure how to respond, I stand with my neck back, shoulders down, chest out, eyes front.

"You will follow cadet Zadak, Level Bravo. He will ensure you are prepared to continue your training."

"But, sir, I'd like—"

"You are dismissed, new cadet."

"Yes, sir."

I want to tell her I'd like to participate in the day's events with my peers. But maybe I'll learn more during in-processing, whatever that is. As a new cadet, I can't just roam around the place, so maybe Zadak will answer some of my questions.

I stand at attention until the inspection ends, at which point Zadak steps in front of me, the letter B glowing dimly between his thick eyebrows. I'm getting used to seeing the different letters that glow on cadets and officers of different levels. Do I have an A on my forehead where that bully cadet poked me? There are no mirrors in the bathrooms I've used.

Most cadets are hard to identify in their matching uniforms and speed-walking, but I recognize him as our rehab escort from the previous day. I wonder why he's been reassigned to me.

"Follow me, new cadet Ing."

"Yes, sir."

He does a foot maneuver which turns him to the left, away from me, and moves toward the door. I follow, glancing back to see the rest of the cadets formed in a line for physical training.

"Eyes forward, new cadet," says Zadak.

Why are they letting me get away with disobeying the doctor's orders? It makes no sense. They made it seem like it was their idea to arrange my day differently. I'm an anomaly. An alien in their world.

Are they afraid of something? *Of me?*

———— ❧ ————

"Hope you can read fast and remember what you read even faster, new cadet." Zadak's pace slows. At the end of a hallway that leads to rehab, he stops and turns toward me. "That's where the rehab clinic is. I'm assuming you recognize it."

"Yes, sir."

"I don't know how you managed to get out of going there today, and I guess for the rest of the week, but it's best if you never have to go there again. You'd be marked as a fall-out." He stares at my hair, scrunches his eyebrows together, and apparently makes a decision. "First things first. Follow me. You need to meet the barber."

After several left and right turns along stark metal hallways which—like the cadets—all look the same, we arrive at another windowless door with BARBER etched over its top. Three scissor-wielding men all stop mid-cut and stare at me. So do the cadets in their chairs. One of the cadets nods to an empty fourth chair.

"Take a seat. I'll wait here," says my escort.

As soon as I sit in the surprisingly comfortable seat, my reflection in a large, unbroken mirror shocks me. I'm a mess. Whatever hair was left after I butchered it stands out in random clumps. I can only imagine how it looks in the back.

The letter A glows softly between my eyebrows. Weird.

The barbers seem to enjoy their work, and the cadets seem to enjoy chatting with them. I listen while I wait.

"Maybe someday they'll figure out how to cook beef."

"Won't matter. Don't have time to eat anyway."

"Hey, leave at least a *little* hair on top, would you?"

"Anyone else feel like something's about to change?"

"Everything in its time, they say."

"Crazy energy near the tubes . . ."

"I had the weirdest dream about Calyxar . . ."

I gaze around the shop surprised by walls painted bright yellow, large pictures with scenes from land before the Halt hanging here and there, and upbeat music filling the room with a feeling of happiness. How different from every other place in Ironhold. I get the sense that Ironhold is far larger than the parts belonging to the academy.

The barber next to me brushes off his seated cadet and moves to stand behind me.

"So, what brings you here, *new* new cadet?" He laughs, not in a mean way, but as if what he's looking at has truly amused him.

I smile at him in the mirror's reflection, and decide I have a nice smile. "I guess someone didn't appreciate the way I styled my hair, sir."

He laughs even harder, and I allow myself to chuckle. "Ain't no 'sirs' workin' in this room, little lady. Relax. I'll take care of this mop you call hair."

He brushes and clips and fluffs and finally says, "Well, that's about all I can do with what I had to work with. No playing with scissors anymore, promise me, and next time we'll get you lookin' more like they didn't just catch you in a net." He pats me on the head. "Welcome to USMA, new cadet."

"Thank you, s—" I peek at his nametag—"Rolph." I don't want to leave. I'd really like to ask Rolph the questions clogging my brain. I bet he'd give me honest answers.

"Let's go, new cadet Ing." Zadak looks me over, and I follow him into the cold hallway. "You'll be scheduled for barber visits as required. They're good guys in there."

I didn't ask Zadak anything yet, so his offer of information about the barbers is a good sign.

"Sir, may I ask a question?"

"You may."

"You were supposed to be the rehab escort this week, sir. Why were you reassigned to escort only me today?"

He looks surprised. Embarrassed, even. He keeps walking as he answers. "They needed a volunteer. I volunteered." Nothing hostile in his tone.

I frown. "But why, sir?" I didn't just imagine his lingering glance yesterday. He's either being protective or he's . . . interested?

He doesn't know about Aiden.

"That's two questions, new cadet." He turns another corner and opens a door. "This is Study Hall. Every evening you'll work on your lessons here."

Beyond the windowless door are rows of tables. Beyond them, row upon row of bookshelves, all stacked full and high.

"Wow. So many. I thought they were mostly—"

"Mostly what?" Zadak stands in front of me, close in front of me. I feel his attraction. No way.

"Mostly destroyed, sir."

"Who are you, new cadet Ing? How, and why are you here?" He speaks softly. His deep brown eyes hold my gaze.

In a moment of weakness, I let myself imagine what it might be like to have this attractive, kind cadet kiss me. After staring at his lips for too long, I look away.

"Permission to—"

"Just talk to me, Ing. Please. I know I shouldn't be talking to you like this, but I have to know. I've heard rumors of someone being brought in, barely alive, through the death tubes. Was that you?"

"Death tubes? I . . . I don't know. I was swimming, there was a huge wave, I went under, and then I woke up somewhere down here. What are death tubes, sir? Is it something I need to memorize from my *USMA* book?"

"So it's true. What did you see when you woke up?" He doesn't answer me. I'm not sure I should answer him.

Pushing my luck on assuming a level of familiarity with him—after all, he practically begged me to talk to him—I ask again. "Please, will you tell me what the death tubes are?" If they're what I think they are, then I bet my father's body, and Joshua's, and who knows how many other bodies of the dead are being kept or disposed of somewhere in Ironhold. My entire belief system about our Farewell ritual hangs on his answer.

I can tell he struggles with whether or not to answer me, but he finally does. "In the outskirts of Ironhold there are special rooms where our dead are taken. Cadets aren't allowed there, only doctors, the Singers, and the priest. We all learn about the death tubes when we're young." He scrunches his eyebrows.

"What did they teach you, sir, about what happens to the dead?" My mantra starts softly in my head.

"The family selects an option, they pray with the priest, and the final option—ashes or full flesh—gets sent through the tubes to a sacred place."

Everything is upside down in this underwater hold. I inhale deeply while searching his eyes again and recite the *Aveyah* in my mind. We continue to stare at one another. The curious expression on his face tells me he wants to ask more.

He looks away first. "I'm sorry, new cadet. I shouldn't be asking you these things, and we have a lot more to cover before dinner formation."

I exhale.

We leave Study Hall. Just around the corner from it a long hallway—I can't see its end—is lit so brightly I squint.

"This is the sun belt hallway. See the six moving platforms? Keep your eyes squinted. You step on here." He gently takes my wrist and leads me onto one of the platforms. It's like the one I used in rehab except we just stand on it and let it carry us through the warm hallway. "Before P.T. every day you'll do this treatment. You'll see at the end that it leads to the P.T. arena."

I close my eyes and remember sunshine.

"So you *did* come from the land." Zadak still holds my wrist. "We were told . . . never mind. Is the sun up top like this?"

What can I say? The hallway is bright, but this is no sun.

"Close enough," I fib. Are all the cadets as ignorant as Zadak about life on land? Am I putting him, or myself, in danger by talking openly about my reality?

My sun belt exposure is way too short, but it does improve my mood. Before we get to the end, I hear unusual sounds coming from beyond the huge open doors leading to the arena. The massive space booms with hundreds of cadets all participating in various physical activities—running around an enormous circle, jumping through tubes, climbing ropes hung from a dizzyingly high ceiling, wrestling, walking across narrow lengths of wood—so much sweat. A huge fan rotates slowly overhead, and rhythmic music blares. Other than songs we sing in our village with an occasional handmade instrument as accompaniment, we have nothing like this music on land.

"Every morning you'll train somewhere in this arena. But let's go. You should see a few more things."

Zadak whisks me down more corridors where I see room after room with regular people, *civilians*, he calls them, sewing uniforms, washing clothes, gutting fish, and in the most amazing rooms of all, larger even than the P.T. arena, tending to chickens and goats and cows grazing on what appears to be healthy, green grass. I notice different symbols on their foreheads, not letters. Maybe they identify what their job is, but I don't know.

And fruit trees. How are trees growing under the sea? And how far under the sea are we, really?

There's so much to learn. So many exciting possibilities.

"You won't need to come to any of these sectors, but you should know they're here. Our citizens keep USMA running." Zadak takes me through more endless hallways to the Mess Hall and grabs a few tubes of the stuff Dez smuggled in to me. "Here. I was told you'll need to eat more so you don't get sick again. Take this chew with it. You got out of going to rehab today, but the Doctor said you'll need this supplement for a while. Something to do with elevation adjustment. You'll get one like the rest of us once you're good to go."

So he retrieved my chews for me. Interesting.

Maybe being below sea level could affect my health, but I wonder why everyone else needs to take something. Must have something to do with living in such an unnatural environment.

The ever-present thrumming constantly reminds me this is no place like home.

I can guess, but I ask anyway. "Sir, what is that noise?"

"What noise?"

"That . . . thrumming noise, sir."

"Oh, that. I don't even hear it anymore. It's the air circulation system for Ironhold. You'll get used to it."

I chew the slightly sweet medicine. It's time to see where the classrooms are. More long, cold hallways with desk and chair-filled rooms for learning whatever it is cadets need to learn. Cadets in the rooms have odd devices they poke at. I learned about the computers and typing machines they used before the flooding Halt, but we've never found an unbroken one in the Heaps.

Everything about this new world overwhelms and enthralls me. They have everything down here we've been told was destroyed.

"Where are the death tubes, sir?" I finally ask.

"You won't ever need to go there, Ing." He drops the "new cadet."

"But I need to know where they are, please. I need to know how I got here."

He looks into my eyes. I can see concern—and maybe a touch of fear. "We're not supposed to go down those hallways. But listen. If I show you where they are, you can't tell anyone I showed you. We'll go to the chapel first. We'll need to walk faster, before classes let out."

My heart skips at least one beat.

11

THE CHAPEL SURPRISES me in many ways. First, that it even exists. Chapels are for those who pray to gods, and not many in my village believe in supreme beings anymore. This chapel is filled with people kneeling in silent prayer. Not a single one turns to look as we enter.

The greatest reason for the awe I feel when we enter through the elaborately carved doors is what I see above.

"Holy—"

"I know, right?" Zadak misinterprets my next word.

The impossibly lofty surface of the chapel ceiling looks like it's made of a flexible, transparent substance that seems to breathe. The water beyond the gently undulating membrane glows a vibrant turquoise, which fills the interior with soothing light.

The intense silence in the space scares me. How can all these people be this quiet? I can't even hear the irritating thrum. It feels like all sound is being absorbed by the mysterious matter overhead.

"This, sir, is slicken," I whisper. I don't know how I know, but something tells me I'm right.

"Indeed it is, Ing."

Goosebumps rise when he whispers my name, and my thoughts turn to Aiden. He knew I wanted to discover the truth behind the funnel that takes our dead. I hope he won't put himself in danger . . . again. He's already done so much for me. Aiden, Tulip, Mom, they all seem so far away. I've lost track of time down here.

And there's nothing I can do about any of my worries right now. I hold my breath. It feels like I might float away.

Suddenly, tingles run down my spine.

"What's that?" I ask.

"Shhhh! Just listen. There must be a ceremony today," Zadak whispers, as if that explains anything.

The singing starts softly, a trio of voices from a room beyond us. The first two syllables leave me breathless.

"Ahhh . . . veyyy . . ."

It can't be. They can't be singing the chant of the Swimmers.

They're not.

"Maria, Gratia plena."

I stand unmoving, mesmerized by lyrics I don't understand, feeling like at any moment I might burst into tears. But I don't cry.

Neither of us moves. We stand there by the chapel doors behind the kneelers, who pay us no attention. By the end of the song, tears wet Zadak's face. The guy's got a sensitive side.

"Please tell me, what is that?"

"You don't know the song? The Ave Maria? The song sung at weddings and funerals?"

Funerals? Of course they have funerals and chapels and believe in a divine being.

"No, sir, but it feels familiar."

"Tell me." When he turns toward me and takes my hands, I look around in a panic. "It's okay. You're safe here. Please tell me, what do the land people do when someone dies? And what's it like up there? And how many people are there, really? Most of us have been told that no one on land survived when the planet stopped spinning, but there are lots of doubters. You're proof that the doubters were right." He sounds desperate to know more than I want to tell.

He keeps hold of my hands as I whisper about the Swimmers and their responsibilities for our Farewells. I tell him I just lost my father, but he doesn't need to know about my decision to become a Swimmer. I give him some basic facts about our village with its thousand'ish people and how every day is a struggle to survive. I tell him about my belief that the bodies of our dead are being transported from the surface of the sea to somewhere below—even though we've all been taught the bodies are being returned to the sea—and about the funnel I saw. I say nothing about my coin.

He listens with raised eyebrows, his mouth slightly open. When I finish, he says, "The tubes."

I slide my hands from his. "Tubes? What are they? Where are they?" He's been generous with his time and information, but he wants more from me than I'm willing to give. He's a nice guy, but I don't appreciate how he seems to be using his position of power over me. He's too familiar, and too fast. I have to keep up my guard.

A look of embarrassment flashes across his face, but he schools himself quickly. "I thought they were just for transporting our dead from Ironhold back to the sea, but if that's how you were brought in, then—"

"Then maybe my father's body is somewhere down here. But why?" A brief dizzy spell forces me to sit on one of the few empty benches at the back of the chapel.

"Right. Why?" He shakes his head as if to make sense of the idea and sits next to me.

We're quiet for a long time. How long can these worshipers kneel, heads bowed, eyes closed? It creeps me out.

"Tell me about the Singers." I startle him from his thoughts. They must do more than sing.

"Well, you just heard them. They live in the chapel and help the priest, Father Malachy." His eyebrows crease.

"Maybe they're like our Swimmers." The idea intrigues me.

What is it about the chapel that makes us whisper, aside from the fact that no one else is making a sound? It felt only right to whisper when I first entered the Swimmers' lodging. But this is different.

It feels as if we don't want to wake some sleeping infant . . . or monster. And just as that thought crosses my mind, a shadow slowly darkens the chapel.

"Ummm," Zadak whispers, his gaze directed upward, "it can't be."

I follow his gaze and hold my breath.

"Can't be what, sir? You're scaring me." I slide closer to Zadak on the bench as the shadow grows larger. Still, no one else in the place moves.

"It's coming. At least I think that's it."

"It?" Something in the water heads directly toward the dome above us.

"Calyxar. Father Malachy is the only person still alive who's seen it before, when he was just a boy, during the funeral for the previous Academy commander. Commander Cameron created slicken and designed our crest. All this time, I honestly thought Calyxar was just a story grownups told their kids to keep them in line. 'Better behave or Calyxar will come for you.' Scared the crap out of us when we were little."

"But . . . seriously? Calyxar?"

"Shhhh!"

My heart races as the shadow grows. Should I say something aloud? Scream for everyone to look up, look out? But I can't breathe.

Suddenly, there it is, an enormous multicolored octopus, tentacled arms stretching out in all directions just beyond the membrane high above us. At any moment, it might pull apart the slicken, and we'll be crushed instantly by the water and the weight of the spectacular creature. At least I'll be awestruck in the brief moment before my death.

Zadak stares at me, his eyes wide.

"What?" I whisper. I want to run from the chapel.

"I think it's here . . . for you."

Another wave of fear.

"That's ridiculous. Why would you say that? Hey, get me out of here, you're freaking me out!" I rise to leave the bizarre chapel, the massive awesomeness of the octopus still looming above, but he grabs my wrist and pulls me back onto the bench.

"Don't go. Please. I don't know who you are, but if it's here because of you, and something tells me it is, then you need to stay. It can't break in. Slicken is impenetrable—you should know that from your *USMA* book knowledge. I think it's curious about you. This is unbelievable."

Nothing is unbelievable anymore. I close my eyes and try to calm my trembling. *Ahveyah, ahveyah, ahveyah.* I focus my thoughts on my mantra until I can hear the word more clearly than my heartbeat. Before I open my eyes again, I hear, **"YESSS. HERE FOR YOUUU."**

It's . . . the voice.

"Did you hear that?" My heart racing, I look at Zadak and then at the monster above us, noticing for the first time that it has three eyes. It is, indeed, the creature on the Academy crest, without the trident and scroll. Its body ripples hypnotically. All three eyes appear to focus on me. Still, no one in the chapel moves.

"Hear what?"

"Those words. Was it you?"

"I didn't say anything, I swear it."

"What do I do?"

"I don't know!" He's not whispering anymore.

"Should we call for help? Should we get the people from the ceremony to come in here? Maybe it's here for them. Maybe it—"

"NOT THEMMM."

"Did you hear that? How could you not hear that?"

"It's talking to you?" His eyes practically pop out.

Both scared and thrilled, I want Zadak to leave me alone. If he can't hear what I hear, there has to be a reason for it.

Tulip is right. I do have to have reasons for things. Good reasons. Oh, my dear, sweet sister, how I wish you were here with me.

Time to backtrack. "Sorry! I'm an idiot. The voice came from that other room. My hearing is so much clearer down here without the constant noisy wind on land. A talking octopus, right?" I hope my snark settles him. "It's probably just a regular old octopus, maybe there are hundreds like it down here. The whole ridiculous Calyxar story is obviously a myth." And maybe all octopuses can communicate magically. How would I know?

"But look," he says, "It has three eyes—"

"And I have two that are different colors. Lots of irregularities in nature." I'm no expert on irregularities in nature. I have even less knowledge about anything relating to deep sea creatures. I only learned about octopuses in scary stories about how they pulled huge floating vessels into the sea.

"We should go," I say.

But Zadak holds fast to my wrist. I can tell he's trying to decide what to do, trying to decide if what I said might be true. His agitation makes me panicky, but I can't tell him to leave me. He's my escort. He's supposed to show me where the tubes are. We'll have to get back before dinner and study hall and taps and—

"YOU WILL FIND A WAYYY." It's definitely the voice I've been hearing at home. It's Calyxar. The octopus spins around gracefully and thrusts away into the darkening sea, leaving me breathless.

Just as it's out of sight, a door opens at the far side of the chapel, where the singing came from. A man in long robes looks at us across the sea of silent kneelers. Zadak jumps up, and so do I.

"That's our priest, Father Malachy, the one who saw it when he was a kid. They say he snuck into the chapel during the commander's funeral when he was, like, three years old. No one believes him today."

The priest opens his arms, and in a booming voice, announces, "Go in peace. Your sins are forgiven."

Sins? An entire chapel full of sinners? What have these people done?

Much like the cadets did in the Mess Hall, the people all rise as if sprung from their knees and swarm from the chapel. They all wear dazed expressions. Definitely freaky.

When everyone else is gone, the priest strolls toward us. Tufts of gray hair stand out against his dark skin, and deep crevices outline his eyes, nose, and mouth. There's no way he could obey a "shoulders down, neck back" command anymore. He barely lifts his feet as he approaches.

"Father Malachy, we were just leaving. I'm assisting with new cadet Ing's in-processing." Zadak finally releases my wrist.

I learned about priests from the old days. My father certainly didn't have anything good to say about them, but Father Malachy looks like a nice man.

"You are the girl from land, is that right?"

"Yes, sir." Should I curtsy? Bow? I stand at attention.

"No need for such formality in this house, my child. Do relax."

I don't move, don't know what to say. I've been a total failure at my attempts to blend in with my new environment. At home, my real home, I wanted nothing to do with blending in, conforming to what others expected of me. But here? It might be a matter of survival if I can't. And if they don't already know, everyone soon will know that I'm the freak from above. The freak that Calyxar just visited. Maybe even spoke to. There's no way Zadak will keep his suspicion a secret.

"I was just telling new cadet Ing that cadets were welcome to come here and—"

"Thank you, Zadak. Will you kindly get me a glass of water?" The priest cuts him off and squints toward the sea above us.

I feel Zadak's eyes on me, but I keep mine on the priest. "Yes, Father, of course," he says. He walks away, though he seems reluctant to leave me. When Zadak is out of sight, Father Malachy places his hands on my shoulders.

"Calyxar visited you just now, yes?"

How does he know? I don't think I should lie. I notice he has no letter or symbol on his forehead.

"I saw a three-eyed octopus, Father." Blend in. Talk like they talk. Call him Father. But don't provide any other information.

"Most unusual. Is there anything you'd like to share about your visit?" The intensity in his eyes makes me take a step back from his grasp.

"I've never seen an octopus before, Father, I've only heard about them in stories. This one is really big, but Calyxar is just a myth, right?"

He doesn't answer. Instead, he stares at me, unblinking, until I look away. He can probably tell I'm not sharing everything. "Your eyes," he says. "I think perhaps you will see things differently from those in Ironhold. I must attend to my obligations now, but you will return here very soon." A statement, not a request. "Welcome to your new home."

My new home. I shudder. I'm sure he saw it. "Thank you, Father."

He turns to leave just as Zadak returns with the water. "Good boy. Give it to the young lady. She appears to need it now." He pats Zadak on the shoulder and whispers something in his ear—I can't hear what—before glancing above again and walking away as slowly as he had approached us.

As soon as the priest closes the far door behind him, Zadak's facial expression changes. "I think your tour is over, new cadet Ing." His sudden formality surprises me. The priest must have reminded him of his superior rank. It makes me uncomfortable thinking he was watching us somehow.

"But, the tubes! You said you'd show me where they are."

"Remember your place, new cadet. Follow me." He turns abruptly and speeds toward the large chapel doors. I have to follow him. I try to remember how many rights and lefts will take me back to the barracks room, where I'll have to change into appropriate clothes for dinner. I don't want to be caught alone and lost in the maze of hallways with unfriendly older cadets just waiting for new targets to stumble their way.

"And what about Calyxar?" I shout after him. "Am I in trouble? Are you going to—"

"Listen." He stops short and I bump into him. He pushes me away gently. "I don't know what just happened, but it would be in your best interest not to talk about it, to anyone. Any of it. You got that?" There's that fear again.

"Yes—yes, sir."

We don't speak a word as we blast along mostly empty hallways except to acknowledge those in officer's uniforms with a "Good evening, sir" when we pass. Sooner than I thought possible, we're back at the barracks.

"They'll be back from drills soon, new cadet. If you have any other questions about expectations, ask your classmates tonight. And here, you're to take one of these every day until they're gone." He hands me the bottle of chews and stares at me like he did earlier. Looks like he's about to ask me something, but the awkward moment is interrupted by an announcement about the uniform for dinner, followed by the rushing of feet as my roommates return.

"Thank you, sir. Good evening," I say. After another moment's pause, he does an about-face and departs.

My roommates swarm the room. Dez punches me playfully, stripping off her day clothes along with the others who jostle for space under the cold showers before returning to change into the dinner uniform. She's back in a flash, and I copy how she dresses.

"Follow me, kiddo. Time to down some slop. I told Mette to sit at another table so you could sit with me. My table cadets aren't too bad, but I hope you memorized the menu since this morning. We can talk about everything before taps. But first, let me adjust that dress-off for you."

Before I understand what she's talking about, she walks behind me, grabs both sides of my shirt at the waist, and yanks the excess material to the back. "Now tuck it in and try to keep it like that as long as you can or they'll harass you. Nice haircut, by the way."

The upperclass cadets have no lack of reasons for harassing new cadets. I line up behind Dez and we march off to the Mess Hall. As hungry as my stomach tells me I am, I really wish I had some time alone to process the events of the day.

In the chapel, and unless I've been hallucinating, Calyxar told me I would "find a way."

A way to the tubes? Are they my way out? Do I even want a way out? The thought of staying makes me queasy. I'd trade the ominous thrumming for the whistling wind on land in a heartbeat. Still, the resources down here blow my mind.

I can't leave yet.

12

DINNER IS TOLERABLE, but I attract way too many basic questions from the older cadets at our table. I respond to "How's the cow?" appropriately and learn not to take big bites. New cadets have to be prepared to respond immediately. No wonder I notice few new cadets with more flesh on them than absolutely necessary to hold their bones together. I'm already noticing changes in my own body, and I've only been here for . . . how long? A few days? A week, maybe, counting my unconscious time on that cold table?

Back in the barracks, Dez jumps onto my cot. "Tell me everything! Is Zadak as nice as I think he is? Word's out he has a thing for you. Did you get to see everything? No way you saw everything. But the cows? Did you see the cows? When I was little, I wanted to be a farmer, not anymore, and the sun belt? Is it like—"

"Whoa, slow down. How about I answer one at a time?" I laugh at Dez's enthusiasm, but her comment about Zadak worries me. It's pretty clear that any kind of romantic situations are frowned upon at USMA, especially between new cadets and everyone else.

Even though I want to, I don't tell Dez *everything*. "Zadak is nice, I saw the cows, and the sun belt felt great!"

I tune out the end-of-day turmoil surrounding me.

"Hey, Dez, how *did* you find me that night?" She never answered that question when I was strapped to the table.

Mette plops next to Dez. Her whiteness always makes me stare too long.

"Mette . . . heard you." Dez's answer surprises me.

The two exchange a private glance before scanning the rest of the room. I look around too. Cheered on by several of his followers, Lou wrestles a guy next to him, someone throws sweaty underwear at their neighbor, secrets are whispered, Dash grumbles and scratches his bandaged leg—typical releases of stifled energy. I laugh at the good-natured clowning. Dez and Mette finally turn back to me.

"You *heard* me? How?" Where they held me was a distance from the cadet areas.

I notice something peculiar in Mette's pink-gray eyes when she speaks. "I can't really explain how, but I felt you. I knew where you were. It's something I've been able to do since I was little, and I'm not exactly great at going unnoticed." She twirls her hands around to indicate her general whiteness. "So I sent Dez."

Dez nods, and I wait for Mette to continue.

"We all know where the scientists work, and Dez is the only one I trust to get away with going there and back without getting into trouble."

"Everyone knows me," Dez says. "People feel sorry for me, so I've learned how to use that for my benefit."

I look at my two new friends in awe. "Why do people feel sorry for you?" Aside from the scar on her face, I see nothing unusual in her appearance other than the impish expression, which always seems to lurk behind her proper cadet façade.

"Supposedly, one of our farmers found me under a tree and brought me to the chapel. Said I'd been deserted, and no one knew of any recent birth. Father Malachy named me Dez—clever, right?—and when no one claimed me, he tasked the Singers to raise me. Talk about a boring life. As soon as I could, I volunteered to be a cadet."

"The Singers? The women who taught Mette how to sing? I heard them in the chapel."

"Yup. Three women with lovely voices who kept me safe and isolated and tried to teach me how to harmonize with them, but to this day, I couldn't match a pitch if you lit a match under my pits. Ha!" Dez mimes lighting a flame under an armpit, and we laugh. "Don't get me wrong, they kept me alive and fed me well, but they never quite learned to be nurturing. You won't catch me going to chapel services anytime soon."

I understand the desire to flee from boredom. Maybe I really have finally found where I belong.

"Why are you here, Mette?" It makes sense to me that with her abilities to "feel" others, she'd be more suited for life as a scientist, a doctor, or a mother rather than a cadet.

"I dunno. My parents always told me I'd make a great leader. I didn't understand what I could do with my mind until I was about ten, and it scared me. I always felt like my parents were a little afraid of me too, like they knew I could do things they didn't understand. I could never explain it. I wanted to make them happy, and they were thrilled when I told them I'd think about the Academy."

I nod. "Do you think you made the right choice? Do you believe what your parents said about being a leader?"

"Should I show her?" she asks Dez.

"Do it."

Mette places her hands on Dez's and my head and mumbles something I can't understand. Her touch makes me feel slightly faint, but it passes when she lets go. Then she stands and closes her eyes in the chaos surrounding us and speaks, softly at first.

"Oh Spirit, our creator, you have searched our hearts, now help us be closer to you in our hearts and minds. May our mutual gathering be filled with gladness and may our worship of you be genuine and universal." She starts the cadet prayer from our *USMA* book. "Strengthen and increase our desire to choose the harder right over the easier wrong and help us to overcome our deficiencies." With each word, her voice grows louder, and then she says something really weird.

"Now join me and twirl!"

One by one, everyone in the room starts spinning around while reciting the prayer with her. Everyone but Dash, who glares at Mette with fingers in his ears.

They continue while spinning. "Encourage us in our endeavor to go beyond and to rise above conventional expectations, and never to accept deceitfulness because we know truth will always win."

A chill runs down my spine.

"Grant us the courage to do right, and guard us against disrespect in all its forms. Gift us with friendship and opportunities to serve those less fortunate than ourselves. Let us find joy with those who are joyful, and compassion for those in need . . ."

Mette opens one eye and looks at me as if to say, *"See what I can do?"* I don't know whether to thank her for sharing her gift with me—and evidently protecting me from it—or fear her for what she can do with it.

". . . Help us to act with honor and to live our lives with the ideals of the Academy foremost in our actions, that we may serve you and our planet. We ask this in your name, our Master, in whom truly we believe."

When the prayer ends and Mette opens both eyes, my roommates stagger unsteadily. Some fall over. They look around at one another and giggle. They look confused. Their expressions remind me of how the worshipers looked when they left the chapel. I don't like it.

Dash glares at Mette. Lou scratches his head, his eyebrows furrowed, and grabs the closest guy in a mock choke hold, rubbing the top of his victim's head with a knuckle.

And I worry about a young, new leader with the ability to control others. Trickery or magic or whatever it is she can do isn't leadership, though. It's manipulation.

"Asshole!" Lou's victim shouts.

———— ✎ ————

I think about the words in the prayer. They focus on decent ideals, but now I'm really worried about cult behavior. One reason I want to get back to my village, beyond comforting my family and friends with the knowledge that I'm okay, is to let them know, they deserve to know, about this advanced civilization under the sea.

But this prayer, the chapel, the blind conformity? Again I question how an advanced civilization prays to a "Master."

When we were children, in addition to hearing the story about the first man and woman getting kicked out of a garden, we learned several other stories of creation. The stories were supposed to teach us how humankind craved mystical answers to impossible questions.

One story sticks with me, maybe because it's our mother's favorite. She used to repeat it at bedtime frequently throughout our childhood, and it goes like this.

Before time, all was dense, gentle, motionless mist. It was neither happy nor sad, it simply was. No one can say where the lightning bolt came from, but it struck with fury into the mist, and when it did, the mist recoiled. Shattered in dispersed directions, the mist careened away from the shock faster than laughter from a tickle—at this point in the story, Mom would tickle us, and maybe that's why I loved the story so much—*until what remained was a multiverse of compressed, vaporous, rotating spheres spinning and swirling around a barren center point, held in their orbits by their oneness.*

But the lightning was not satisfied with its one great disruption, and so it spread its spikes out to each of the spheres, shocking them over and over until each was forced to harden itself against the assaults. Crusts grew on surfaces, and as winds around each sphere cooled the mist, water dropped to form lakes, rivers, and oceans.

On one such sphere, static from a particularly powerful strike sent tiny particles of crust rolling across its surface leaving heaps of egg-shaped formations scattered across land and tossed into waters. Sparks from subsequent strikes ignited life within the eggs, and when the lives within grew too great for their protective homes, the eggs cracked, releasing creatures of all types. This planet became known as Eyopia, and its inhabitants lived together in harmony.

A sphere in a universe parallel to that populated by creatures hatched from eggs evolved similarly, but with egg shapes more malleable and membranous than those on Eyopia.

This planet became known as Earth.

But there were countless spheres in the multiverse. On each one, different species evolved in diverse ways. Very different ways.

At this point in Mom's story, she would ask Tulip and me to imagine all the possibilities that could exist far beyond the stars. The challenge was enough to send us into dream-filled slumbers. We never believed the creation stories were true.

The "Lights Out" announcement blasts its warning that taps will soon play.

"Guess we'll catch up more tomorrow night." Dez smiles, squeezes my shoulder, and jumps under her covers.

"Good night, Ing." Mette touches my shoulder, her hand light as a feather, and whispers in my ear before heading to her cot. "We will help you, Dez and I."

Another chill.

And then those saddest of notes echo through the room. Grateful for the darkness, I remind myself that we don't cry.

What's Tulip doing now? Who will remind her to keep her tears inside even though she won't? Will Aiden comfort her and my mother as they try to make sense of my disappearance? Aiden. Heat spreads through my body as I recall his touch, his kiss, his body entwined with mine. What the hell am I doing playing soldier in an undersea world?

I feel lost.

———— ∿ ————

The things I imagined as a child about life beyond our stars are nothing like the wonders I'm imagining now. I toss and turn, unable to silence the chaos. Did a three-eyed octopus actually visited the chapel? Yes. Zadak confirmed it. Did it talk to me, and just to me? I'm way less certain in the stark surroundings of this dark room than I was while awestruck in the shimmering chapel.

Doctor Vesper gave me chews. Could they be making me see things? Hear things? But I heard the voice at home, too. The medicine is supposed to help me adjust to the difference in pressure from land and make up for some lacking nutrients. Maybe that's all it's doing, but maybe the doctor doesn't know about weird side effects.

"Holy hell, Ing," Dez whispers. "You got someone in bed with you over there?"

Is that even allowed? In addition to the usual choir of irregular breathing, I can't block out the other guttural groans and moans. Hey, we're a bunch of horny, repressed teens all locked up together. I can't imagine any of us not taking the time now and then to release ourselves, so to speak. But I don't know the rules for bed-and-body sharing.

Aiden, his body on me, in me . . .

"No way. Sorry. Can't sleep." The girl on my other side snores lightly. "Hey, Dez?"

"What."

"How'd you get that scar?"

Silence, and then I notice her vague silhouette sitting at the side of her bed. I sit too.

"I'm coming over," she says, and then she's by my side. "They told me it was because I wasn't *adjusting* well."

"They?"

"Yeah, the Singers. I told you they weren't very emotionally supportive. Guess I kept trying to run away. I remember going back to the farm, must have been about five, and I hid in one of the cow stalls. Amazed I didn't get crushed that night, but the cow was sweet. Farmer found me in the morning and brought me back."

"They did this to you when you were five?" I struggle to keep my voice down.

"No, not then. They weren't total monsters. But I kept trying to find a happier place to live, and a few years ago, they found me at the tubes."

My heart jumps at this revelation. She knows where the tubes are.

"What's so bad about being near the tubes?"

"I wasn't just near them. I was about to get inside one of them."

"So . . ."

"So they taught me a lesson."

"The Singers did this?"

"No, the psych docs. Started seeing them when I was about ten. They were supposed to help me 'adjust to the lifestyle expected of me.' Neurofeedback, they called it. They'd stick electrodes to my head and supposedly fix whatever they thought was out of whack. They apologized to the Singers after, said one of their techs accidentally bumped the lever that controls the intensity of the electrodes, but I never did believe it. I used to think they actually wanted to kill me. Stomp out the little troublemaker. Make it look like an accident. That's how I got the scar. But I'm tougher than I seem."

Her story makes me shudder. "And now?"

"I don't know. But I've never been back for treatments, as they call it. I think Father Malachy might be watching out for me."

"But what was your plan? What were you going to do in the tube? Zadak said they shoot out the dead into some isolated place underwater. Were you trying to—"

"Kill myself? Hell no. We've all heard rumors about bodies—dead ones—coming to Ironhold from the sea top, no one will confirm it, so I figured if they could bring bodies in, it could be a way to get out. I want to get out. Something's been weird here these last few years. I can feel it." She leans against me. Must be exhausted. I get it.

"I thought you all believe there's no life on land. Didn't that idea scare you?"

"They've told us that since we were kids, but a lot of us don't believe it. And once we started hearing stories now and then about the bodies, I figured there had to be people up there."

"How would the Singers handle it if you found a way to leave?"

A funny thought strikes me. Dez's curiosity took her from her adoptive family of three Singers. My curiosity took me from three Swimmers. Well, three if they took on the young novice as soon as I disappeared, which they probably did. I have to believe Aiden is safe with Sebastian.

"I already left. When we come here as cadets, we voluntarily give up our families. It was easy for me to make this decision. If I couldn't escape through the tubes, I could find a different kind of family here. We're basically all orphans at the Academy."

Just like the Swimmers. But I must still have a mother and a sister at home. Guess I never really did become an official Swimmer.

"What if I asked them to send me back? Sure, they rescued me from that tidal surge, but it's not like I volunteered to come here. Maybe they'll let you go back with me. The people in my village should know about Ironhold. If you saw how we live up there, you wouldn't be in such a hurry to leave. Can you swim?"

"Ha!" Dez's exclamation is loud, and several cadets flounce in beds near us. "Oops," she whispers. "Of course I can swim. Every civilian community in Ironhold has a pool. Swimming's one of the first skills we're taught as kids. Be pretty messed up living underwater and not knowing how to swim, don't you think?"

So different from people on land.

"But it's not like you go into the ocean to swim, right? So why is it so important to learn?"

"Huh. I dunno. Guess I never really thought about it."

"Are you ever afraid of it? Of the sea?" I want to ask about Calyxar.

"Nah. The founders and engineers who built Ironhold were the smartest people from around the planet. They knew what was coming before the planet paused, and they were ready for when the waters shifted. They built this place in a huge crater on land. Supposedly, they knew it would end up way underwater. I guess they were right. There was no damage at all to anything down here. We're pretty far down, you know."

I really don't know.

"But why didn't they build bunkers on land?"

"I dunno. I'm no engineer. Probably because things on land couldn't stand the impact or whatever. Slicken can handle pressure changes. And there's a constant source of energy from tides in the water. That's what we're told, anyway."

"So do you think I could get back home? Let everyone know I'm okay? Maybe bring the people in my village back here? This would be like a dream for them. There's nothing up there, Dez. It's a mess. Spotty electricity even though it's constantly windy, no medicine, long seasons that either burn or freeze or depress you, and some people don't live"—the words catch in my throat—"they don't live as long as people down here." The priest and many of the officers appear to be decades older than my parents and in far better health.

"You're dreamin', new cadet. You're in the military now. And listen. You have a big day tomorrow." She pats my leg. "Lots of classes. I don't suppose you've learned how to compute differential equations yet up there, have you?"

"I have no idea what those words mean. I'm a fast learner, though." *Differential equations?* "But hey, I'm not giving up on the idea of getting back home or getting a message to my family somehow. Will you help me?"

"With an impossible challenge? You're on. Now get some sleep, will you?" Dez stands.

"Just one more thing," I say.

She sighs and plops back down.

"What's the deal with the three-eyed octopus?"

13

DEZ YAWNS. "Are you asking about the symbol on our crest? Because I know you're not asking me if there's really a three-eyed, trident-wielding octopus out there. Please tell me you don't believe that. Did Zadak tell you about the whole Calyxar nonsense? Octopuses don't live very long, you know."

So many things I don't know. It could have been a trick. Maybe Father Malachy performed some illusion to validate his belief in the creature. But if that's true, how could he make it talk only to me? I can't tell Dez about my experience in the chapel. At least not yet.

"He told me Father Malachy was the only one who saw it when he was a kid. Why does USMA still use it on its crest?"

"Holy hell, newbie. You're killin' me." Dez leans against me again. "The bottom line is that a long time ago, someone convinced someone high up the eight-legged suckers were really smart and strong. Cadets are supposed to be smart and strong. Gotta admit, it would help to have more than two arms most days."

"I get the motto and the date, but what about carrying the spear thingy and having three eyes?"

"The spear thingy. You crack me up. It's called a trident, a weapon some ancient sea god used to carry, something like Posey or Poison—no, Poseidon. We obviously don't use those anymore, but they look cool. And the three eyes—now that I think about it, seems like everything in the old myths comes in threes—the three eyes mean we should be able to learn from the past, apply what we've learned to the present, and make intelligent decisions about the future. And now I'm going to make an intelligent decision about my future. I'm going to sleep. Reveille's gonna suck."

"Good night, Dez. And thanks."

Dez grunts, shoves my shoulder gently as she rises, and soon I hear the slow breathing of her slumber.

I still can't sleep.

Three eyes. Three points on a trident. Three Swimmers, three Singers, three spinning rings on my coin. Who has it? I have to convince Dez to help me find it. In her explorations of "happier" places in her youth, she probably knows more about Ironhold than most.

The memory of my coin—it's mine, it belongs to me, it should always be with me—makes the skin over my heart sting. Without them, I feel incomplete. A feeling that time is running out nags at me, as if time is some physical object that will soon be used up. Depleted. Gone. A quickening in my blood reminds me to control my breathing.

What was the Elder Swimmer's concern about time? Something to do with when the coin reappears, it'll be time, but he never finished his thought, and I didn't stick around long enough to press him on it.

And the bodies. Are they really returned to the sea from here? Why take the dead from land? What could the people of Ironhold be doing with them. Sure, bodies are merely flesh and bones, perfect for providing food for scavengers, but a place with abundant sources of plants, animals, and water shouldn't need dead bodies to supplement their diets. The thought makes my stomach clench.

I don't understand my role in any of it.

"LET IT GO NOW. BREATHE. YOU MUST CONTROL YOUR EMOTIONS. YOU MUST CONSERVE YOUR STRENGTH."

Blind in the darkness, I bolt upright and whisper, "Why are you talking to me? What do you want from me?"

"SOON. YOU WILL KNOW SOON. SLEEP NOW."

A three-eyed mythical octopus needs me for some reason. My brain feels like it's going to explode.

———— ❧ ————

Still awake when reveille blares, I roll from my cot and wait for the uniform announcement. Can Calyxar see me? Does it hear my thoughts? Would it be rude to ask if it's a *he* or a *she*? Can't imagine that matters.

When I hear "swimsuits under battle attire," I feel both dread and excitement for a day filled with physical activity and real school. The uniform makes me wonder again about the idea of battle.

Where, and who, are the enemies?

Glad I don't have long to ponder.

Confident in my memorization, I stand ready at the end of my tightly made cot when the inspecting officer asks me to recite words from General Douglas MacArthur, some ancient military leader. His whole long speech is in my little book.

"Sir, Duty, Honor, Country. Those three hallowed words reverently dictate what you ought to be, what you can be, what you will be. They are your rallying points, to build courage when courage seems to fail, to regain faith when there seems to be little cause for faith, to create hope when hope becomes forlorn."

I understand courage, faith and hope. The words don't really matter, though. All the officer wants to hear are the right words in the right order.

"New cadet Ing, why aren't you dressed for rehab?" His eyes pierce mine as if he can snag the truth from my pupils, but his expression quickly changes as his focus fluctuates between my right eye and my left. The grass green and the sky blue obviously fluster him.

I'll never blend in.

"Sir, I was released from rehab yesterday." It's true. I stare at his chest, avoiding his scrutiny.

"New cadet, what is the cadet honor code?" He seems eager to catch me in a lie.

"Sir, a cadet will not lie, cheat, steal, or tolerate those who do." I keep my face expressionless. At least I think I do.

The officer stays silent for too long, not moving away. If he asks me to recite The United Survivors Military Academy Song, I'm in trouble. Nothing. No movement, no demand. I'm nervous. Move on to the next cadet, sir, I think, and he frowns before moving along.

Did I do that? Nah. He's probably as uncomfortable as I am. But still. It's a bad idea to make people feel uncomfortable, curious, or even fearful around me. Like Mette with her fair features, I'm different. I try to imagine how people in my village would react if a stranger floated into our village from the skies above us.

We'd freak out. We'd protect ourselves. We'd want answers.

When the officer asks Dez to recite the Academy Song, I concentrate on her words. I'm pretty sure Dez speaks slowly and loudly for my benefit. Never knew I'd need to remember everything I heard. If I want to stay out of trouble at USMA, I'll have to.

The rest of the morning's inspection passes quickly, and we march off in step to the rhythm and lyrics of an upperclass cadet—Dez told me to call them uppers—echoing each short phrase in time with our steps.

"A yellow bird—*a yellow bird*

"With a yellow bill—*with a yellow bill*

"Was sitting on—*was sitting on*

"My windowsill—*my windowsill*

"I lured him in—*I lured him in*

"With a piece of bread—*with a piece of bread*

"And then I smashed—*and then I smashed*

"His little head—*his little head.*"

Flooding shite. If the purpose of these disgusting lyrics is designed to motivate and inspire us, it fails. Several new cadets snicker. After marching and echoing three other equally offensive songs, a change in the atmosphere tells me we're near the pool. The air feels thicker. The thought of swimming again excites me.

"Platoon, HALT!" The upper's command surprises me, and I march right into the cadet in front of me.

I don't know her name. She catches her balance, turns, and glares at me. I jump back and stand at attention, happy the upper hadn't noticed. Three rows behind me, Dez giggles. That gets his attention.

"Laughing? You think this is funny, new cadets? Who thinks this is funny?" He marches down our line toward me. I feel his eyes on me, but I keep my face a blank and my eyes straight ahead. "Was that you, weirdo? Hey! I'm talking to you." He pokes my arm.

"No, sir," I say, my voice even, my neck back, shoulders down, chest out, eyes ahead.

"Then who was it, new cadet?"

"Sir, I do not know." It could've been someone other than Dez, so I'm not really lying. After all, I don't know what everyone's giggle sounds like.

"Who knows, new cadets?" He walks past me, looking for another target, but no one speaks up. That makes me feel good. No snitches, not even Lou.

A man in the pool doorway clears his throat. The upper stops and says, "Platoon, fall out."

I don't move until everyone around me races for the door. I follow.

The pool opens at the end of a hallway beyond the gym, and the sight of it thrills me. It's not as big as the sea above, but its length and width make me itch to jump in and swim, and swim, and swim.

If only I could swim out of here and back into my world.

This is where we'll learn Survival Swimming. Dez points to a ladder leading up to a platform on a ridiculously high tower. Her eyes open wide. For the first time, I sense a hint of dread in my otherwise fearless friend.

"New cadets," a fit young officer shouts. "You will line up single file along that edge. When I blow this whistle, you will jump into the water, surface, place one hand on the edge, and await further instruction." He doesn't look at any of us when he barks his orders. He sounds annoyed.

There's no time to wonder why we're leaping into the pool fully clothed. The whistle makes me jump—I think I'm the first one into the water—and the weight of boots and uniform pull me under. I can't find the bottom of the pool. When another cadet's boot smacks my head, my brain flashes back to being out of control when the tidal wave sucked me under. *Panic.*

I try to kick, my arms thrashing around sluggishly in the soaked uniform jacket, but the angle of my feet in the tight boots do nothing to propel me. I look around in the sting of the salt water and see wavy images above me. My heart beats in my ears and I almost inhale, but a lifetime of practice holding my breath finally pays off.

You're fine, I convince myself. *You love the water. Swim.*

I surface to the sound of gagging and coughing as other cadets bob back to the surface. Evidently, this exercise is a first for them too.

Where's Dez?

"Today you will practice bobbing and traveling," the oblivious officer shouts.

Where's Dez?

"You will submerge, releasing air from your lungs slowly until you touch bottom, at which time—"

"Sir!" I yell. "New cadet Dez is—"

"Did I give you permission to speak, new cadet?"

I ignore him, I ignore the snickering of my classmates, I ignore my decision to blend in. Dez is in trouble.

Below the surface, I see her motionless shape at the bottom of the pool. I'm used to the sting of salt water in my eyes from countless hours of practice in the ocean. I swim toward her as fast as my cumbersome clothing allows. My heart pounds in my ears. *PLEASE-be-alive-please-be-alive-please-be-alive* I think, scooping her into my arms and pushing off from the hard surface.

It seems to take forever to resurface with one hand around my unconscious friend and the other stroking furiously, my boots making it nearly impossible to kick with any efficiency. Before reaching the top, I see another shape approach the side of the pool. Someone lifts Dez from my arms.

I breach the surface and gasp for air just as Lou raises Dez's body out of the water to the waiting officer.

Huh. Of all people, it's that obnoxious jerk who came to my aid.

Mette helps me from the pool, and we all watch as our instructor straddles Dez, alternately pressing on her chest and blowing into her mouth.

Come on, come on, come on, Dez. Breathe, dammit.

The air in the pool room presses in on me.

I think we all hold our breath.

The officer turns his head away and jumps up when a gush of water spews from Dez's mouth and her cough declares her return to consciousness. Scattered nervous laughter follow our group exhalation, and then all eyes are on me. I stand at attention as the officer approaches me, though my instinct is to rush to Dez's side. She pushes herself up slowly and looks more frightened than when she pointed to the high platform.

"New cadet, what you did demonstrates courage." The squint of his eyes warns me not to smile. "But it was also foolish. This is *survival swimming*, and all of you have grown up with pools." He gazes around at the class, "Not everyone will—"

"But sir, she—"

"Enough, new cadet." He spits into the pool. "Back into the water, all of you. New cadet Mette, escort new cadet Dez to sick call and return immediately. New cadet Lou, I'll speak with you later."

I stand dazed, unable to move, until Lou grabs my shirt-sleeve and pulls me to the pool's edge.

"Suck it up, Ing," he mumbles. I'm not sure if he's being helpful or just being a jerk again.

For the rest of the class, we submerge until our boots hit the bottom and then push off at an angle, "bobbing and traveling" across the length of the pool. Once I get the hang of it, it's easy. I can't stop worrying about Dez, though. Maybe like me, she was kicked in the head when another cadet jumped in after her. Or it could have been something else. Her talk about thinking the techs wanted her dead fills me with dread. I hope she'll get some rest and gentle treatment with Doctor Vesper.

Which reminds me, I'm due to return to her office. I'll use that as a reason to check on Dez once class ends. "Doctor's orders, sir," I'll say. I've lost my enthusiasm for being in a classroom.

"There will be no discussion or mention of today's unfortunate incident once you leave this room," the officer says at the end of class, his voice strangely hushed. "Is that understood?"

"Yes, sir," we answer in unison, though without enthusiasm.

"I said, is that *understood?*" Hands on hips, he glares at each of us in turn.

"Yes, SIR!"

What the flood? No mention of a girl almost drowning in class? There's no way this can be kept secret. I've heard how cadets talk before taps. Another kind of test, probably.

At least we don't have time now to jump from the high tower. I wasn't exactly looking forward to that either.

An upper arrives and marches us through a tunnel lined with powerful machines that blow water from our uniforms. The blast makes it hard to breathe. We push the person in front of us to end the abuse. Survival Swimming will be our first class of the day for the next few weeks, so I have to toughen up.

"Hey! New cadet! Where do you think you're going?"

An upper stops me when I turn toward the sick call clinic rather than toward the barracks to change for breakfast. I stand at attention again and recite my doctor's orders, keeping my eyes lowered.

"Show me the note," he demands. He stands inches from my face. His words leave a spray of spit on my face. So gross. I flinch.

The note. I have no note. Doctor Vesper didn't give me a note, she just told me to come back in a few days. "Sir, Doctor Vesper, she, uh—"

"She UH, new cadet? What do you mean, she UH? Are you spazzing on me, new cadet?" His nose nearly touches mine, and I step back. "Did I tell you to *move*, new cadet? Are you gonna run away crying now?"

He wants me to. I feel it. He wants me to break down, to run from him, to give him a reason to continue his abuse, to report me for disobeying a superior.

No way. I look him straight in the eyes, and he recoils slightly before regaining his stiff-back composure. Not sure why my eyes have such an unsettling effect on some and not others, but I like how this guy reacts.

"Sir, I'm to report to Doctor Vesper. I don't have the note because I've just come from the pool." I don't have the note for other reasons, but it seems like a sensible explanation.

"Then get there ASAP, spaz." Without another word he turns and walks away faster than necessary for his rank. I hurry to the clinic, relieved not to be stopped again. I'll miss breakfast, but I'm more accustomed to minimal meals than anyone else in this bizarre world.

A soft, sorrowful sobbing stops me when I enter the clinic. It's a female in the back room, but not Dez. I recognize Shayla's voice, the girl who appeared to be quite pregnant. With no one in the front office to acknowledge my arrival, I start toward the room when Doctor Vesper appears.

"Oh. Ing. You've come back. I see you're looking well." Her eyes dart from me to the back room several times. "The chews are helpful, yes?"

I won't tell her my decision to stop taking them. I have to know if they're possibly causing me to see and hear things, even though I believe Calyxar is real and has been communicating with me. There's no way for me to know about other side effects. I haven't felt faint again.

"Yes, Doctor, I'm feeling much better." I glance toward the room. "Is that . . . could I go see Shayla while I'm here? And I'd like to check on Dez, too."

I don't miss a flicker of fear in her eyes at the mention of Dez.

"No. That would be against protocol. Shayla will be just fine, and in a few days, she'll be back with her class. And Dez? Why would Dez be here?" She busies herself with papers on a countertop.

Oh, shite. "She was . . . Mette brought her, was supposed to . . . there was an . . ." I can't say the word accident, was ordered not to mention it, and don't know what might happen if I do.

"Sit down, please. Perhaps we should increase the dosage on your prescription. You look flushed." She glances at my chest, maybe looking for the glow. I have to get out of here.

"No. I mean, no, Doctor, I think it's just that I've missed breakfast, and survival swimming really wore me out. Bobbing and traveling today in full battle uniform." I indicate my partially damp clothing and try to ignore Shayla's weeping.

"Well, then, let's take another blood sample, just to be sure, and I'll send you with a note back to the Mess Hall." She preps a needle while she speaks, and I pull my arm from the sleeve.

"Doctor Vesper, would you please give me a note to return for my follow-up this time? An upper hazed me this morning for not having one." I'll find a way to use it to my benefit, and not for returning to a place I once thought was safe.

Dez is in trouble. I feel it in my blood.

"Of course." She removes the needle, all doctor-like again. Maybe I'm just being paranoid.

"Sir, may I ask a question?" I button my shirt.

"I'm a doctor, remember? Not an upper." She smiles, back in control. "What's on your mind?"

"Is this the only clinic for USMA cadets in Ironhold? I mean, is there another doctor I might have to see if you're not available?" What I really want to ask is why Shayla is still crying. Did she deliver her baby? I know nothing about the survival rate of babies born in a place like this. I just want to run in and hug her.

"This is the cadet clinic, but I'm not the only doctor. We rotate between several clinics. There's a large civilian population here. It's not all about the Academy, though some of *my* uppers would have us believe so." She pats my arm. "And then there are the animals. But let's get you on your way. Go to the table just to the right of the door inside the Mess Hall and give them this." She hands me a note. "I'll see you again in a few days. Keep taking your chews, and here's a note for your return."

I thank her, and before leaving the clinic, ask her to say hello to Shayla for me. "I hope her baby is okay," I say, and there's that flash of fear again. I leave her office and close the door behind me. Doctor Vesper needs to work on her poker face. My father taught me to practice my poker face if I ever found myself in trouble with another person, and it's already come in handy. I mastered it as a child. Tulip never could. Those eyebrows of hers.

Tulip. Mom. Aiden. Javier. I'll find my way back to them somehow, but I don't think my earlier idea of bringing them to Ironhold is a good one anymore. If the doctor is afraid of something, there has to be more to the place than anyone is letting on.

And now, Mette. Where did she take Dez? Standing with my back against the clinic door, I close my eyes and picture the route to the horrible room I woke in after my rescue. The room where Dez first found me. The horrible room with the hideous nurse where Dez just might be waiting for rescue.

I'm not going to the Mess Hall.

14

I GLANCE AT Doctor vesper's scribbled notes and smile. She forgot to date them. She was certainly eager to get me out of her clinic. Because she claimed not to know anything about Dez or what happened to her, I scramble for a plan.

The hallways should be free from uppers with everyone in the Mess Hall, but I don't know what Academy officers might be doing before classes start back up. Our swimming instructor is probably devising plans for covering up Dez's accident. The "unfortunate incident," as he put it. I can always use being a newbie and not knowing my way around as an excuse if someone stops me. It isn't a lie.

With a pretty good feel for how to find that cold, scary first room of my arrival, I speed-walk down the hallways—two rights, a left, a right, straight for a long stretch, then another right—and nearly slam into the horrible nurse, who just stepped out from the room.

Flooding shite.

"Well, if it isn't our little land dweller." Her sneer terrifies me. "What brings you back to my lab, new cadet? Shouldn't you be serving your cadre at breakfast?" She locks the door behind her and then shoves me against a wall.

ShiteShiteShite. *What do I do?* I could run. I could definitely outrun her.

"Sir, may I make a statement?" I remind myself to keep a poker face. Don't show any fear. Don't give her the pleasure. Keep my back straight, shoulders down, neck back. Easy to do against a wall.

"Oh, my. The perfect little cadet, aren't we now. How I would love to hear your statement, soldier, but you see, I have a job to do, and so do you." Inches from my face, she glares at me. "I would suggest you find your way back to the cadet wing." She pulls me off the wall by my collar and presses her forehead against mine. "And unless you'd like another little nap in my office, stay, the hell, away." She *kisses* me on my cheek—what the flood?—before pushing me away and slinking down the hallway like some satisfied cat.

Gross. I wipe the nasty nurse's saliva off my cheek and recall a saying about curiosity killing cats.

I left my mother, my sister, everyone, to satisfy my selfish curiosity. Mom was kind when she told me I wasn't being selfish. I know the truth.

And now I'm trapped in a fascinating undersea world where people live like those in pre-Halt days. And even though I know of no enemies—except, possibly, some uppers—there's a military academy for training young people how to be soldiers. There's a chapel with a barrier made of slicken and a three-eyed octopus who talks to me. There are clinics for sick or injured people and animals, so health isn't perfect, and accidents happen. Accidents kept secret. Secrets, and lies.

"A cadet will not lie, cheat, steal, or tolerate those who do." The cadet honor code doesn't seem to apply to officers.

I was selfish in my decision to join the Swimmers and selfish when I allowed Aiden to follow me out to sea. I'm selfish now, enjoying Ironhold's luxuries and challenges, even though the whole cadet business is weird. I'm still selfish in wanting more than life in a windy, struggling village.

It's time to think about someone other than myself.

I don't move until the wretched nurse turns a corner.

"Dez?" I whisper into the locked door. "Are you in there?"

Nothing. I rattle the doorknob. "Dez? I'll find you. If you're in there, I'll get you out. Chin up, friend. I'll be back."

I can't risk hanging around much longer, and as I hurry away, I mistakenly turn down an unfamiliar hallway. Already in an unauthorized place, I figure it won't hurt to explore. How much more trouble can I get into? Maybe I'll find Dez in one of the other clinics Doctor Vesper mentioned.

Near the end of the hallway, my chest aches. An unsettling sensation tugs at me, but maybe it's just because I'm lost. Who might stop me next?

Despite my better judgement, I follow the tug until I come to an unmarked door. I place my hand on the doorknob. Just as I'm about to turn it, I hear a commotion inside the room. Several voices. People excitedly speaking over one another. I remove my hand from the knob and back away, the glow on my chest hurting more than ever.

It's calling me. My coin. I'm sure it's in this room. It has to be here, sensing my presence somehow and pulling me toward it. Whatever it's doing, it's attracting the attention of people in the room. I'm not stupid enough to burst in.

I need help.

Bells and muffled conversation in the distance guide me back to the cadet area. I wait until there's silence, everyone seated in class, and hurry to the barracks to see which uniform is missing from my roommates' wardrobe. I'll change and find my classroom.

"Welcome back," a voice from the far side of the room stops me.

"Oh! Hey, Dash. Don't people with crutches have to go to classes?"

"Don't people *not* on crutches have to go to classes?" He smiles, and I relax. "I thought maybe you and Dez and Mette snuck off to the creamery or something. Dez gets caught there too many times, but she always smuggles back something for me. Where are they, anyway?"

"They didn't come back here after breakfast?" I play dumb. Dez told me Dash was one of the good ones, but I don't know how far to trust him. "I had to go to see Doctor Vesper for another blood test. I missed breakfast, and I didn't know which uniform to wear next."

"It's the *as for class* uniform. You'd be in math now. It's not far. I'll be cleared to put weight on my leg tomorrow, no more crutches, so it's back to the grind for me then. It's been nice just hanging out here, though. Nice and quiet. I'm already ahead in math, if you need any help."

Boy, do I need help.

"Thank you. I'll probably take you up on that. I have more catching up to do than you can imagine. No fancy classrooms where I come from."

"Must be nice. Hey, can I ask you something?" Dash swings his legs to the side of his bed and sits.

"Sir, may I ask a question?" I mock him, and we both laugh. "Of course. Ask whatever you want, and I won't lie."

"Why are you here? I mean, not here in this room, but here, at USMA. Don't take this the wrong way, but you just seem, I don't know, different from the rest of us. Like you're not supposed to be here. Like, I don't know, you're more important or something." He lowers his eyes, looking embarrassed.

Wow. I continue to dress as I answer.

"Huh. I'm not sure where to begin, but you're right. I'm not really supposed to be here. I should be back on land helping my mother and sister and making babies, but I ran away. Funny you should use that word, *important*. I wanted—no, I want to do something important, but I never expected to find a world like this."

I give him the short story of my journey here. I don't leave out the evil nurse and the torture table.

Dez could be on that same table, another victim of a water accident. I weigh whether or not to tell Dash. I need help.

"And now can I ask *you* something?" I button my shirt, and he nods. "Did you hear anything about Dez when everyone returned after breakfast?"

"What do you mean, did I hear anything about her? What happened?" He straightens.

Not wanting to say the words aloud across the room, I walk over to his bed and sit next to him.

"She's missing," I whisper. "I pulled her from the bottom of the pool, she was unconscious, and the instructor revived her. Mette was supposed to bring her to sick call, but she's not there. Doctor Vesper said she hadn't seen her."

Dash's eyes grow wide. He shakes his head and mumbles, "Dammit, Dez. She just can't catch a break."

"Shhh!" I put a finger to my lips.

"Why are you whispering?" he asks. "We're the only ones here."

"Because the swim instructor warned us not to tell anyone about it. What if people are listening to us right now?" Paranoid or not, we glance around the large room. "With what I've seen down here, I know they could find a way."

"What are we going to do about Dez and Mette?" he asks.

I want to hug him. He said "we."

We look at each other, neither of us knowing what to say next.

"Now I'll share something," Dash says, and to my surprise, he stands without his crutches before sitting again, seemingly in no pain. "I'm not proud of it, but I've been milking my med profile. I've been fine for a while now. This leg's probably stronger than my other one since I've been working on it here in the room."

"But why? Why would you want to be harassed every day with the rehab cadets?"

"Because see?" He spreads out his arms. "I have the room to myself for most of the day, and I don't have to put up with any of the shit. I had some kind of weird virus, too—don't worry, it's gone—so it made sense to keep me out of the classrooms."

"Look," I say. "I should probably get to class, but do you think we could search for Dez and Mette after taps? Are there guards or anything that might stop us? We'll have to be quiet. Wait for everyone to fall asleep. What do you think?"

He frowns. My heart sinks.

"You should get to class. Your schedule will pop up on your tablet when you open it every day. They probably didn't tell you that. And I'll think about tonight. Hey, what'll be your excuse for being late for math?"

I pull out the two notes from Doctor Vesper. Both are barely legible. One says, "follow-up in 3 days," and the other appears to say, "To Mess." My stomach grumbles.

"Here, give it to me." Dash holds out his hand. "It's already messy. Let's just change this to look like 'Math.' Easy peasy." He hands it back to me, but something feels wrong.

"Isn't this kind of like lying, though? Changing her word?" I don't want to get in any more trouble than I'm already in. I'd never say that Dash altered the note.

He raises his eyebrows as if the idea never occurred to him. "Wow, yeah, I guess you're right. I was just trying to help you, but you could be in big trouble if someone looked closely. I'm sorry. Here, give it back."

I almost give it back.

"Nope. I'm going to take my chances. And I don't want you to worry. I'll take full responsibility for whatever happens. Just . . . please . . . think about helping me tonight." I turn to leave.

"Good luck, then, new cadet Ing, Level Alpha." His attempt at formality makes us both laugh.

"Thanks. I'll see you later." I grab my writing tablet, a miraculous device, and get to class just before it ends. Students are closing their tablets when I walk in. The instructor raises her eyebrows.

"New cadet Ing, I've reported you as absent." It's the friendly officer who knows Dez.

"Sir, I have a note from Doctor Vesper." I hold out my note to her but before she can take it, the bell rings.

"Well, hurry off to your next class then, and I'll see you tomorrow. You have a lot of catching up to do."

"Yes, sir. Thank you, sir." I stash the note in a pocket and follow Lou down a hall to the next room. "Hey, Lou," I call to him.

"No talking in the hallways." He scowls at me over his shoulder. I stay right behind him.

Inside the classroom, we stand behind chairs like we do in the Mess Hall until the professor enters the room and a cadet nearest the door command, "Take seats." Lou seems irked when I sit next to him. My tablet shows this class is Military Art, but I see no drawings, no paintings, no sculptures of any sort in the stark room.

"Welcome, new cadet Ing. We've heard a lot about you. Welcome to USMA. Know that your peers will assist you in your lessons. All cadets are assets in our mission to protect our species against the possible invasion of aliens from other realms. This is the core of Military Art."

I hate being called out. What did they hear about me? And aliens from other realms? Calyxar comes to mind. Could the mind-talking octopus be an alien? A scary thought.

While the officer drones on about ancient military maneuvers that have no application to anything on our planet anymore, I hunt for the right letters on my tablet to create a message. "Thanks for helping this morning." I turn it toward Lou. He glances at it, but his expression doesn't change. Good poker face. I figure out how to erase that message and write, "Dez and Mette missing. Do you know where they are?"

Direct hit. He flinches and shakes his head once before turning away.

"New cadet Lou, I see new cadet Ing is asking you for assistance. Do not turn your back on her. You must cooperate to graduate, yes? Now, World War Three found soldiers who were . . ."

Shite. Didn't mean to get him in trouble.

The day drags on and my head throbs. New terminology, classes with questions I can't answer, and too much attention on "the girl from land," as everyone calls me. My presence upsets the story that there are no humans above, although there are already plenty of rumors that I've really lived here all along in some hidden section of Ironhold.

Finally, time for the end-of-day pre-taps ruckus. Lou marches up to me with fire in his eyes, and I hold my ground.

"What are you tryin' to do, huh? Do you know what would've happened if the P saw what you wrote?"

"No, I don't, and what's the P?"

"The professor, dumb-shit! Both our asses woulda been, hell, I don't even know, but you can't mention it. We can't talk about it, okay?" He paces back and forth between his cot and mine. He's afraid.

Everyone in the room hushes. They all know what happened at the pool. I glance at Dash, who gives me a thumbs up. Leg brace off, crutches gone. Ready for our rescue mission.

"Okay, okay, I'm sorry," I say. "I'm still getting used to everything. I didn't mean to get you in trouble today."

Lou stops and stands with his hands on his hips, but his eyes look sad. No more poker face. "Let's all just get some extra sleep tonight, okay? No messin' around now." He scans the room, and I watch as each person tucks themselves into bed. Even Dash.

So Lou's the leader of this group. If only I could trust him.

I stare at the two empty cots and want to shake him, want to shake them all out of their beds and insist they follow me in a search for our missing peers. What happened to cooperate to graduate? Is everyone afraid of what might happen if they disobey an order?

Maybe I should be afraid too, but my blood boils. Dez already has scars for something she did before becoming a cadet. How could anyone punish her for nearly drowning? I hold out hope for a different scenario. She could be in a special clinic for water-related accidents. But if that's the case, Mette should be here now to lead us all in an amusing performance of the Cadet Prayer.

It doesn't feel right having both of them missing.

"Goodnight, Lou," I say, and he grunts.

Taps plays. I'll never get over the knot in my heart and throat each time I hear its mournful melody. I wait. And wait. The silence nearly lulls me to sleep, but the pounding of my heart as I anticipate my search with Dash keeps me awake.

Finally, a tap on my shoulder. "Let's go," he whispers.

———— ❧ ————

Our uniform is gym clothes with head lamp, and bare feet for maximum stealth. We sneak from the room without disturbing a single sleeper.

"I think they might be in the same room where I woke up after my rescue. Follow me." The hallways are darkened. Not completely. Every surface gives off a weird glow. The path to that horrible room is seared into my memory. I run, light on my feet. Dash stays right behind me.

The atmosphere feels eerily quiet except for the *thrum, thrum, thrum,* as if every being in the entire undersea world is straining to hear our movement. I consider turning back. I stop—too quickly—and Dash grabs onto my shoulders and spins me around to prevent us both from falling.

"Sorry! Sorry. A little warning next time?" he says.

"Oops! Yes. Listen. I don't want to get you in trouble too. Maybe this isn't such a good idea. Maybe they'll be back in the morning, and I'm just overthinking things."

"You're not." He releases his grip on me. "There've been rumors of cadets disappearing over the years, but no one talks about it openly. Dez is tough, sometimes too tough for her own good, but Mette's never been in trouble. Something's not right. Lead on."

"If you're sure, okay."

He nods and turns me back in the right direction. We make it to the room without incident. Like before, the door is locked. I hold up one finger and press my ear to the door, listening for any voices or movement. Nothing.

"Any ideas?" I ask.

Dash retrieves something from a back pocket. He holds up a small tool. "It's one of my hobbies." He kneels by the door.

I hold my breath and keep watch while he fiddles with some strips of metal in the doorknob. Before long, I hear a *click*, and exhale. He looks up at me before turning the knob slowly. The door opens. I see the table and cringe.

The room is empty of all but my memories.

I motion for Dash to follow me inside, and he closes the door. "Maybe there's something here. Notes or charts or something." We search through drawers and cabinets. The countertops hold nothing except what I assume are surgical tools and needles filled with liquid. No notes, no mention of Dez or Mette or a swimming accident.

"Well, I'm actually glad they're not in here," I say. "This is no place for healing, and the nurse who works here? I hope you never have to meet her." And then, another thought comes to mind. "What about the chapel? Dez said the Singers raised her. Maybe they just sent her home." The Singers might not have maternal instincts, but I can't believe they'd be purposefully cruel. Maybe Dez will be reassigned to one of the stables. I can't imagine Mette milking a goat, though. She just seems too . . . proper.

"Huh. That's a good idea. It's worth a visit, and if we get caught, we can always say we're searching for enlightenment so we can be better soldiers." He grins. I appreciate his humor.

"One more thing before we leave," I say. "There's another room I need to get into first, before we go to the chapel."

"Sure. Where is it? And how do you know so much about the rooms in these hallways?"

"If you don't ask, I won't have to lie."

He smiles and jogs next to me to the room where I know they're keeping my coin. It tugs at me before we even get to the long hallway.

"Whoa! Are you all right?" Dash stops me. His eyes reflect the glow beneath my shirt. "We need to get you to a doctor." He forgets to whisper.

"No. Shhh. I'm okay, really. I'll explain later, but right now we need to—"

"There they are!" A familiar, loud voice echoes from down the hallway.

Lou. Flooding snitch. Two others accompany him. I can't tell if they're cadets or officers.

"Run!" I yell, and even though I have no destination in mind, I think we can outrun our pursuers.

"To the chapel." Dash punches something into something into his wristband and takes the lead.

I see the chapel doors. Just as they crack open, a searing pain in my back takes my breath away. And then, nothing.

———— ❧ ————

My hands tremble when I wake, and I'm afraid to open my eyes. They feel like they might be stuck shut. A horrifying thought.

"Hello?" My voice sounds raspy. I keep my eyes closed. Where am I? Why am I afraid. I can't remember . . .

I can't remember.

Someone places a cool, wet cloth across my eyes. A soft voice says, "You'll be all right. You've had a little mishap, but don't you worry."

"Who's there? Mom? Is that you, Mom?"

"Shh," the voice says. "It's Mette. Here. Let me take this cloth away. Open your eyes slowly, okay? You've been asleep for a long time."

It's not like me to sleep long, is it? I barely lift my lids, don't want to tear the skin off my eyeballs, and a ghostly face comes into focus. Not the creamy brown skin of my mother, but a girl with skin like a cloud and white hair. She said her name is Mette, but I don't recognize her.

"What happened to me? Why am I here? Where am I?" A horrible fear that I've been here before makes me fling my hands upward because I think they might be strapped down. *Why?*

"You don't know how you got here?" Mette asks. Something about her voice mesmerizes me. "You were swimming, remember? There was an incident, and you nearly drowned. Good thing we saved you."

The explanation seems right, but something doesn't add up.

"I want to go home. Will someone please take me home?"

Mette looks over her shoulder at an approaching figure. "Hello, Father Malachy. She's just woken up." The man wears long robes. My heart beats faster at the sight of him.

"Welcome back to the world of the living, child, we—"

My head pounds and my stomach lurches. Mette and the old man jump back when I puke.

"Oh, dear. Get the mop, please, Mette. I'll watch our patient. Do you not remember me? You visited with cadet Zadak. You saw Calyxar. I believe the creature spoke to you." He raises both eyebrows and waits for me to say something, but I stay silent. "Come. Perhaps you'll feel better in the chapel." He extends his hand to me, but I get up on the other side the bed and walk around it by myself, avoiding the mess I made.

"That girl, Mette, said I've been asleep for a while. How long?"

"Don't trouble yourself about that right now."

I shake my head and keep myself from rubbing my dry eyes. Still dizzy, I take several slow, deep breaths.

"Come," the man coaxes.

I follow him out of the small room. If anything will clear up the fog in my brain, I'll give it a try. As it is, I struggle to make sense of the sights and sounds around me. I'm nowhere near home, that's for sure, but the place doesn't seem entirely foreign to me, either.

Once inside the chapel, I hold my breath. "I remember this," I sigh into the overwhelming space. How could I forget the undulating membrane far above us? "Calyxar, the octopus, right?"

"Yes! She visited you here. Most unusual. No one has seen it for—well, for decades—and then you came along, dropping into our little world like a gift from the heavens." His words are nice, but they don't match his tone. He sounds worried. "Do you remember where you are now?"

I have no reason to distrust this man, but my instincts tell me to be careful. "Only this space and the octopus, but I don't know how I got here and what I'm supposed to be doing." It's not a lie. What is it about lying that triggers a memory?

"Now don't you worry. You'll get your memory back in time, I'm certain of it. And I'll be here to take good care of you. You see, there's been a mistake in your assignment. But we'll fix it. Let's get you some food. You look like you could eat a meal fit for an army."

An army. Cadets. Military art. Sweat trickles between my shoulder blades.

I shouldn't be here.

15

"**WHAT DO YOU** mean, there's been a mistake in my assignment?" Flashes of events evaporate as quickly as they come to mind. It's dizzying. Or maybe it's the subtle movement of the translucent barrier between us and the sea above. This place is underwater.

"You see, you came to Ironhold by most unusual circumstances, and the, ah, leadership decided you would be an asset to the Academy." He says *leadership* as if the word were smeared in shite.

I squeeze my eyes shut, glad they weren't injured while I was unconscious, and try to recall my sister's face, my mother's face, my father's . . . my father is dead. He's dead, and I swam with his body out to sea, and there were others, another dead body and—

"But I believe you're here for a reason. A very special reason. Don't you feel this is true?"

I don't know what's true.

"Where's my father?" Like the uppers do with new cadets—I remember that—I get right up in his face with my hands on my hips and look him straight in the eyes. I don't even hold my breath as I wait for his reply.

He stares at me like I'm an injured animal brought to him for care. Maybe that's what I am. My body aches and my brain's still fuzzy. Father Malachy—I remember now, he's a priest—opens and closes his mouth several times before saying, "He's . . . dead, child. Do you not know this?"

"I know he's dead, I know, but where is he? Where's his body? He's somewhere down here, I just know it. Don't lie to me. You know he's dead, so you must know what they did with him, and with the other Swimmer's body—the Elder who died out at sea, and with all of the others who died and ended up here." Everything comes back to me in a rush. What are they doing with dead bodies in Ironhold? I shudder.

"Oh, my. This is what I'm saying. It seems you know more than you should. This does not surprise me. It merely validates my belief you were brought here to serve a special purpose. The scientists down here are playing with fire. But I've said too much." He says *scientists* like he said *leadership*.

"No, you haven't said enough." I act bolder than I feel.

"Excuse me, Father Malachy. Lunch is ready." Mette approaches. I suspect she overheard our conversation.

The priest doesn't bother to look at her. "Wonderful, Mette. Ing and I will join you in a moment."

I glance from Father Malachy to Mette, and other memories, other faces, try to pull their way from the haze. I struggle to attach names and faces.

"Chicken soup with fresh bread." Mette smiles. "Just what the doctor ordered, right, Father?"

The doctor. Doctor Vesper. Will she be searching for me? She wrote notes for me, passes, and another cadet, a nice one, Dash. Yes, he altered one of the notes and helped me look for someone. A friend. I stare at Mette, and a memory of her sitting next to a girl with a scar on her face comes into vivid focus.

I know where I am. I remember what happened.

"Mette, where did you take Dez, and where's Dash?"

Mette's eyes flash surprise. She looks at Father Malachy for guidance. He nods, ever so subtly, and she starts to sing. It's the song I heard when Zadak brought me into the chapel, the one similar to the Swimmers' chant.

"Ahhhveyyy . . . Mariii . . . iahhh."

Mette is a Singer. Her voice made the cadets in our barracks recite the Cadet Prayer while spinning around like fools. I can't allow her to hypnotize me.

My head spins, and my legs wobble. I tilt toward Father Malachy. "Stop it! Stop it, Mette." I push away from him and lean against the back of a bench. She won't stop, though, so I block my ears against the beautiful, sorrowful melody.

And then I sing the Swimmers' chant while staring into her eyes as my *Ahveyah* fills the luminous space and I can hear only the vibration of my own voice. I walk toward her, feeling stronger with each step, and when Father Malachy grabs my arm, I push him away.

Mette takes several steps back and stops singing. I close the distance between us.

"Where . . . are . . . my friends?"

Mette looks beyond me to the priest, who says, "Come with me. I'll take you to Dez."

As I follow him toward a door at the other side of the great space, a thunderous voice in my head stops me.

"STAY." It's Calyxar. I freeze.

"Father Malachy, I don't know what's going on here with you and Mette and the Singers and why people either want me here or want to hurt me, but I need some time to think, so would you both just leave me alone here for a while? Please."

He looks down his nose at me. I think he might refuse my request. "How much time will you need?" He glances at the dome above us.

"Where will you be?" I counter. "I'll come to you. If you understand everything that's happened to me since I left home, you should be able to understand why I just need to think for a minute. And pray. By myself." This is where people come to pray to their Master.

He nods, almost smiles, and points to the room we left. "We'll save you some lunch. You really do need to eat." He and Mette leave me alone, and I walk to the center of the chapel. I have no reason to believe they won't be watching me, maybe even listening.

Should I run? Too many mixed messages. Mette already tried to influence me with her song, but why? And Father Malachy seems concerned about my health and my importance in Ironhold. But then he gave Mette some signal to hypnotize me. Why? I know of no safe place to run.

Dez would know. I fear for Dash, though. He was with me when we ran to the chapel. The priest didn't mention him. He said he'd take me to Dez. Maybe my accomplice is back in class after a reprimand for being off-limits. I hope so.

It feels good to sit quietly, alone, with no one yelling at me, spitting in my face, asking me stupid questions.

I want to go home. Mom somehow knew I'd be a "new cadet," but how? I don't believe she ever lied to me, but she did keep the coin hidden for too many years. My father must have agreed with her decision.

"ING." Calyxar's rumbling voice. **"DO NOT LOOK UP. CLOSE YOUR EYES."**

But I want to raise my eyes to the curious dome above, want to see the mythical octopus, want to scream, "Get me out of here! Take me home!" Instead, I do as it says. I close my eyes. I'm guessing it doesn't want anyone to know it's close by. For me.

"THE PRIEST IS CORRECT. YOU ARE IMPORTANT. TIME GROWS SHORT. SOON I WILL ASK YOU TO CHOOSE. YOU WILL NOT BE ALONE."

Choose what? Tempted to look up, I squeeze my eyes shut and bow my head. If anyone's watching, they'll think I'm praying. How do I talk to this creature, though? It mentioned time. Sebastian, the Swimmers' new Elder, appeared concerned when he spoke of time and my coin.

I have to get it back.

"I HEAR YOUR THOUGHTS. YOU WANT TO GO HOME, BUT YOU CANNOT. OUR PLANET IS IN PERIL, AND YOU MUST—"

"Hello? Is someone out there?" A voice from behind the far door. Dez.

Despite my better judgment, I bolt from the bench and run toward the door.

"Ing, wait! You don't understand!" Father Malachy shuffles out from the other room—I was right, they've been watching me—but I'm faster and closer.

"Dez, open the door." I call to her, but it stays closed. I slam into it and turn the knob. Locked. "Dez? Are you okay? Open the door."

Father Malachy slows to a walk until he stands behind me. I feel his hand on my shoulder. "Please. She's been through a lot." He unlocks the door.

"Hello." The door opens and Dez smiles at me. Her head is shaved. "Who are you?"

———— ❧ ————

I glare at the priest but soften my expression when I see the pain in his eyes.

"What . . . happened?" I turn back to Dez, who's still smiling at me with a vacant expression in her eyes. "Hi, Dez. My name's Ing. Father Malachy said I could visit with you, maybe because we're the same age. I'm new here." I want to throw up again. This isn't the feisty friend who brought me food and helped me adjust to being a cadet. If not for the scar on Dez's face, more pronounced without hair to hide it, I might not recognize her.

She smiles at Father Malachy, and then beyond him at Mette, who pushes past me into the room. "Come in. All of you come in," Dez says. "I'm hungry. Is anyone else hungry?"

I'm always hungry. "Yes, I am. Maybe Father Malachy will bring us some sandwiches." I look at him, challenging him, wanting him to leave us alone, if only for a little while.

He hesitates and narrows his eyes. "Of course. Sandwiches. Dez, you will eat if I bring them?"

Dez's expression changes, as if the question baffles her. "Why wouldn't I?" She pouts.

"Of course you will. Foolish me. I shall return momentarily. Mette and Ing will visit with you while I'm gone." He and Mette exchange glances, and I prepare myself for another song. I'm not about to let that happen. As soon as the priest leaves, I grab Mette by her sleeve and pull her to the back of the room away from Dez. "Give me a minute, Dez. I just need to ask Mette something, okay?"

Dez nods, and I watch her clear a small table for our meal.

Mette yanks her sleeve from my grasp and whispers, "What do you think you're doing? You have no idea what's about to happen."

"Then fill me in, and be quick about it. What happened to Dez after the pool? You were supposed to take her to sick call. Who did this to her, and who the hell are you? You're not a cadet."

"Listen, that's not important. Something big's about to happen, and you show up just as we're trying to prepare."

"Prepare for what?"

"For something really bad. Another catastrophe, I think. I don't know exactly what, but the scientists are working on something, and Father Malachy's been trying to find out what. He doesn't trust them, and the feeling's mutual, so he thought maybe Dez and I could infiltrate their labs and find out what they're not telling us. Dez knows more about Ironhold than anyone our age—"

"And you can hypnotize people with your song. These scientists, are they the ones bringing in the dead from above?" The horrible nurse's face comes to mind, and I shudder.

"I don't . . . I don't know what you're talking about."

She looks genuinely confused. I believe her.

"I *did* bring Dez to the clinic, she was breathing fine, really, and then Father Malachy came and signed us out. He warned Doctor Vesper not to let anyone know. She's a good doctor, above board, and doesn't get mixed up in any of the politics. There aren't many safe places for people to hide, and the chapel is one place the scientists won't visit. Father Malachy might seem intense, but he's a good man."

"Then how'd she end up like she is now?" I want to ask about Shayla's baby, but I don't have much time before the priest gets back, and Dez is looking at us.

"The scientists, they got her. You see what they did to her before. Anyway, I think she was trying to get back to the cadet area. She talked to Father Malachy about you, how you saved her life—that was amazing, by the way—and she must have been going to get you. I didn't know she'd left, and—"

"I'm ready," Dez says. "Enough whispering." She stares at me. I notice a flash of recognition, a flicker of the real Dez. "You're really pretty," she says, "but someone did a real number on your hair."

"Yeah," I say. "I don't care, though. Hair's overrated."

Father Malachy returns with sandwiches and two bowls of soup for Dez and me.

"And look who's talking about doing a number on hair!" Mette says, running her hand gently over Dez's bald head.

"Yeah." Dez looks thoughtful. "I guess I cut it off so I wouldn't have to fuss with it."

Someone must have planted that memory in her brain. Would the Singers do that? Who were they?

We eat, and Father Malachy smiles genuinely. Maybe I've misjudged him. Maybe I've misjudged them all. They must care about Dez. And despite lacking natural maternal affection, the Singers raised this abandoned girl.

Dez should be with them instead of in a room alone, recuperating from whatever the scientists did to her. If in fact it was them.

It's all exhausting. My body feels primed to run, to hide, to scream. Something dangerous looms in the atmosphere, something invisible yet palpable.

Calyxar knows. It told me the planet is in peril. It was going to tell me more. Will it speak to me in places other than the chapel?

"YES."

I flinch.

"This has been lovely." Father Malachy gathers the empty dishes. "Our guest needs to rest now, Dez, but we'll check in on you again soon. You rest up too. We all need to be strong for our next adventure." He makes it sound like we'll be going for a long walk around Ironhold later. Dez walks with us to the door.

"I enjoyed our visit, Dez." I take her hands in mine and stare into her eyes, trying to find her, trying to remind her she knows me, trying to break through whatever barrier has dampened her fighting spirit. I lean in close and whisper, "And thanks for making up my cot that first morning in the barracks."

She grips my hands tightly. She remembers. "She can stay with me, Father Malachy. We'll rest. Promise."

"Maybe tomorrow," he says. "When you're feeling stronger." He must have a plan that will make sense to me.

"I'll see you tomorrow, Dez," I say.

She releases my hands, and after we leave her room, Mette locks the door.

"Why?" I ask.

"To keep her safe," she says.

We walk through the chapel to the other side. I stop myself from looking for Calyxar. Back in the room where my puke has been cleaned up, I sit on the bed.

The priest explains, "They left her outside the chapel door as a warning, we think. I don't know what she might have told them. What they might have forced her to tell them. She's a fighter, but I think you experienced some of their methods when you first arrived, yes? I'll never understand why the scientists handed you over to the Academy, though."

I wonder about that too.

"Well, if they're working with—or for—the uppers in the Academy, then they know they can keep me in line. And if you're right about me, Father—"

"I am," he interrupts.

"Then I need to figure out what I'm supposed to be doing down here. When I left my home, I had an emerald-green coin with me. When I woke up, it was gone. Do you know anything about it?"

He and Mette shake their heads slowly.

"Dash and I were on our way to find it before coming here to look for Dez. By the way, you never told me about Dash. Is he okay?"

Father Malachy bows his head. My heart skips a beat. "I'm sorry. We couldn't save you both."

From another room, three robed women emerge. The Singers. One of them speaks.

"They stunned you both. We were returning from visitations with the believers." Her voice is like the fragrant breeze in my forest above. My senses fill with longing for home, for my family, for Aiden, even for the struggles we endure. "You were closer. We lifted you inside but were not swift enough. He was gone when we returned for him."

"If you let us," says another, "we can ease your grief."

"No! I don't want you to do anything to me." *How do they sense my grief?* "But if you have the kind of power I think you have, then bring Dez back."

Father Malachy puts an arm around my shoulder, but I shrug it off.

I hate being treated like a child.

My irritation shifts to anger. "Why didn't you stop those attackers with your song? Did you think Dash just wasn't important enough to save?"

"Sadly, we could not," says the eldest, but she doesn't look sad at all. Maybe the Singers aren't capable of emotion. "Knowing our ways, they came prepared with sound-blocking devices."

"We have faith Dez will come back to us when she's ready." The youngest of the Singers places a cold hand on my knee.

My eyelids feel like the tarps over our windows at home. So heavy.

"You must have faith. Do not push her too quickly," says another.

Faith in who, in what? "But what if we don't have time to wait? It's no secret something bad is about to happen. Even Calyxar—"

Shite. I said too much. My head is a dustbin.

"Yes?" Perched on the edge of his seat, the priest leans toward me. "Even Calyxar?" He tilts his head and raises his eyebrows, encouraging me to finish.

"What did you do to me?" The soup. They must have put something in the soup.

"Go on. Calyxar told you something? What did . . ."

I hold my breath. Father Malachy's words fade. I stop fighting, close my eyes, and let go.

———— ⮑ ————

Why would they do this to me? My last thought as I fall away from my surroundings.

"BECAUSE THEY BELIEVE YOU HAVE AN ABILITY THEY DO NOT UNDERSTAND. THEY WANT TO KEEP YOU SAFE UNTIL THEY LEARN WHAT YOU CAN DO. THEY HOPE FOR MORE TIME." Calyxar's voice may be my dream's imagination, but we're together, somehow, in a place where no one can hear or hurt us.

"What is this ability? Do you know?" All I know is my coin wants, needs, has to be with me.

"I KNOW MANY THINGS, FOR I HAVE BEEN HERE SINCE THE BEGINNING."

"The beginning of what?"

"THE BEGINNING." No explanation.

"But you have to know about my coin. I'll get it back, I know where it is, but what then? Will it help me get back home? Will I find my father?"

Everything I've done since leaving home suddenly feels like a mistake.

"WHEN IT UNITES WITH YOU NEXT, IT WILL BE TIME."

Calyxar must know exactly what will happen. I grow impatient. *"What aren't you telling me? Why aren't you telling me?"*

"YOU WILL DECIDE THE FATE OF THOSE REMAINING IN YOUR WORLD. THERE IS MUCH AT STAKE."

What the flood! *"The fate of . . . what the . . . no. That's insane. I'm just a . . . a girl . . . I can't . . . I can't . . ."*

I don't know how my brain disengages from the terrifying voice and what it told me, but it does, and for what must be for hours.

I wake slowly, purposefully, listening to the whispers around me before opening my eyes. I hear Mette's voice first.

"I told you it was too much. What if she doesn't wake up?"

"Nonsense." The priest's voice. "Dez is already awake. It shouldn't be long, and in any case, she needed sleep. Look. Her color is already coming back. Poor girl. None of this is her fault."

Well, I could've stayed home.

The Singers speak, one or two or all three. Their mesmerizing voices blend together. "Do you truly believe she speaks with Calyxar?"

"Yes."

"Then the prophesy soon will transpire. This bodes poorly for the human race."

The Singers' voices sound strangely mechanical. I keep my eyes closed.

Prophesy? I wait, hoping to hear more, hoping they'll leave me alone, hoping—

No such luck. "Ing? Wake up, child." Father Malachy nudges me gently. I can't pretend I'm still asleep.

"Why?" My voice sounds far away. "Why did you drug me? What do you want from me?" I sit slowly, my head pounding. I want to be back at the Academy. At least there I don't have to think about what I'm supposed to do, to wear, to say.

But Dash paid for my disobedience—I still don't know where he is—and Lou was with the bastards who hunted us down.

The priest speaks softly. "You have done too much too quickly. When I saw how weak and pale you've become since your visit with Zadak not long ago, I had to intervene. We need you to be strong, Ing."

"Why? For the prophesy?"

He inhales sharply.

"How . . . what do you know about the prophesy?" Mette asks.

"I know you're afraid of it. I know it's not a good one."

Father Malachy looks at Mette. His forehead wrinkles.

"Stop hiding what you know," I demand. "Who's actually in charge down here? Is there a Council? Who's the upper of the uppers? Maybe that's who I need to talk to. And thanks for your concern about my health, Father, but I'm beginning to think your motives are more selfish than you want to admit."

He stares at his sandaled feet.

"You are correct," he admits. "I have been selfish, and for a good reason. You see, it is my calling to protect and save as many believers as I can."

"Believers in what?"

"Why, in *God*, child. In a better life beyond this troubled sphere. It has always been my calling. But now, there is a new urgency. A different urgency." He looks at the Singers. "The prophesy, as passed down since before the Pause, when scientists and community leaders came together to create this entire spectacular metropolis"—he waves his arms out wide—"told of a time when we would no longer be safe on this planet, despite the technology that went into creating this specialized ecosystem."

"But what's the danger?" I ask. "Why won't you be safe?"

"I suppose you must know. The Pause is about to end. Another impact is imminent. According to the prophesy, the collision shall release a species farther advanced than any we've encountered in the history of our planet. Aliens."

"But . . . isn't that a good thing?" I ask. "Isn't that why there's an academy here, so young people can—"

Oh, flood. So young people can battle the aliens. Defend against the unknown. Protect they ways they've been trained to believe are the right ways.

Mette answers. "There's more." She looks at Father Malachy, eyebrows raised, and he nods. "The prophesy also says that the species will look upon us as vermin. They will destroy us and claim our planet as their own."

I shudder. "And you believe that time has come?"

"I do," says the priest.

"So you're going to save the believers. What about those who don't share your belief?"

"The choice is theirs. It always has been."

"Is it really, though, Father?" I look directly at each of the Singers and then glare at Mette. "I've seen how you influence people. Do your *believers* honestly have a choice if you're hypnotizing them into following you?" Now I know why all those people in the chapel had such dazed expressions.

"It's not that simple," he says. "What's important now, though, is that you are here. The prophecy told of a way to safety, a way that would be delivered by one from above.

Your arrival in Ironhold can be no coincidence." His eyes pierce mine.

"How is it, then, that a *non*believer might be your only hope for surviving whatever catastrophe you think is coming, even if she has no idea how she's tied to any of this?"

He stares at me open-mouthed. And then, the sound of feet running through the chapel turns us all toward the door.

"Ing? Talk to me, Ing—where are you?"

It's Dez!

16

"IN HERE!" I stand too quickly and grab onto Mette when a wave of dizziness hits. Our eyes meet. I can't tell if she's angry or scared.

"Sorry," I say, pushing her away gently. I open the door just as Dez bursts in, and we collide.

"Ing!" Her face brightens before she collapses in my arms.

"Someone get a doctor, fast!" I pull her to the bed. She's ghostly pale. Sweat covers her face. "And someone get a cold cloth." One of the Singers floats from the room. I hope she's going for a doctor.

Mette disappears and returns with a basin of cool water and a cloth. The priest takes Dez's hand and mumbles a prayer.

Dez opens her eyes and tries to sit.

"Wait," I say. I wring out the cloth and drape it across her forehead before thanking Mette.

"What happened?" she asks, looking from me to Father Malachy. "What am I doing here? What's Ing doing here?"

"Tell us what you remember." Father Malachy pats her hand before letting it go. "You've been through quite an ordeal these past several days. Do you remember the swimming pool?"

Her eyes open wide. "Yes! I totally freaked! I mean, I know how to swim, but I've never been in a pool that deep and I kept waiting to hit the bottom and I never did and then I tried to swim back up but my lungs were screaming and I couldn't kick right with the boots on and I wasn't even sure which way was up anymore and someone bumped into me, hard, and I lost it."

"Shhh, slow down, Dez. You're safe now." I press my hand to her shoulder to keep her from jumping up.

She looks at me. "And then Mette told me you saved me. Is that true?"

"Well, I brought you back to the surface and Lou helped lift you out—"

"Lou? What the—"

"Yes, he pulled you out, and the instructor resuscitated you. He told Mette to bring you to sick call, and then—"

"I'm here." Doctor Vesper enters and practically shoves me aside. "What seems to be the problem?" She places a hand on Dez's forehead and examines her eyes with a small light.

Dez pushes her hand away. "I'm fine! Really, I'm fine. I'm just . . . what happened? I had a weird dream we were having some kind of lunch meeting, and then I woke up locked in the room over there." She points in the general direction of the other room. "Oh, and sorry, Father, I might have dented one of those monster candle holders when I broke the door handle."

I chuckle. Dez is back.

Doctor Vesper scans the room. Her nostrils flare. "What's going on here?"

"We were—" I want to tell her the priest drugged us to keep us from leaving, or to keep us safe, I don't know, but she interrupts.

"I released Dez with meds and a bed rest recovery profile for a week. Mette, you were to take her back to the barracks. Why aren't you girls at the Academy?" Her sharp tone disturbs me. She lied to me about not seeing Dez after the accident.

Father Malachy glares at her. "You know why, Doctor."

"But . . . no. You mean . . . then it's true?" Her voice trembles, and her wide eyes betray her otherwise professional appearance. "Are you certain?"

Father Malachy is locked in a staring contest with her.

Dez pushes away my hand and sits. "Enough already. Mette? What are they talking about?" She scratches her head. "And no offense, Father, but what in holy hell happened to my hair?"

Mette speaks. "They got you, Dez. I didn't think you'd leave on your own. You were safe here in the chapel. Why'd you leave?" Her upturned hands make her appear vulnerable, but I don't trust her. At any moment she and her Siren sisters could attempt some form of control over the room.

Dez scowls at the Singers, her childhood caretakers, who stand mute against a far wall. Finally, she says, "I've been manipulated my whole life. There's no way I was gonna go back to being their little project." She stands and walks toward the door, rubbing her bald head, and then turns around to face the room. "Time to tell us what's going on, Father. And Doctor Vesper obviously knows something too. What do you expect Mette and me to find when you send us on these secret missions to the science labs? Do you really think they'll let us just walk right in and ask what they're up to?"

"And are we really safe here in the Chapel?" I ask. Every nerve in my body vibrates. I scan the room for other possible exits.

"CALM YOURSELF," Calyxar booms. I glance around the room. No one else appears to hear it.

I take a deep breath and hold it, waiting for more. But nothing. I exhale.

"Yes, you are safe here." Father Malachy's voice doesn't convince me. "From the beginning, all branches signed a contract of cooperation and noninterference."

"All branches? What does that mean?" I ask Dez.

"Like, the chapel is one branch," she says, "and the labs and the farms and the maintenance and the Academy and each neighborhood wing, they're all independent. They cooperate, for obvious reasons, but they're all self-regulated, and violations aren't tolerated."

"But who's in charge? What's keeping the scientists from barging in here right now and, I don't know, killing us or drugging us?" I glare at Father Malachy.

"The worst kind of banishment," he says.

"The tubes," Doctor Vesper mumbles.

The room falls silent. I still don't understand. "But if no one's in charge, how, why would any agency follow the keep-to-yourself rule?'

"Fear," the Elder Singer breaks the silence. "Rumors are powerful, are they not, Father?"

Father Malachy nods, his eyes downcast.

The Singer continues. "The first generation living below the sea heard a warning, every one of them, in the same dream and by the same voice. The voice said that if any agency encroached on another or planned any harm upon another's territory, this entire metropolis would be"—she looks at each of us before delivering her final word—"crushed."

"Calyxar," I say, stupidly.

"What did you say?" Doctor Vesper straightens in her seat.

The priest's eyes light up. "You heard her, you did. Tell us what she said to you. What do you know?"

What do I know. The tension in the room tastes bitter.

"I don't *know* anything for sure, but I can guess. You've all been living with this vague threat that if any group of people harms another, the consequences will be death for everyone. And yet you have a military academy training to defend against some alien enemy from an old-ass story, scientists you don't trust, and people in the medical field who are into torturing young people." I glance at Dez's scar. "And even though you all seem to be living healthy lives, you lie about the conditions on land." The weight of water above us and the constant *thrum* suddenly oppresses me.

"Why lie?" I continue, my face hot. "I came from there, from a community struggling every day to tolerate the constant wind, the insufficient food, the endless months of brutal sun or depressing shade or frigid darkness. There's life above. Why deny it? Why stay down here? And why deprive us of all you have? What's the purpose of any of this?" I throw my arms out wide.

"The purpose, child, is to keep humanity alive." Father Malachy paces the room, hands clasped behind his back. "The architects of Ironhold came from all of the military services and the brightest minds. They anticipated the Pause and built our habitat to withstand its effects. They knew there would be survivors, though scarce, upon the land, and that not everyone would join them in their plans for moving to a homeland that would end up submerged. The plan has always been that after surviving the next prophesied impact, we all would return to land, and our soldiers would destroy the aliens."

"And do what with those barely surviving above? Confine us? Kill us? Enlist us in your military? Will anyone above even survive if what you say is true?" I panic. No one in my village knows about this prophesy, unless Sebastian has kept it a secret among the Swimmers.

Where are you, Aiden? Do you know about this? Is this how I will lose you again? A sour taste rises in my throat. I swallow it down. The gray walls press in on me.

"CLOSE YOUR EYES. SLOW YOUR BREATHING." Calyxar's thunderous voice shakes me from my dread. **"THEY DO NOT HAVE ANSWERS."**

Dez moves toward me and takes my hand. With her other hand on her hip and defiance on her face, she addresses the room.

"Yeah, how about telling us what *you* all know?"

With Dez by my side, the room's oppression eases.

"Maybe start by explaining what happens with your dead and with the dead from above, like my father, who was just sucked down here somewhere by a massive funnel." I challenge Doctor Vesper. "You're involved too, I think. Father

Malachy, you and the Singers must know something. When Zadak brought me to the chapel, you were all in another room. He said there was a death ceremony going on. What happens after that?"

The doctor and the priest exchange a glance, but neither speaks.

"Well?" Dez demands. "She has a right to know. We all do." She addresses the Singers. "But you three already know. I can tell by your expressions." Their poker faces remain unyielding. Dez must be able to see some slight change in their expressions that I can't see. They make me feel uncomfortable. Cold.

Doctor Vesper slumps in her seat. "Like Father Malachy said, we don't encroach on other agency domains, but I will admit to being troubled by snippets of conversations. I'm not one to encourage rumors, but the disposition of Shayla's baby—"

"Careful, doctor," the priest cuts her off.

"Why should I be careful anymore if what I'm hearing is true?" She straightens, her tone sharp.

"What happened to her baby?" I shout, releasing Dez's hand and marching toward her. "I heard Shayla crying the last time I was in your clinic. What did you do with her? With her baby?"

The doctor puts up her hands as if to keep me away, and I stop right in front of her.

"They took her. The baby." She squeezes her eyes shut, a pained expression on her face.

"Took her where? Who took her?" I look around the room at the others, who don't appear to be surprised at all by this news.

"Shayla is fine," the doctor says. "She's back at the Academy. And the baby, well, they take all of the babies born to cadets. It's what they've always done."

It's Dez's turn to march up to her. "Who takes them, and why?"

"Who else, Dez?" The priest's face, like his body, wilts. "The scientists. I thought—no, I made myself believe they were placing the newborns in civilian homes to be raised until they were old enough to join the Academy, but now, now I suspect the rumors are true."

"Go on," I say.

"When the time comes to return to the land, repopulation will be, for lack of a better word, purposeful. Training at the Academy is meant to develop a population of strong, obedient citizens."

"Oh, wow," I say. "Is that why you—or someone—assigned me to the Academy? To make me obedient?"

The priest shakes his bowed head slowly.

"But the babies," says Dez. "If they're not being raised in families, then—"

"Then who do you suppose is raising them?" Doctor Vesper stands and moves away from us, turning her face to a wall.

Dez shouts at Father Malachy, "Did you know about this?"

He raises his head but doesn't look at her. "I had my suspicions."

"And all these years, the mothers just let their babies get taken away?" Dez places both hands on her head as if to contain her emotions.

"No. Of course not." The doctor turns around and leans against the wall. "We're ordered to sedate them when it's time. When they waken, they're given the sad news of their infant's failure to survive." She mumbles the last words. "Cadets have come to believe they can never bear a live child, though many still try . . . and hope."

"This is beyond cruel," I say. "How can taking babies from their mothers be considered anything other than actions that inflict harm? And you're all in on it."

"No, we're—"

"Aren't you, though?" I cut off the doctor's protest. "You're providing newborns to the scientists for hell-only-knows what wicked purposes, and you just wash your hands of it? How could you?" *Does Calyxar know about this?*

"I KNOW. AND SOON, YOU WILL RIGHT MANY WRONGS. TONIGHT, WITH DEZ, YOU WILL FIND AN-SWERS."

Maybe the priest and the doctors had no choice when faced with a smarter agency, even one that agreed to a doctrine of noninterference. Scientists probably have more available resources. I suspect they recruit only the cleverest citizens. They found ways of manipulating the doctrine to their advantage, and without fear of dooming the entire metropolis to being crushed.

I shake my head in disgust at Doctor Vesper. She participated in procedures she knew were wrong and didn't do anything to stop them.

Couldn't, maybe.

"But that doesn't explain the dead. Where's my father's body?" I look from the priest to the doctor to the Singers waiting for someone to answer me.

The priest starts. "We can only suspect he and the others are being used for research. For what, we honestly do not know. With the grieving family and our Singers, I preside over somber, respectful reflections on the departed, after which the family says goodbye, and the Singers transport the body to the tubes."

I cringe at the mention of the tubes, my way into this increasingly corrupt place and, possibly, my way out. "And then what?"

The youngest Singer finally speaks. "And then, someone from the scientific community presents us with a document confirming disposition of the body to the sea, and we are asked to depart. We never witness the final disposition."

"So they're probably keeping those bodies too," Dez says. "But why? And . . . ick." She throws herself back onto the bed.

"That's another thing we were hoping you and Mette might discover for us," says Father Malachy. "And now, it would appear, you too, Ing. But I fear there's no time for that now."

"What do you mean?" I ask. My chest tightens. It feels like a glow might start where my coin should be. The spot aches.

The priest answers. "There's talk that the rogue viscous body that caused the planet to pause a century ago is already on a collision path back to our planet with its invaders. It is roughly the size of our Earth, and it is close. I believe that's why you are here."

I try to imagine such a thing. A planet-size ocean filled with some advanced species in a speeding bubble. I think about slicken, the impenetrable skin that keeps our ocean from drowning the entire population of Ironhold. "Is the chapel the only place with a ceiling made of slicken?" I ask, not that the answer would matter.

"Why do you ask?" Doctor Vesper looks at me as if I'd asked how to pull the plug on this place. What a thought.

"Well, I guess I'm wondering what might be able to puncture it."

Mette looks horrified. "It's impenetrable," she nearly shouts, her eyes wide, and I think she might spout off the definition of slicken.

"That's right," Father Malachy agrees. "Slicken was installed in several places around Ironhold. You haven't been here long enough to have visited every sector, not that you would be required to. The substance was bioengineered to be even stronger than most of the metals used in construction. Its design qualities allow for flexibility when there are pressure fluctuations in the environment, both inside and in the surrounding ocean. Quite brilliant, actually. And like many creatures in the sea, slicken is engineered with regenerative properties. No need to worry about it failing."

Thrum, thrum, thrum. If only my breathing was as steady as Ironhold's.

"Oh, good. It's just that I've never seen anything like it, and it makes me nervous." I wonder if that approaching rogue thing might be surrounded by slicken. If something the size of our planet were tough enough to crash into us without bursting, then maybe it's similarly engineered. Maybe it will burst. How else will the aliens get out? I keep these thoughts to myself. "So what do we do now?"

"Yeah, and if you're sending us out to snoop, what's in it for us?" Dez asks. "Seems like we should be given some kind of incentive to put ourselves out there again. I haven't exactly had great luck lately." She points to her bald head.

Father Malachy places an arm around her shoulders. He looks at her with kind eyes. "You are as precious to me as a daughter, Dez. I don't ask you to do this lightly. Your incentive would be the same incentive for all of us. Survival. The scientists know something about this collision, and you can be sure they'll take whatever action is necessary to protect themselves. But they're not sharing their information. They've been more secretive than normal lately and won't respond to our queries."

"Keeping secrets?" I ask him. "That sounds pretty childish. Have you gone to them in person and asked what's going on? Or are you afraid of them?" Too bold.

Father Malachy looks at me and shakes his head slowly. I feel ashamed, but also angry.

"I'm sorry, I didn't mean it that way. It's just—"

"No, child. Don't be sorry. Your question is valid. The truth is, I am an old man. I have witnessed much since growing up in this unnatural world. My parents were not pleased with my decision to follow this calling to become a priest, the only holy man in a population possibly destined never to feel the sun or gaze upon nighttime stars, never to see the heavens above. I've heard stories of such things, things you have witnessed, praise God. But those in the scientific world think little of me and what I do. They would just as soon see me flushed through the tubes rather than entrust me with their knowledge."

Dez looks at her feet. "We'll get answers," she whispers.

"What about you, Doctor?" I ask. "Wouldn't they tell you if you asked? Aren't doctors kind of like scientists?"

She meets my gaze. "You've been in my clinic. You've seen what I'm allowed to do. No. I have no friends in the scientific community."

"All right then. When do we leave?" I ask.

"After the darkened hours is safest," Dez says. "We should sleep a little first and then eat something that'll give us energy." She emphasizes energy when she looks at Father Malachy. "Ing can come with me, there's an extra bed in that room, and we'll come for you, Mette, when we're ready."

All I've done lately is sleep, but Mette looks exhausted. Being a gopher for the priest, the Singers, and probably the doctor, she must feel pulled to shreds. Maybe she deserves my sympathy, but that's all I'm willing to give her.

Dad used to tell me, "When you're old enough, you'll get to make your own choices. Don't let anyone make 'em for you." Huh. Maybe like Mom, he also anticipated my choice to leave the life I was expected to lead. Mette doesn't seem to have choices.

"I'll be ready." Mette stares at Dez as if pleading not to be forgotten.

"I know you will. Let's get some sleep. Food in two hours, Father?" Dez takes charge, and I immediately breathe easier, despite the sour taste in my mouth.

"Of course. And I hope you know how much we love and appreciate you. All of you." He glances from Dez to Mette and finally, to me. The moment weighs heavy. I turn to leave the oppressive room. "And Ing,"—I stop but don't look back at him—"I'm sorry, I truly am, for these circumstances and the less than hospitable treatment you've received since your arrival."

I nod and flee from the room with Dez right behind me. I search the dome above as we cross through the expansive chapel, but no Calyxar. Once we're inside her room, Dez closes the door and spins me around.

"What in the name of Calyxar's spawn? I thought my life was crazy before you dropped into it. Tell me I'm not making a big mistake by taking you with me now."

"Now? I thought we were going to—"

"Yeah, now. You think we're waiting two hours and taking Miss Pink Eyes with us? She's like a beacon. Never really did trust her. Spends way too much time with grownups."

"Well, I can't say you're making a mistake, but I also have no idea what I'm . . . what we're going to find. Isn't it dangerous to leave before the dark hours?"

"Danger-schmanger. I know ways around places beyond the Academy the rats haven't even found yet, and yes, there are plenty of rats in Ironhold. I'm not just talking about the cadets."

I remember Dash. "They have Dash, you know. At least I think they have him. I still want to find out what they've done with my father's body, if anything, but he's dead. If Dash is still alive, we need to find him first, right?"

"Hell, yeah, and I have a pretty good idea what sector they all might be in. Your father, Dash, and who knows who else. Haven't been down that way in years, but I know the way. It's not where Father Malachy wants us to go." She looks down. "Why are you barefoot?"

I explain the stealth outfit Dash and I chose for our mission before Lou and crew took us down. Dez rustles around in a compact closet and pulls out a pair of shoes.

"These should fit. Too tight for my clodhopper feet. Put 'em on while I grab a few things. That bastard Lou. But he pulled me from the pool?"

"He did. Maybe just to get praise from the instructor. Who knows."

Between the excitement and the unknown, my queasy stomach threatens a rebellion. After all the crazy things I've done since running—and swimming—away, the thought of finding my father's body in some lab doesn't settle well.

I pull on the shoes, glad they fit and that we'll be leaving the chapel before anyone suspects anything. Before they bring food.

"Hey, newbie, you okay?" Dez grabs both of my hands and searches my eyes. Her concern shakes the doubt from my mind.

"Yes. Yeah, I just . . . let's go. I'll follow you, okay? Is there anything I should know before we leave? Like, are we going to be crawling through slimy tunnels or anything?"

"Why? You afraid of slimy tunnels?" Dez smirks and shoves me toward the door. "You're gonna love our first stop. There's some things I want you to see, especially now that I know Father Malachy believes our population's fate has something to do with you. Holy hell, Ing."

Snarky, like my Tulip. I miss her terribly.

"Should I be bowing to you or something?" Dez scratches her shaved head.

"You're a jerk." I return the shove. "Lead the way. And no slimy tunnels."

17

"BEFORE WE GO, I have to tell you something."

"Make it fast," Dez says. "We need to beat feet before someone decides they need to check on us."

"Okay, okay. I know you're going to think I'm ridiculous, and I know how you feel about the whole Calyxar story, but you're wrong." No sense in keeping this secret.

Dez puts her hands on her hips. "This better be good."

Her scar stands out in the unnatural lighting. My admiration for her, and all she's endured, grows. She's the kind of friend I wish I had at home. She'd understand my rebellion.

"Calyxar's real. It's been talking to me. And I'm not crazy."

Dez shakes her head. Her hands drop. She stares at me until I feel uncomfortable. "Holy hell. Are you taking your meds?"

"Yes! Well, no, but that's not it," I stammer. "I'm telling you, since Zadak brought me into the chapel during my in-processing, it's been telling me things. And I saw it. It swam right near the top of the slicken." I point toward the expansive membrane beyond our little room. "It left when Father Malachy came in."

Dez looks perplexed. "And what am I supposed to do with that info? Take you back to the Doctor? Pretend you didn't just tell me something ridiculous? Leave you here and lock the door?" Her words are critical, but she speaks softly.

"But you can't. You broke the lock with that big candlestick." I point to the bent thing on the floor.

Dez looks at the broken candlestick and, after a heartbeat, bursts out laughing. "You are one crazy I-don't-know-what. Look me in the eyes and tell me you really believe Calyxar— an ancient sea god or whatever—chats with you."

"It does. Listen. Weird things are happening, right? I heard cadets talking about it at the barber shop. Everyone's been acting all mysterious, and Father Malachy believes a big space blob is about to invade the planet. Honestly, I don't know what he expects us to find, but I'm telling you the truth about Calyxar." I wish the creature would talk to Dez right now.

Breaking the stare-off, Dez looks at her feet before talking again. "So what's it saying?" Tiny wrinkles on her forehead make me feel bad for making her anxious. I don't want to tell her. I do, but I don't.

"Not now. Like you said, we need to beat feet, but if for some reason I stop or it looks like I'm thinking about something, it might be because I'm listening to it. I just needed you to know that. And Dez," I hold her shoulders, "Please trust me."

She shakes her head again. "Okay, fine. But if some voice in your head tells you to turn on me or do something stupid—"

"I wouldn't. Never." I mean it. I step beyond the door. "Let's go. Let's figure out if Father Malachy is freaking out for nothing."

Dez leads me along the chapel wall to a doorway hidden behind a length of cloth heavily decorated with brightly colored images of fluffy clouds and banners with prayer snippets and angels. Before leaving, I glance up at the murky sea, wishing Calyxar would appear so I can prove myself to Dez. No luck. The weight of the water above makes my skin feel tight. I remind myself to breathe.

We move along a wickedly narrow, winding hallway with no obvious end. No doors. No windows. So narrow I can press my hands against each wall. It feels like we're somewhere between other hallways and rooms. Like we're in a maze that might end in a trap. Worse, the air smells like it did in the room where I first woke. It stings my nose. I sneeze.

"What is this place?" I whisper, crouching, though I don't need to. I want to make myself small. Invisible.

"I'm guessing the ones who build Ironhold used these passages for something sneaky. You'll get used to the smell." Dez whispers too. She strides ahead of me as if avoiding an unseen threat. "Keep up!" She looks over her shoulder at me. "And what in holy hell are you doing? You look ridiculous!"

I feel ridiculous. Matching her swift steps, I shrug and straighten.

The hallway curves sharply and branches in several directions. We turn right. The walls, ceiling, and floors are all the same dull gray with that weird dull glow like many of the other hallways. Eerie. As we walk on, a damp mustiness replaces the stinging odor of the first hallway. Worse, for sure. I don't need more reminders that we're in a closed environment below the surface of the sea.

Thrum, thrum, thrum. I hate the reminder that this air is unnatural.

Dez stops and turns.

"I was gonna show you where they found me and a few of my hideouts, but I don't think that's important anymore. The labs are down there." She points toward one of the passages. "I know what's in a few of the rooms, but I'm pretty sure there are lots more I haven't found yet. We need to be really quiet now. Like, no talking, walk softly, and whatever you do, don't sneeze again. I'll go slow."

I grab her arm as she turns. "Wait. What do we do when we get there?" We've made no plans.

"Chill, girl. Just follow me. There's a way to see into some of the rooms, and once we know they're empty, I know how to get in."

"What if they're not empty?"

"Then we wait. And we listen. Got it?"

"Got it. But—"

"But what? You asked me to trust you. Now you gotta trust me. Let's go." She removes my hand from her arm.

Now I really feel like crouching. Moving like sea slugs, we slither along. My heartbeat matches the damnable thrumming, making me momentarily dizzy. Dez doesn't see me stop and reach out to the walls on either side to keep my balance.

And it happens. First, an ache in my heart, and then the glow. This time, the tug prickles my skin. My coin calls to me.

Pulls me. What am I supposed to do? I can't call out to Dez, but I need to stop her.

As swiftly as I can, I shuffle up and tap her shoulder. She turns around, and my expression matches hers when I see the reflection of my glow in her wide eyes. Eyebrows arched, mouth open, she points and stares. She mouths the words *holy hell* before grabbing me and whispering, "Are you okay? I need to get you back!"

"No, I'm fine." I whisper, thinking I should have mentioned my coin and its attraction when I told her about Calyxar.

"Do you know what's in whatever room we're close to now?"

"I think it's a chemistry room, but I usually just go to where the scientists hold meetings. I haven't been down this far in years. Why?" Her eyes shift back and forth between my eyes and my glow.

"They took something from me when they brought me in. A coin. It's important. And it's supposed to be . . . here." I point between my breasts. "I think it's in that room."

"Damn, girl, you're just one big mystery. Come on." She turns and slides a hand along the wall as we creep. She stops short, turns to me, and puts a finger to her lips. Slowly, she moves something on the wall, and a small shaft of light enters our space. She peeks through the tiny gap, then steps away so I can look.

My coin. There it is, surrounded by five people in white coats and dark eyeglasses. The coin shoots a bolt of green light straight up, making the scientists jump back as if shocked. I know what that feels like. I jump back too when the coin flies from the exam table to the gap, slamming against it. It sticks there. I reach my hand toward it, but Dez yanks me away and pulls me farther down the hall before stopping.

A loud clink, my coin dropping onto a hard floor.

"What the hell!" A man's deep voice.

"Quick, get it!" A woman.

"I'm not touching it!"

"Well, someone needs to pick it up!"

Excited voices from the lab overlap and echo in the space where Dez and I hold our breath. And then, a sound that tugs at my heart more than my coin ever has.

Babies. From somewhere far away, the soft, sorrowful sound of babies whimpering.

—————— ⤸ ——————

My coin sits just beyond my reach. With the sound of those tragic sobs, my glow vanishes, my coin's pull stops, releasing me, if only temporarily. Releasing me to discover something awful, I think.

Dez looks like a lost child. "Holy—what the—"

"Let's go." We have to move. "Do you know where it's coming from?"

"I don't. I told you, It's been years since I've been down this far."

Dez and I shuffle through the increasingly claustrophobic passageway. The air smells stale and thick. My breathing quickens, and I feel lightheaded again. *Shake it off.*

Babies. How many will we find, and who's caring for them? I imagine little old ladies rocking them, cuddling them, doing their best to hush them. Maybe there are too many babies and not enough little old ladies. Maybe this is the time of day when all babies get fussy. The last baby born in our village had something called colic and cried all the time. Maybe my sense of dread is silly.

We stop at an intersection and listen. Left or right? The sound seems to come from both directions.

Dez closes her eyes and turns in a slow circle. "This way." She turns left and slows her pace. The crying grows stronger, my anxiety with it. We're finally on the other side of a wall to a room with no apparent way in.

I tremble with each sob. Something doesn't sound right. I've heard babies wail and whine and carry on. Their complaints never sounded like this, though. Never sounded so meaningful.

What I don't hear are the calming voices of caretakers. No shushes, no sweet talk, no lullabies.

"We have to keep going," Dez whispers. "Gotta go around and get into the main hallway." Her eyes lock onto mine, questioning. Like she wants me to say, "Forget it, let's go back." Like she's afraid.

I hold her shoulders, feel her shake.

We could retreat and report the sounds to those waiting in the chapel. Could demand an explanation or at least a safe escort back to see what's happening in what might be a legitimate nursery. But I don't trust anyone anymore. I don't think Dez does, either.

"You know Shayla? Her baby could be in there," I say.

Dez nods, looking as frightened as when she pointed to the high platform at the pool. "It sounds weird, though, right? Like it's not just babies?" She senses it too.

"Yes. We have to find out what's in there, but what if someone sees us? I mean, can we just show up in the hallway and walk into the room?"

Before she can answer, a series of clicks and whirrs followed by silence startles us. The sobbing stops. The sudden hush makes me hold my breath. Dez mouths her favorite words again, *"Holy hell."*

We stand unmoving for what seems like hours before the first whimpers start again.

"I know you're not into slimy hallways, but how do you feel about ventilation ducts?" Dez looks at my hands still holding her shoulders and pushes them away.

"Umm—"

"Follow me. You'll be okay," she says.

Claustrophobia already threatens my breathing in the narrow hallways. I've never seen a ventilation duct, but the idea of crawling through something that might be even more confining rattles me. If it's the only way to see what's on the other side of the wall, though, I'll suck it up. I follow Dez as she searches for an entryway, glad to see her confidence return.

We don't go far before she finds a panel midway up on the wall. She lifts it slowly, pulls it out, and sets it on the floor. She looks at me and nods before hopping up into the opening and standing inside, her feet resting at about my chest level. With a subdued grunt, she disappears.

"Come on," she whispers.

Before I can talk myself out of it, I hoist myself into the opening, wondering what the heck we're doing.

As I pull myself up into the shaft, my foot bangs against the metal wall. The crying stops. Are the babies listening? Dez looks over her shoulder and raises her eyebrows. Neither of us moves.

I think I might suffocate. I close my eyes and imagine floating in the sea with *Ahveyah* calming my mind.

The whimpering starts again, and we crawl cautiously toward it. Something delicious-smelling floats past us, and I wish we'd eaten something earlier. I hope my stomach won't growl.

Dez freezes, and I nearly smack my head on her shoes. Laughter from a room below us. I hold my breath. It's not *nice* laughter. There's no joy in it. Sweat tickles my upper lip, and I squeeze my nose to suppress a sneeze. I catch snippets of conversation.

"Ghosts again, Pablo?" Laughter.

"Probably just rats."

"Varmints are great swimmers, unlike some of those cadets!"

NoNoNoNoNo. There's no way I'll be able to keep it together if a rat—or rats—decide to join us in the ducts.

Dez doesn't make a sound as she passes over the vent that opens over the room below. I stop to look down. White-jacketed people shove food into their mouths. So much food. My mouth waters. Better keep it closed so I don't drool onto one their heads.

Following Dez's lead, I take advantage of the lively discussion to move a little faster. When we stop again, Dez stays over the crying room for such a long time, I wonder if she's come to a dead end.

Nope.

Before continuing down the duct, she turns her head toward me. My heart skips a beat. Two beats. Through the vent, light from the room below illuminates her tear-streaked face.

My turn to look. *We don't cry.* Babies cry, sure, but what would make Dez cry? I don't want to know, but I have to look.

Row after row of tiny naked bodies, infant to near-toddler size, their heads, limbs, and bodies suspended by straps of different sizes, each wearing a cap with wires disappearing into an adjoining room, each little face contorted into expressions of fear and disgust. They look . . . old.

Click, click, whoosh. Rails along each row spray water on the children, hosing them down. With a *whoosh*, another spray of water runs across the floor under them, washing away the waste.

One of the babies stops sobbing and stares up at me through the vent.

I clamp my hands over my mouth to silence a gasp.

Her deep brown eyes plead with me. I stretch out a hand on the vent, wanting to touch the child, desperate to let her know I'll rescue her and the others.

"We have to get in there, Dez. Have to find out what's in that next room." I don't want to know what's in there, either. How can it be anything good? Wires hooked to captive babies. What the flood?

Dez nods and wipes her cheeks with the back of a hand. I follow her farther down the duct until she stops above the adjoining room. This time when she turns to me, I have a hard time reading her expression. Fear? Wonder? She slides beyond the vent so I can look in.

Rows of tables with full-grown bodies covered in sheets, head to toe. I can't tell if they're breathing. Wires from one end of each sheet lead back to the infant room. And tubes filled with something green. Are they sleeping or—

"Looks like an exit chute about twenty more feet," Dez whispers. Without waiting for a response, she crawls toward it. I follow until she disappears down an opening, then lower myself after her. We're back in the between-space hallway. That stale, trapped feeling prickles the hairs on my neck.

"What now?" I ask, as if she'll have any better idea of what to do than I would. "This is seriously messed up."

"I didn't see any workers or doctors in either of the rooms." Dez shakes her head slowly. "It's like they're all on some kind of automatic system. Did you see those things in racks by the babies?" I nod. "It's like some kind of robotic feeding system, and the straps? They turned the babies from face down to face up before I let you look in."

I can't shake the expression on that tiny baby's face. " If we can get in, what then? I mean, we can't just disconnect everything. Who knows what that could do to the children? And the ones under sheets, are they even alive? I'm scared, Dez."

"Yeah, me too." She reaches out and squeezes my shoulder. "We could go back and get Doctor Vesper, but I really wanna get in there and see if we can figure out what's going on first. You with me?"

"Of course." If only I felt so sure. "But if someone sees us?"

"I'll think of something. Come on." She hesitates, looking in both directions, before practically running down the passageway. Guess she's not worried about stealth anymore.

She finds a doorway out of the narrow passage, and when I step into the wide hall, I inhale deeply, releasing the tightening I've felt in my chest ever since we left the chapel. We're not in a safe space, though. Dez waves me on, and we hurry toward the room with sheet-covered bodies. The door is un-locked.

"Ready?" Dez opens the door. We step inside. So far so good. I count twenty-six beds, thirteen on either side of the room, nineteen of them occupied. Far too cold for comfort. No signs of life.

We approach the first bed as if a rattlesnake lurks under the cover. Are there snakes in Ironhold? If there are rats . . .

A sickly-stale smell makes me gag.

"I'm gonna be sick," I whisper, desperately scanning the room for a sink, a bucket, anyplace to catch the rising burn. No such luck. Snake or no snake, I raise the sheet at the end of the nearest bed and puke on a petite pair of pale gray feet.

"Damn, girl." Dez pats me on the back before replacing the sheet to cover my mess . . . and those gray feet. "You gonna be okay now?"

I wipe my mouth on my sleeve and nod, even though I'm not convinced. "Pretty sure she's dead. Maybe they all are." It's time to see what's happening at the other end of the bed.

On either side of it, we walk to where the wires emerge. Together, we lift the sheet. She'd been beautiful recently, this older woman. Her skin, though gray, looks flawless, her lips still full. Pads with wires sprout from patches where her thick, silver-black hair had been shaved.

I wonder how she died. And what's happening with the wires.

Dez touches one of the wires and starts to ask, "Should we—" when someone approaches the room, their footsteps loud in the hallway. Laughter. Two men.

I grab Dez's hand and pull her two rows back, where we drop behind a sheet-draped table just as the door opens.

"Oh, gross! What's that smell?" One of the men says.

"Really? That smell? Oh! Right. Check it out, old lady's toe's sticking out."

Flood. I thought Dez covered it up. I squeeze my eyes shut. My knees feel bruised from slamming onto the cold metal floor. Nothing but cold metal everywhere, and the taste of metal in my mouth.

"Oh, man! Sombitch Dash puked on her feet."

"Hey, cut him some slack. How long did it take before you weren't creeped out?"

"Yeah, whatever."

Flooding shite. They have Dash. But what does that mean? He's alive, so . . . it takes everything in my will to stay put. Who are these men, why are they here, and what are they doing with these bodies? How is Dash involved in any of it? I open my eyes and see anger flare in Dez's face.

"Think we should wake him up and make him clean this shit?"

"Nah. What difference would it make? He's still in pro-gramming. Come on. Let's get this batch to the tubes."

This batch, to the tubes. As if they're cooking something. How many tables are in a batch? We're only two rows back.

"You first, lady. Hey, how 'bout I do the slime this time, you do the wires?"

"Yeah. Whatever."

A sickly sucking sound and the rough tearing of tape and wires from scalp make me queasy again. I plug my ears. My fingers can't block out the crude laughter, though.

I want to scream.

18

AS SOON AS they roll the dead woman from the room, we stand. I rub my sore knees and Dez rubs her scalp.

"Shite, Dez, they have Dash. What did they mean, he's still in programming?"

"I don't know, but it can't be good." She covers the scar on the side of her face with a hand, as if trying to protect herself from another injury. "We have to find him."

"Where do you think they're keep him?" The thought of how they might be programming him makes my heart race.

"I obviously haven't been everywhere, but he can't be too far from here if those assholes were going to make him clean up your, ah, stuff."

Click, click, click, whirrrrrrr.

We stare at one another again, our eyes mirrors of fear and disbelief. The babies. The wires. My head feels like it's about to explode.

I hold my stomach. "Those men just ripped the wires off that woman's head. Look, they're just lying on the floor now.

We don't know where Dash is, but we do know something wicked is going on here. Let's take them all off."

Dez raises her eyebrows. "Now you're talkin'. What about the green stuff?"

We move to where the old woman's table was. The tube on the floor sits in a tiny dribble of fluid. "Looks like it stops once it's . . . out," I say.

"Yeah, maybe some kind of automatic pressure system. We'll learn about those things in engineering classes when we're uppers."

I keep my opinion about my future as an upper to myself. Automatic pressure systems. We collect rainwater to supplement pond water back home. Electricity is glitchy. Everything we do up there, we do to survive, and yet . . .

A pang of guilt and homesickness seizes my heart. *Pull it together. We don't cry.*

I look around at the other bodies and wonder how long it'll take the two sleazebags to deliver one to the tubes. And then I gasp.

"What's wrong? You're not gonna hurl again, are you?" Dez winces.

"No." I walk to a table two rows in from the back of the room. I couldn't see the last few rows when I was in the duct above. A once strong, slender arm hangs from the side, a long, jagged scar down its forearm reminding me of the day it happened. The last day my father worked the Heaps. Flying debris is always hazardous, and when a gust knocked him onto a rusty shaft of rebar, we thought we might lose him.

I lift the sheet from his face. "Hi, Dad," I whisper, and Dez's arms are around me.

"Oh, Ing."

"It's okay. I wanted to find him. Now I know." Same weird green liquid in a tube inserted into his neck, same wires attached to his shaved scalp. I rest his arm back onto the table. "What kind of monsters are running this place, Dez?" I stare at the face of a man I once loved. Still love. Thought I delivered him to his final resting place, his perfect, peaceful plunge.

I slide out the green tube. I peel the tape and wires from his scalp. My hands shake. "Monsters."

Have they done this to the infants? My own scalp prickles. "Let's do the rest together, and fast. This is sick."

"If they come back, though—"

"If they come back," I say, "*when* they come back, I've got enough rage in my body right now to tear them to pieces."

"Damn, girl. I'm with you. And yeah. Let's start back here in case we hear them in the hall, we can still hide."

"I'm not hiding. I'll fight before I let them near my father's body again. Near any of these bodies again."

"Okay then. And hey, I'm really sorry you had to find him like this." She pats my arm.

"Me too." I look at my father again, grateful for all he did for me while he was able. Then I raise the sheet back under his chin. When those bastards return, I'll make them look at him. I'll make them look at every face. "Any idea how far we are from the tubes?" I want to know how long we have to free the bodies from this violation.

"I'm really not sure, but I can't see why those assholes would be in any hurry to get back here. It's not like these people are going—"

"Stop!" Too harsh. "Sorry, Dez. Didn't mean to bite your head off. Let's do this. Looks like the tubes are inserted into their necks. They slide out pretty easily. I'll remove the wires. Ready?"

"Yeah. Hey, I'm not hearing anything from the kids' room, are you?"

"Just that clicking sound earlier. Guess they're being rotated or fed or who knows what. We've gotta get in there next, and then find Dash, or do you think we should get back to the chapel and tell them what we found?"

"I don't know. Something doesn't feel right, and I'm not just talking about this." She spreads her arms out, palms up.

"Like what?" I ask.

"Like, why wouldn't Father Malachy know about this? Why wouldn't Doctor Vesper?" She frowns.

"Probably that 'you do your thing, I'll do mine, and we'll stay out of each other's way' policy."

"Maybe. But still. How could this be kept a secret for so long? I know you don't know. But I don't think we should go back to the chapel. Not until we find Dash."

"Agreed. Let's start here." I lift the sheet from a body opposite my father. It's Joshua, the Elder Swimmer who perished at sea during my father's Farewell.

"You knew this man, too," Dez says. She must see something in my face as I look at the man.

"Yes. It's strange seeing them like this—people from my world who didn't know this place existed." At least I don't think they knew about Ironhold.

We free his body, tuck the sheet under his chin, and start toward the two tables nearest the wall before I stop short. Something about one of the shapes—a large body—scares me. For some unexplainable reason, I don't want to see it yet.

"We should do the ones nearest the door next. I think they've been here the longest." Without waiting for her, I stride to the table opposite where the old woman had been and lower the sheet. A man, maybe about fifty, but it's hard for me to judge age in Ironhold. "What do people down here die of? I mean, other than being dead, this man looks like he was pretty healthy."

"Never really thought about it. Seems like dying's a private thing. If there's a family, they'll go to the chapel. The Singers will do their thing and then they'll be taken to the tubes—oh! Or maybe not right away. Like these people. Wow. This is really creeping me out now."

Glad I'm not alone. "Hey, we're going to figure this out. Let's get this shite off of them."

We work fast.

"I wonder how these people died," I say.

Dez glances around the room. "People die all the time down here. Up on land too, I guess, right?"

"Yeah. It's harder to stay alive up there than it is to die. My father would still be alive if we lived down here, and my Mom wouldn't be blind."

"Holy hell. I don't know anything about what you've lived through. Glad you have, though, and glad you're here. I feel pretty stupid right now." She hangs her head, shaking it slowly.

"Hey, you've been through some shite too, right? And probably more than any other cadet at USMA. Maybe we were supposed to find each other and make some things right. And maybe we can find a way to get back to land. I won't lie, though. I don't think you'll like it up there. Now let's finish these last two people."

Finally in the back row, the row that somehow repels me, Dez pulls back the sheet from one of the bodies, leaving me with the one I don't want to see. I lift the sheet, and my legs go numb.

"NO NO NO NO NO!" Someone—I—scream.

"Hey! What do you think you're doing in here?" They're back.

"What the hell?" Gruff voices and the sound of shuffling feet barely make an impression on me as I stare at the man on the table.

"I said, what do you think you're doing?"

I've never been a violent person, but something snaps inside. As my vision constricts with my heart, the room spins, and all control leaves me.

"Yeah. Hey, what the hell? Check it out, Vlad, they're all unplugged."

Rage. Pure, simple rage. Without thinking, and with a scream that rises from somewhere so deep inside it scares me, I charge at the closest man—who watches my approach with dumbfounded surprise—and knock him to the floor, slamming into the guy behind him in the process. Dez is on that one in a flash. She delivers a punch to the face that knocks him out cold, and in a flash, she has one of the green liquid tubes from the floor around the guy's neck beneath me.

I jump off of him just as he goes limp.

"Is he . . . is he dead?" I ask.

"Nah, just low on oxygen for a bit. Nice job, by the way. Didn't know you had it in you."

"I didn't, either." My voice sounds like it's coming from someplace far away.

"Here, help me tie him up." She rolls the guy onto his stomach, and I hold his hands together as she secures them with a length of wire. "He won't try too hard to pull out of this before feeling the wire slice into his wrists. Now, his ankles." She amazes me with her quick response.

We finish tying up both men without speaking, but she keeps looking at me as if waiting for me to tell her something.

Still shaking with fury and fear, I stagger back toward the two unfinished bodies when the man Dez punched wakes up.

"Satan's fury! You two bitches don't know what you've done, you—"

"Shut up or I'll knock you out again." Dez stands over him, fists clenched.

Torn between the action near the door and the tables at the back, I return to Dez's side. Whatever we're in, we're in it together. We'll get answers from the despicable men before I go back—

The one Dez choked out groans before opening his eyes. He looks scared.

"You're gonna pay for this," he says, his voice raspy.

"No, I don't think so," Dez says. "Now, tell us where Dash is. We know you have him in programming."

"I'm not tellin' you nothin'." He spits on Dez's shoe.

"Wrong answer, dimwit." She raises the fouled shoe under his chin and, after wiping the glob of spit there, kicks him in the stomach. "Let's try this again." She turns her attention to the man she punched. He flinches. "Where, is, Dash?"

"Tell her and you're a dead man, Doug."

"You just don't know when to be quiet, do you. You must be Vlad." Dez looks at me. "Think you might find something in here to shut him up? He's obviously not in the mood to be helpful today."

I nod, scanning the room but avoiding the far end. I pull a sheet off the nearest body and approach Vlad.

"Don't you dare! You wouldn't! That's disgus—"

Before he can finish, I jam a balled-up wad of sheet into his mouth. He gags a few times, but finally settles, staring at me with murderous eyes.

I stare back.

"What do you say, Dougie. Are you going to be more helpful than your buddy?" Dez steps toward him, and he flinches again.

"Hey, listen, we don't have nothin' to do with the programming, okay? He ain't even done yet, so no big deal, okay?" He scooches away from Dez until his back brushes the door.

"No, Doug, nothing's *okay* here. Just tell us where he is." She raises a foot near his face.

"Yeah, yeah, he's down the hall, five doors down that way, but I didn't tell you nothin', right?"

"Right." Dez eyes all four corners of the room. "Any cameras in here, Dougie? Any alarms?"

"Nah. Why would they put security in here? It's not like anybody in here's gonna—"

"Shut up!" Dez cuts him off. "What about five doors down?" She looks at me. Assessing me.

"Nah. Nobody bothers us down this wing. We're just doin' our jobs, okay?"

Dez ignores him, her attention still on me. "I'll stay here and watch over these scumbags. You go get Dash. Be quick." She leaves no opening for argument.

I help her shove Doug away from the door and leave the room.

An empty hallway. Empty, cold, dimly lit, and entirely lifeless. The rhythmic *thrum* only adds to the sense of desolation. Of death.

Were my eyes mistaken back in that ghastly room?

Focus. Find Dash. Bring him back, and then . . .

And then, what? Face that unbearable reality?

I run down the hallway. One, two, three doors down and I skid to a stop. Youthful voices. I wait, ear to the door, heart pounding, trying to determine if an adult might be inside. My curiosity has to be satisfied, even if it kills me.

I crack open the door and peer inside to see a room with about twenty uniform-clad youngsters, no adults. One of them points at me with a frightened expression.

Shite.

I close the door and run two more down, bursting into the fifth room without hesitation. There, strapped to a metal chair, a cap sprouting wires on his head, Dash stares at a wall-size screen where images of dead bodies being prepped for "information retrieval and safeguarding" accompany a soothing woman's voice discussing the procedure and how patriotic citizens "like you" will help to produce the greatest civilization ever. The images and words repeat.

"Dash." I stand in front of him, hurriedly unfastening the straps. His blank expression frightens me. "Dash, it's me, Ing. Dez and I are getting you out of here."

Nothing.

"Come on, buddy. You don't belong here." I shake him, but he continues to stare ahead, right through me. "Dash! I need your help. Dez needs your help. Get up." I grab his hands and pull and pull and finally, he stands. Memories of helping my father out of bed on his final day flash through my head, and I can hardly believe his body lays five doors away.

"Look at me." I take his face in my hands and tilt his head toward mine. "We're going down the hall now and we're going to get Dez and then—" There it is again. The *and then*.

"Where? What the?" He glances around, life slowly returning to his eyes.

"I'm right here. I'll explain later. You need to come with me now, and everything will be all right." I have no reason to believe that's true, but I don't need him to freak out.

"Ing?"

"Yes! You remember me? We were running to the chapel and you—"

"Something knocked me down. Next thing I knew, these two guys were telling me I wasn't a cadet anymore, I failed something, and my new assignment was in the morgue. Why do I feel like I'm in some kinda nightmare?"

We all are. He stares at the chair and cap and wall with its distressing video.

"Just . . . come on." I take him by the hand and pull him toward the door.

"Wait. What if they're out there?" He squeezes my hand, his face a mask of fear.

"They're not. Dez has them tied up in the morgue, and we're going to get answers."

He grins. "Dez is a badass."

"Yes. Yes, she is. Now let's go."

I open the door, check that the hallway is still empty, and Dash runs behind me back to where Dez waits.

When we open the door, though, Dez isn't alone with the two bound men. Mette stands behind her, nostrils flared, hands on her hips.

"You left me behind. Do you know how embarrassed I was, how humiliated, when I went to your room with Father Malachy, and you were gone? I thought we were friends, Dez." Mette scowls at me. "This was *your* idea, wasn't it."

"Maybe it was. How'd you find us?" I glance at the bound men, who appear to have lost their fighting spirit.

"Hey, Mette," Dash says. "Did you know about this place? Seems maybe you did since you're here now."

Mette looks flustered. She drops her hands and gazes around the room before looking at her toes. "I heard rumors, but I've never been here. I found you guys the same way I knew where Ing was when she arrived. I . . . felt her."

If she met with any opposition while looking for us, she would have squashed it with her power of persuasion. I have to keep my guard up if she tries to influence us to do something against our wills. Despite her apologetic expression, I still don't trust her.

"So, what now?" Dez says, her chin held up in a rebellious attitude. "You thinking about sending some special signal to the chapel? Is someone gonna bust in here and drag us to a programming room like what they did to Dash?" She puts a hand on his shoulder. "Are you okay, buddy?"

"Yeah. Yeah, I think so, but can we get out of here? This room makes me feel sick."

"At least you're not on a table," Doug murmurs, and without missing a beat, Dez grabs a sheet off of another body and shoves it in his mouth.

She gets right up into Mette's face. "So? What's gonna happen, Mette? Are we still friends?"

Mette steps back. "Of course, Dez, but I don't know what I'm supposed to do with all this." She gestures around the room.

"You're supposed to look around and say, 'What the hell?' You're supposed to help us stop whatever they're doing in here and in the next room—have you seen the babies in the next room?"

Mette shakes her head, her white eyebrows crease. "Babies?"

"Yeah, babies. See these wires?" Dez picks one up from the floor, then grabs Mette by the hand and walks her to the end of a table. "See all these patches of ripped hair? These wires were stuck onto all these scalps. See where they're all going?" She's relentless. "They're going into the next room where I'm pretty sure they're hooked onto babies' heads."

"And there's more," I say. "A room with children in uniforms, there were images on the walls and a voice coming from somewhere else, like in the room where they had you, Dash. I don't even know what's happening there."

"I think I do," he says. "I think they're supposed to be some kind of great new civilization. That's what I kept hearing." He points to Vlad and Doug. "They said we'll be going back to land pretty soon, repopulating it after some big thing that's supposed to happen soon." He looks at me. "You said it's pretty rough up there, though."

"It is." The thought of returning to land makes my heart leap. But then, reality hits, and I hold my breath. I know too much. Too much suffering. Too much exertion for little gain. Too much sadness over things lost.

"What do you mean, something big?" Dez yanks the sheet from Doug's mouth. "Tell us. What do you know?"

"I'll tell you, but you gotta untie me." He ignores Vlad's glare. So much for loyalty.

Dez looks around, probably figuring four-to-one are good odds, and asks me to untie his feet.

Doug rubs his wrists but doesn't stand.

"Talk." Dez stands over him. "And don't leave anything out."

"Fine. Whatever. All I know is something's gonna start the planet spinning again pretty soon," he shakes his head as if trying to imagine what that means. He knows about the prophesy. "I guess it used to spin a long time ago, and after things settle down up top, whatever that means, we'll be going back. Not that any of us want to, right, Vlad?"

Vlad looks away, shaking his head, and gags. I can't stand the sound of his heaving, so I pull the sheet wad from his mouth.

"I ain't tellin' you nothin', and you're a dead man, Doug." He turns away from all of us.

Dash looks pale. "We have to tell someone. I don't even know who. Can we leave now?"

"Not yet," I say. Slowly, I walk to the back of the room. To where we didn't finish our work. To the two remaining bodies still plugged with wires and tubes.

How I wish they had, but my eyes had not deceived me. I place my hand on Aiden's cold chest—*I won't cry, I won't*— and then slide out the green tube. I feel Dez behind me.

"I don't recognize him," she whispers.

"He's from my village. He was in the water with me when the wave—" I can't finish. Something hard sticks in my throat. I try to swallow. Can't. Can't move. Start shaking and can't stop.

"Oh, no, I'm so, so sorry. Come here." She turns me around and locks me in an embrace. I cling to her.

"They lied." My words come out strangled. "They said they didn't know anything about him. I was the only one saved from the wave."

I pull away, thoughts returning to what that monstrous swell could have done once it reached land. "Do they know about my village, Mette?"

She looks away before speaking. "I'm not exactly sure. I heard something about some kind of special drones that can't be detected."

"What's a drone?" I ask.

"It's a little machine that flies and can see things. They could send them up through the tubes."

The bizarre birds. The clackers that hover over us in the Heaps. The strange sound they make. How long have the people down here been watching us? Watching us suffer. Why?

I turn back to Aiden, the breathtaking man who loved me and made love with me. I remove the wires from his skull—*what did they steal from him?*—and smooth my hands across his face. Every muscle in my body tightens. Every voice in my head wants to scream. I kiss his forehead and turn away. *We don't cry. We don't make a fuss over death.*

I barely knew him.

Dez continues her interrogation. "Tell us about the babies, Dougie. Whose babies are they? Why aren't they with their mothers? And what's the deal with these wires?"

"Listen, I just do what I'm told, okay?"

"No, it's not okay, and who's telling you what to do? Who's your boss?" Dez grills him.

"I don't know who he is, but I see some old dude in a long robe walking toward the lab sometimes."

Dez shoots me a look, and we both turn to Mette. With eyes wide, mouth agape, and both hands over her heart, she shakes her head.

"Your turn to talk, *friend*." Dez saunters toward Mette. Her fists are clenched.

19

"DEZ, STOP, PLEASE," I say. "Let's not jump to conclusions. There could be lots of older men in robes down here, right?" I don't believe it, but there's already been enough violence in the room without Dez knocking out Mette's teeth.

Dez looks at me like I'm an idiot—*ouch*—and Mette mouths a *thank you*.

"Pretty sure he's that priest at the chapel," says Doug. "I don't go there, but I heard Vlad call him Father M, ain't that right, Vlad?"

On his side facing the wall, Vlad doesn't budge.

"Say it's not true, Mette. Tell me he's not involved in this." Dez's shoulders droop.

"I honestly don't know. You have to believe me. He never lets me know where he goes when he leaves, he just tells me who to study and when I should use my, you know, abilities to get people to do things." She seems to be telling the truth. "I can't believe he'd be involved in something like this." She glances around the room, a look of revulsion on her face.

"So we can't go back to the chapel," says Dez. She turns to Doug. "Who's in the lab, and how many? You didn't tell us who you work for."

"Only three that I know 'bout. They control the machines that adjust that green juice and the wires. It's pretty great, really, being able to take memories and stuff from dead people and put 'em into new brains. Those kids'll be way smarter than me, that's for sure."

No question about that. I suddenly understand why the babies look so pitiful. So old. So sad. So burdened.

The idea is brilliant. The practice, barbaric. How many of those infants will grow into adults with memories my father never had a chance to share with me? So much knowledge and personal memories, many that should remain private, forced into the brains of helpless children. It makes me sick.

Where is Calyxar? Why hasn't the giant spoken to me during these discoveries? How much does it know about the inner workings of Ironhold, or has the three-eyed octopus really just been some fantasy I've worked up?

"We have to unhook the babies." I run from the room, careless and uncertain of who will follow me. I step inside the infant room and gag in the heat and humidity. I control myself just as the clicking and whirring rotates the children toward what appears to be a feeding device with nipples.

"This is revolting." Dash puts a gentle hand on my shoulder.

"I don't know what to say," Mette whisks past me and removes a wired cap from the closest baby, stroking the child's little head.

I look around for Dez.

"She'll be here in a minute. Had to make sure those thugs wouldn't leave and report us." Mette continues to stroke the child, who turns from the nipple and gazes at her.

It gives me an idea.

"Mette, can you do something, hum or sing something that might calm these babies, release them from their thoughts while we remove their caps?"

She nods with an expression filled with gratitude. "Yes, but—"

"But keep us out of your head," I say, "and no tricks. I really want to trust you, okay?"

"I didn't know. Really, I didn't. I want to help. Nothing about this is good." She beckons Dash and me to where she stands, puts a hand on each of our heads, and murmurs something that feels like a breeze. Then she hums a tune so beautiful it makes my heart ache, as if it isn't aching enough already.

The infants all turn away from their food toward her, and I watch as their faces soften. She continues to hum while the three of us rush through the room, removing wired caps from the babies and stroking their little cheeks, looking into their eyes, giving them each a tiny taste of human contact.

Another *whoosh* and a stream of water washes across the soiled floor, pushing it all into culverts around the edges of the room and soaking our feet in the process. A slight floral aroma almost camouflages the lingering smell of waste.

"This is inhuman. That's not even a strong enough word." Dash's cheeks are wet with tears.

"We'll fix this, okay?" If only I knew how.

"Look," he says, pointing to my chest and its glow.

"I know. My coin—I know where it is. I just don't know how to get it back or what to do with it once I have it. Hey, shouldn't Dez be here by now?"

The door bangs open and Dez enters, hands behind her back, pushed into the room by three men in white coats.

"Sorry, guys," she says, her head hung low.

"Cease what you are doing immediately," the largest of the three demands. "Put your hands behind your backs and do not resist."

"No. We won't." I surprise myself with my boldness, stepping right up to my captive friend as I confront the coats. "Now, release her and leave us alone. We're here under orders from Father Malachy." It's true.

The three burst into laughter. "Oh, really?" says the obvious leader, the one who keeps a hand on Dez's shoulder. "And why do you think the good Father sent you here?"

Why, indeed. Why send us to spy on scientists if he already knows what's happening in the labs? Does he want us to be captured? Are we simply in his way? The thought chills me.

We're in Hell. Ironhold is the Underworld of stories I learned as a child.

Visions of my father, of Aiden, of all the other desecrated bodies beyond the wall, and the helpless babies make everything in my body vibrate. The glow on my chest burns more brightly than ever.

The three coats step back, pulling Dez with them. The leader releases Dez and heads toward me slowly, his eye riveted to my light.

"You're . . . you're the one they've been talking about. The coin—"

"What about my coin? Where is it? It's no use to you, so give it back."

"Oh, but you're wrong. It's of great use, and you're going to show us how it works. There's not much time left. You're coming with us now." He reaches to grab me by the arm, but I spin and deliver a swift kick to his crotch—a move my father taught me and Tulip when we were kids, not that we ever had to use it—and he crumples to the floor.

"Mette, do something!" Dez yells.

"You will release the girl," Mette speaks in a voice that tickles my ears, "and you will return to your laboratory."

The man on the floor stands, one hand still cradling his injury, and shuffles out the door. The other two work on the knot binding Dez's hands, and when they finish, they leave the room too.

Either they don't know about Mette's power, or they didn't notice her when they came in. If they had, they would have plugged their ears. Maybe my unexpected boldness combined with the glow surprised them all.

"What happened, Dez? How'd they catch you?" Mette asks.

"Yeah, and what did he mean about not much time left?" Dash cradles the baby closest to him—a bizarre sight, as various straps hold the child between metal contraptions filled with food and hoses. I count more than thirty rows of tiny bodies strung up this way in the huge room.

"I don't know. Maybe when you got here it triggered some kind of alarm. Well, that, and I got into a bit of a scuffle with Doug. Surprised you didn't hear him." Dez rubs her shoulder.

"Are you hurt?" I ask. I don't want her to be hurt.

"I'll be fine. Doug won't be moving too fast for a while, though. Hey, we gotta get out of here. How long will the three coats be gone, Mette?"

"Not long, I'm afraid. And where are we supposed to go? I thought I knew Father Malachy, but I'm beginning to think he might be involved in this horrible experiment. And if he is, the Singers are too."

The Singers. Dez's caretakers. Mette's mentors. They have to be working with, or for, the priest. I recall the cold hand of the younger one and shiver.

"We can't just leave these kids like this," Dash says.

"We don't have much choice right now," Dez says. "Look at them all. There's only four of us."

As if they understand, the babies whimper in a mournful chorus. I look at each of them, several old enough to crawl on their own, and my eyes stop on the littlest of them all. It could be Shayla's baby.

"We need help," I say. "Who can we trust back in the barracks?"

"I was taught never to trust anyone," Dash says, "but I can't believe there'd be anyone opposed to getting these babies back to their mothers."

"Even Lou?" I ask. "He seems to have a pretty loyal following, and if you remember, he's the one who had you, and almost me, captured."

"Yeah," Dez says, "but he helped pull me from the pool, right? So maybe there's hope for the jerk."

It dawns on me that the priest and the Singers saved me the day Dash was captured because of my connection with the coin.

But what's its purpose?

When Dez and I passed by in the narrow between-space, the scientists in the room with it were trying to make it do something, but—

Click, click, whirr. The straps holding the babies rotate their arms and legs in a truly creepy kind of dance, exercising their muscles, I suppose. Dash jumps back from the child he's been holding.

At least the infants appear to like the motion. Some even giggle. In the short time since we removed their caps, I note visible changes in their faces. Loud yawns and sighs sound like exhaustion. Relief.

"So where do we go for help?" Mette asks.

"Well, we can't go to the chapel," Dash says, joining Dez and me near the door. "And the people in these labs are obviously participants in this heartless experiment, so I say we take our chances with the cadets we know."

I consider mentioning Doctor Vesper, but I don't see any way she could have remained completely unaware. Shayla just delivered a child in her clinic. "What about the civilian population? Dez, you know lots of people, right? And you know how to get to places without being seen. How about if you see who you can round up. Dash could get back to the barracks—could you do that without being stopped?" He nods. "And Mette, would you stay here with the children and keep them calm?"

"Of course, but what will you do?"

"I have to get my coin."

"What's gonna happen, Ing?" Dash's question troubles me. "And what's the real deal with that coin, anyway." He glances at me accusingly. "Who really are you?"

Who am I? Ouch.

"Yeah, Ing." Mette's hands are back on her hips. A display of power. "We're sorry about how you were treated when you got here, but no one really knows who you are or why you're here. Everything was normal until you showed up, and now everyone's scared about something. So tell us. What's the deal with the coin you keep talking about? Why should we trust you?"

I look to Dez for support, sure that she'll have my back. She stares at the ceiling.

Betrayal.

Their accusations suck the breath from me. Anger takes over. "Are you kidding me? Do you see what I'm seeing right now?" I gesture to the dancing babies. "Dez, Dash, come on! This is not about me."

They look at me with bodies slightly turned away. I sense their discomfort.

"But it kind of is." Dez speaks softly. "Mette's right. We don't know much about you, and, well, when you told me about Calyxar—"

I shake my head at her, but she keeps talking.

"—I didn't know what to think. I mean, even if it is real, why would it talk to you?"

"I . . . I don't know! Maybe it didn't talk to me, maybe there's something in the chews Doctor Vesper gave me and the octopus is a hallucination. Maybe I want to believe Calyxar talked to me. But if I made it all up, if it isn't real, if it didn't really happen, then why is Father Malachy so interested in it? Oh, and Zadak was there too when it appeared through that slicken ceiling. He didn't hear anything, but he saw it. Go ahead and ask him."

The three of them looked at one another as if trying to decide who will speak next.

"Oh, and another thing." I'm really pissed. "Do you think I purposely came to this hellhole, Dez? You saw me on that table. You—"

"Calyxar spoke to *you*?" Mette's upper lip quivers. "What did it say?"

"So you believe it's real and might have spoken to me." I state it as a fact. I put my hands on my hips when Mette drops hers. "Dez, Dash, you've been really kind to me, and I think you know I'm not here on some kind of evil mission, but I seriously need your help now, and so do these kids. People need to see what's happening in here." I take a deep breath when they both nod. "And Mette, you may be the smartest one here, and I wish I had the ability to influence people like you do, but I don't. We need your help too."

She looks at the babies. "What's going to happen to them? What's going to happen to us? We're safe down here, aren't we?" So much for her tough-girl act.

Moving closer to me, Dez asks, "Why do I suddenly not feel safe here anymore? I'm sorry, Ing, we never should've questioned you. You're right. We need to figure out how to fix this." She looks at me with an expression that begs forgiveness. I nod.

Dash frowns. "I've heard the rumors about running out of time. Do you know what they mean?"

"I wish I did. When I was home," the word sticks in my throat, "the Elder Swimmer—the Swimmers are the ones who bring the dead out to sea, that's how I ended up here—anyway, he said something about when the coin reappears, it would be time for something, but he never said what. He looked worried when he said it."

He looked *more* than worried when he said it.

"So now I don't know what to do. It's here, and nothing has happened yet, so—"

"So you're the one who must have some kind of control over it," Dez says. "I mean, look at you." She points to my chest.

The glow aches. It's like it knows it's time to do . . . something.

Click, click, whirr. The babies' exercise session finishes. We stop talking to watch how the straps roll them all to their left side for mouths to latch onto their squishy food containers.

"We can't let this continue," I say. "This can't be our great new generation, or whatever they're supposed to be. Dez, please. Find their mothers, their families. Tell them about this horror. Bring them here. If they have weapons, they should bring them." *Do civilians in Ironhold need to keep weapons?* "Dash, will our classmates follow you? Can you convince Lou to gather the rest of the new cadets and bring them here? I can't believe he wouldn't help if he knew about this place."

"Yeah. I'll get them here. I'll talk to the uppers, too, and maybe some of the professors." He walks over to the littlest baby. Could be Shayla's. He removes his shirt, and Dez hurries over when she realizes what he's doing. "I'm taking her," he says. "No one'll haze me if I'm carrying a baby. At least, I hope not."

Dez helps remove the infant from the straps and swaddles her in Dash's shirt. She pulls the feeding container from its contraption and hands it to him. "You're one crazy sombitch," she says, and for the first time in a long time, we all take a deep breath. Even Mette, who looks lost.

"Mette, I changed my mind about what I think you should do."

She raises her eyebrows, acknowledging me, but can't take her eyes off of what Dash and Dez are doing.

"It looks like the babies will be okay here. The machines are still moving and feeding them. Will you please come with me?"

She looks like she's been struck by lightning. There's no lightning in Ironhold, though.

"Umm, yeah, no, why? Why me?"

"Because I don't believe I can make it to the room and get my coin without your help. I need you. Listen, I don't know what to expect once I get it, but something bigger than me, bigger than all of us, is at work here. For whatever reason, that coin is supposed to be with me."

We lock eyes. She's trying to find the right answer.

"I'm ready to go." Dash steps between us, the baby nestled contentedly in his arms. "Wish us luck." He looks at the child and smiles. She gazes up at him as if enchanted by some kind of gentle, magical creature. I feel the same way.

"I'm ready too," says Dez. "How long do we have before we need to come back? And what'll we do when we get here?"

Time is running out. I feel it. It's making me jittery.

"Come as soon as you think you have enough people to overpower anyone who might try to stop you. But be quick. With enough people on our side, we'll make sure this barbaric secret gets out. And you might not want to hear this, but once I have the coin, I'm pretty sure Calyxar will tell me what I'm supposed to do."

She hesitates, finally nods, and runs to hold the door open for Dash and the baby.

Mette and I lock eyes again.

"Well? Will you help me?"

20

I WAIT. Mette squeezes her eyes closed, maybe trying to make the madness in the infant lab disappear, maybe asking herself how much she can live with. She'll either go with me to retrieve my coin or run out the door and report me to someone. I could end up on the shock table again. Or worse, on a table next to Aiden.

Pain grips me. Has it been only a few days, maybe a week since he held me, loved me, and gave me hope for happiness together? How is it possible that something so perfect ended so violently? So needlessly?

It's my fault. My fault for allowing him to swim with me. He died in the wave that separated us. I'll have to live with the guilt of his death.

But why couldn't they have saved him too? He had no coin. I'm the coin bearer. I'm the fulfillment of some old prophecy.

I hold out hope that my village hasn't been destroyed.

"Please, Mette. Open your eyes and do the right thing. I know you're scared. I am too. I had nothing to do with this"—I indicate the room—"but I'm pretty sure I'm supposed to do something to stop it, or fix it, or do whatever's making me feel like I need to get that coin back."

She opens her eyes. Tears. She's just a teenage girl like me, living in a world that makes no sense, trying to be tough and wanting to do the right thing, whatever that thing is.

"You're right." She wipes her eyes. "I am scared. I'm scared of you, of why you're here, of what's about to happen, because something big *is* about to happen, isn't it?"

"That's what people are saying." We jump when a whoosh of water sprays across the floor again. The babies all appear drowsy after their exercise and feeding, so that's good. I can't shake the beautiful vision of Dash holding the baby. "But you have to know more. Tell me what you've heard."

"Honestly, just what you heard. Another collision, but it'll be worse than what happened before. No one's talking about it in public, though. What good would it do to have everyone panic?"

Another collision. Ironhold exists because scientists anticipated the Halt far in advance and prepared for it. I try to make sense of it all, of why the original Swimmer—my ancestor—walked from the ocean with the coin. Maybe he was sent from Ironhold to spy on those who managed to survive the devastation, to learn how they possibly could survive. Maybe the Swimmers know about the drones. Know that when they deliver the dead back to the sea, those in charge of snatching them from the surface will be ready to receive them.

The Elder Swimmer knows more than he was willing or able to share—the fear on his face when he mentioned time convinced me—and Aiden hadn't yet been told the truth about his responsibilities.

I thought the word they chanted—and I adopted—was some kind of mystical word that made good things happen. I have to admit, repeating it does soothe me. If my village is okay, please-oh-please let it be okay, what's the Elder doing now that he's alone, or with some ignorant young novice?

A sudden sense of foreboding washes over me. My chest aches with the glow. We have to act.

"Listen, Mette. Maybe I can't convince you not to be afraid of me, but if we don't get going pretty soon—"

The door bursts open, and the three white-coated men enter.

Flooding shite. If their eyes could shoot flames, we'd be ashes. Their ears are covered. Mette has no power over them.

"You will come with us now," the leader says too loudly. Several infants fuss.

I could try rage-charging them like I did with Vlad, but there's three of them, and Mette is no Dez.

"Where are we going?" I ask.

"You will see, soon enough. Let's go. And don't try to run away. We have guards in every hallway."

The leader walks out, and the other two motion for us to follow. They walk out behind us. At least they don't tie our hands.

They don't need to. Sure enough, strong-looking uniformed men and women practically line the hallways we walk through. Not a single friendly face. Bright plugs in their ears. Weapons at the ready. I can't outrun them.

Mette stops abruptly in front of one of the soldiers. "Minu? Really?"

The woman stares right through her, though I note a brief flash of something that looks like sorrow darken her stern face.

One of the coats pushes Mette along. With one eyebrow raised—*one eyebrow raised, my baby sister, is she still alive?*—Mette whispers, "Minu just completed the Academy last year. She was my neighbor. I thought we were friends."

I wondered what happened to those who finished their training. I guess some continue to train as soldiers. They become law enforcers. Doctors. Professors. Farmers. Electricians. Scientists.

Wicked scientists.

I stare at every guard we pass, searching for, hoping for a flicker of humanity in their eyes, but every glance leaves me cold. Most won't meet my gaze. The several who do look at me appear startled, maybe because they've never seen anyone with different colored eyes. What a silly little thing to arouse such a strong response. Have they seen the infant room?

When we turn a corner into another long hallway, the ache in my chest nearly makes me faint. I stumble, and Mette grabs me around the waist. The two coats following us stop on either side of us. They squint. My glow is brighter than ever, and I'm surprised when a rainbow of colors reflects off of the cold metal walls. Hall guards nearest us turn their heads away from the light. Somewhere close by is the room where my coin waits for me.

We're heading there. I'll finally be reunited with it, the ache will stop, and I'll know what to do.

"Here! Stop here!" I lean against a door. This room has to be our destination.

But no. The scientist leading us turns, scowls, and gestures to the other two, who pull Mette off of me and grab each of my arms. At a fast pace, they practically drag me down the rest of the hallway, past where my coin remains captive. The leader coaxes Mette along. She keeps looking at me with a mixture of fear and concern. Once we turn another corner, the ache and glow subside.

My apprehension does not.

Something in the atmosphere feels familiar. A slight difference in pressure. A song? Is someone singing? A waft of incense. They're taking us back to the chapel.

"BREATHE." Calyxar's voice startles, then comforts me. It's not a hallucination. Something inside makes me understand I'll be okay. I'm not as confident about my captors.

"Why are you smiling right now?" Mette asks, but what can I say to her?

One more corner, and there it is at the end of the hallway. The chapel doors open. Father Malachy steps out, flanked by the Singers.

He opens his arms as if expecting us to run into his embrace.

As if.

And Mette screams.

The sound, full of pain and fear, stops my breath. When she falls—hands covering her ears—I catch and hold her up. She trembles. Our captors don't seem interested.

"Stop! Whatever you're doing, please stop!" I scream at the Singers, whose voices resonate in tones I didn't think were possible for humans to make.

"It's gone. I can't feel it. Why can't I feel it anymore?" Mette drops her hands and looks at the Singers with pleading eyes. They stop their eerie chant.

The Singers remain silent. I have no idea what Mette experienced. No idea what seems to have disappeared from her so suddenly.

"Come." Father Malachy beckons us. "Come back to the chapel. We have much to discuss."

The lead scientist shoves us forward. Seeing no alternative, I take Mette's hand, and we walk to the chapel. I want her to stop shaking. Her fear is contagious. These are her people. If she fears them, what might that mean for me?

Father Malachy and the Singers turn and retreat into the chapel as we approach. Our captors push us forward but don't join us inside. Maybe they'll guard the door to keep us from running.

I have to ask. "What's gone, Mette? What happened to you back there?" Tears on her white skin sparkle like ice crystals.

"I don't think I can sing anymore." She holds a hand to her throat. "They said they'd make me one of them, a real Singer. They said I'd live forever! They took away my power. The only thing that made me valuable. They took it away."

I used her for her power too. I'm no better than those who push us around.

"You're way more valuable as a friend, Mette. They can't break your spirit unless you let them. Don't."

"Enough whispering," Father Malachy bellows from deeper inside the chapel. "Come. Sit." No longer the paternal figure I first met, he commands us. We sit.

I gaze at the expanse of slicken overhead expecting Calyxar to appear and let me know everything will be okay. No such luck. I think—*Help us! Something bad is about to happen*—but no response.

The priest smirks at me. "It won't come anywhere near you now. We've maximized the protective shield voltage surrounding Ironhold. Anything attempting to approach will sorely regret it, if they manage to survive."

How does he know what I'm thinking? Of course there's some kind of shield to keep all the sea creatures—many with sharp protrusions—from potentially breaking through into Ironhold. But slicken is impenetrable.

"THEY SPIN UNTRUTHS. EVERYTHING THAT IS CREATED CAN, AND ULTIMATELY WILL, BE DESTROYED."

Way to make me feel more confident. Shite. Flooding shite.

The priest's self-righteous expression makes my rage flare. "What do you want from me?" I take Mette's hand again. "From us?"

"I'll be the one asking questions, young lady. First, where is Dez?"

Dez and Dash will be bringing civilian and cadet reinforcements to the lab hallway, and soon. With Mette's help, I was supposed to recover the coin and figure out what to do with it before something bad happens. I'm seriously in over my head.

"I don't know." Not a complete lie. "She ran away when those *scientists* outside the chapel burst in on us, in that seriously flooded-up room where infants are plugged into dead people." I can't sit any longer. I stand and approach him.

"You've known about this, all of you." I glare at the Singers, whose faces remain blank.

"Return to your seat immediately, young lady!" Father Malachy takes a step back, but I'm not about to retreat.

"No. Now tell us what's making everyone so afraid since I got here. Time is running out. I keep hearing that. I heard it from the Elder Swimmer, Sebastian—maybe you know him?—I guess you've been spying on our village." I see a flash of recognition at the mention of Sebastian's name. "And I've heard it down here. So what does it mean? And what do I have to do with any of it?" I stop about two steps away from his face. He squirms in his robes.

"You . . . the coin . . . the prophesy I told you of earlier." His eyes open wide. He looks like a crazy person.

"Now tell me the rest," I demand. Mette is by my side. My boldness has empowered her, if only a little.

The priest wrings his hands. "It said an act of nature would bring a coin to us, someone from above, and then it would happen again." He stares at me with frantic eyes.

Another collision. Are we all about to die? I take a half-step closer. "Tell me why I'm here. What am I supposed to do about some alien collision. I'm a fifteen-year-old girl, for hell's sake."

"It will start the planet rotating again, a good thing, yes? But—"

"But what?" I press him.

"But details beyond that died with Father Domingo, my predecessor." He bows his head.

"So—" I barely know what to say. "So you don't know what's going to happen when I get my coin back? It's time, you know." I feel it. And I'm suddenly more afraid than ever.

He nods. "That's right. But I'm not ready to give it back to you." No longer playing the loving holy figure.

I step back, wondering where Dez, Dash, and the baby are. What am I supposed to do?

Mette grabs my hand and addresses the priest. "None of what you just said explains the babies. How do they fit into whatever the scientists—and obviously you—are planning? It's cruel and inhuman. They're just . . . babies!" She sobs.

I hug her, and she lets me.

"We thought, maybe if the prophecy was not for our lifetime, we would return to the surface, feel the sun, the wind, the bitter cold, feel something, anything, *different* from down here, and help those who have survived to rebuild. Our children would be resilient, and with the knowledge of ages, would create a better life, a better world, more quickly—"

"Stop!" He wouldn't last a day in my world. "You don't know what you're saying. These are not *our* children. These are babies stolen from their mothers and subjected to torture. Have you seen their faces? And you know nothing, nothing of what it's like to live on the surface." I'm back in his face.

Mette releases me and dries her eyes as I rant.

"You and your people have spied on us from the safety and luxury of your mechanical world, but you haven't experienced our hunger when the brutal months of the Daylight fry our crops. You want to feel bitter cold? You've never shivered for months during the Darkness when it feels like your blood might stop flowing. You've probably never considered ending it all when the Drearies make you drop to your knees and beg for the blistering sun to return." I tremble.

The priest stands with his mouth open, his arms hanging limp. The Singers remain unfazed.

"We thought it would work—" he mumbles, as if to convince himself.

"And what about the cadets at the Academy, and all your *believers*? Do you really think they'll be able to defeat whatever aliens you believe are on their way in this . . . this blob thing?" I suddenly notice the crowd of stone-faced people turning toward us from where they've been kneeling. I shake off a chill.

He shrugs the tiniest of shrugs and shakes his head. "My followers are resilient. And the cadets, they've all been chosen since birth, modified—"

"Modified?" Mette shouts. "What do you mean, modified?" She points at the Singers. "And don't you even think about it." They remain silent.

"We have made advancements in genetic modification. New cadets and those chosen for Academy life, like the new infants, were gifted with enhancements. They will adapt to the challenges above."

Mette touches the glowing A between her eyebrows, the Level Alpha indicator. "Enhancements? What did you do to us?"

I touch mine. I've never given it much thought before, other than thinking it's kind of cool.

"I've ensured your resilience. You will be grateful when the time comes," he says.

"My village. Tell me the truth. Are they still alive?" I hold my breath for his answer. I don't trust anything he says anymore, but when he nods, my heart leaps. "Then bring me to my coin. Now."

He squeezes his eyes shut. "You don't know what you're asking. Perhaps if we can hold off until we learn more, perhaps your father knew something—"

"Don't you dare talk about my father." I seethe. The image of his newly deceased body attached to wires sickens me.

"Can you not see that we have worked for the survival of our species?" No longer mumbling, no longer pretending to be ignorant, he tries to make me back down. "Can you not appreciate the feat of engineering and the vision required to create Ironhold before the collision that destroyed all life on the planet but your stubborn village?"

How could I know the extent of the destruction? Our villagers are the only survivors? The throbbing *thrum* sounds louder than ever.

"Of course I can appreciate it! You've seen how we suffer above, seen it and done nothing to help us. So why are you afraid of another collision? How could it be any worse than the one people prepared for over a hundred years ago? Why not just let it happen and continue living as you have? What's different this time?"

He drops his hands. "You. You are different. Our best minds cannot predict what will happen when you have control of the coin in our world, only that it could—"

A commotion outside the chapel stops him. Shouting and banging on the door—*are we locked inside?*—and do I hear reveille? Is someone playing reveille on a bugle? The Singers glide across the floor to the doors—*what are they?*—and then they stop and turned to Father Malachy, who nods.

Mette and I run toward them as they fling open the doors. The guards are gone. The crowd in the chapel gathers behind the priest, but they appear to be in a trance.

Outside the chapel, I gasp at the vision of cadets from multiple class levels, all dressed in battle gear. All but one—Dash—who stands in front of them with the baby still nestled in his arms. The guards who stood along the hallway while we were escorted to the chapel now merge with the noisy crowd. Former cadets, I suppose. How quickly loyalties adapt to changing dynamics.

And it's not just the baby I believe to be Shayla's. I scan the crowd looking for familiar faces—Zadak holds a child—and I see them. All of the infants from the lab are snuggled safely in cadet arms, and the uniformed children hold the hands of civilians mixed in with the cadets.

"You have no control here," I tell the Singers. Dash must have warned his followers. From what I can see, they all wear earplugs. The three Singers twitch awkwardly before retreating from the door. Father Malachy takes their place.

"What is the meaning of this?" He shouts, but the trumpeter won't quit.

Dash rushes to Mette, who stands with open arms, and hands her the infant. Then he approaches Father Malachy. I stand by his side.

"Where is Shayla?" he asks, and not politely.

"She is in good care. There are women in the outer sections who tend to those who've lost their children, and—"

"Lost?" I blurt. "She didn't *lose* her child. How can you live with yourself? The doctor said she was back at the Academy. How can you keep telling these lies?"

A cadet will not lie, cheat, steal. He's done them all. A professed man of some ancient god, he must never have been a cadet. He ignores me.

I whisper to Dash, "Have you seen Dez?" He shakes his head.

"What are your intentions, young man, and would you please silence that trumpet." The priest glares at the gathering. His followers form a silent, creepy crowd behind him.

Dash faces the crowd and puts a finger to his lips. The immediate silence stuns me. Somehow, the lowliest of cadets has managed to lead peers and uppers to confront injustices hidden from them for decades. He must have told them everything.

"My intention, our intention," Dash gestures to the gathering, "is to stop these cruel experiments you've been overseeing. Your subordinates didn't hold back when we showed up in their labs. We know you've been telling them what to do."

The priest doesn't flinch.

"Take Ing to the coin. You still have one loyal follower who refuses to unlock the case it's in. Unlike you, we're not about torture." He motions to someone in the crowd, and an upper drags a wiry-looking woman behind him. It's the horrible nurse who shocked me into submission when I woke on the cold table. Even though I'm not surprised to see her, I cringe.

When the upper pushes her toward us, she smirks. "I knew you were nothing but trouble." She turns her head and spits. "Little Miss 'Oh, I'm so dizzy'. Little Miss—"

"Shut up!" Dash steps in front of her so quickly she tumbles backward, but an upper steadies her.

"A knight in shining armor," she mocks. "How sweet."

"Tell her to unlock the case, Father."

"And if I don't? What then, new cadet Dash?"

What then. I hold my breath, nausea threatening to empty an already empty stomach. I can't remember the last thing I ate. The last time I slept. *Breathe*.

"YES, ING. BE PREPARED."

I swallow hard and put on my poker face.

"THE SHIELD," it says. **"BEFORE YOU SECURE THE COIN, YOU MUST FIND A WAY TO DISABLE IT."**

As happy as I am to hear its voice, the message makes me uncomfortable. With the shield down, what will happen?

"YOU HAVE NO NEED TO FEAR. YOU WILL BE SAFE."

But what about everyone else?

"Ing, are you okay?" Dash breaks my trance. How am I supposed to make any kind of decision, take any kind of action, with everything pressing in around me?

"Yes. I mean no, not really, but I'll be okay." I don't need to lie.

After gazing into my eyes for several moments as if searching for answers, he turns his attention back to Father Malachy. "The coin is hers. You stole it. Look around you, Father." He indicates the crowd of cadets, officers, and civilians that followed him here. "Do you think we won't find a way to retrieve it if you don't hand it over willingly?"

The priest pulls himself up. "You do not know what you ask. You and these cadets are like an army of ants marching into a trap. A bunch of moths, ready to fly like stupid creatures into a fire. You don't understand the uncertainty of life. Death is sure, sin is the cause, our Savior is the cure, but you're all too ignorant to accept it." He rants like a madman, growing red in the face as he continues. "As it is appointed unto man once to die, but after this, the judgment! Unless a man be born again, he cannot see the kingdom of God, our Almighty Father!" He trembles, and we all stare at him in awe.

He's not done. Glaring at me with frenzied eyes, he says, "We do not know what will happen. I believe it will not be a good thing when you hold the coin. We are not prepared."

I have to stop him. "But I had it in the sea before the wave knocked me into this place, and other than waking up in a cold room with that horrible nurse"—I point at her and return her sneer—"nothing bad happened."

His face brightens briefly before another shadow darkens his expression. "But you were not conscious when we rescued you. You had no control over it. It did not glow until you woke." He holds me in his scary stare, his eyes almost popping from his head.

"Is that why you sent me to the Academy? To keep me away from it? To hope I'd forget about it? To control me like you're controlling those . . ." I point to the blank-eyed crowd behind him, "those believers?"

"We needed more time. We still need more time. You play at being soldiers, all of you, but remember what God said unto those who would be fools. 'Thou fool, this night thy soul shall be required of thee!' And who among you is prepared? Who?" He shouts, his shaky arms raised, fingers pointing. "Are you prepared to meet your Lord, or will the flames of Hell and the lake of fire await you?"

Someone in the crowd shouts, "We're not fools!" Many have removed their earplugs.

"That's enough, Father." Dash steps in front of him.

I shake off the icky feeling the priest's outburst leaves me with. He's deranged.

"And I suppose you thought Dez and I would be held somewhere out of the way when you sent us off to spy." I look at Mette and regret leaving her behind when we ran off. A softness in her expression when she looks back tells me she's forgiven us. "Maybe you planned to have us captured. Maybe even killed." I glare at him, and then the nurse. "But you underestimated Dez." Where is she? Her absence feels wrong.

"I never meant *her* harm. She was like a—"

"Don't say it," I warn.

"Make way! Make way now!" A disturbance behind the large gathering interrupts us. We turn to watch our assembled supporters jostle and squeeze to the sides of the long hallway.

Evidently, someone powerful is pushing through.

The lights go out.

21

AT FIRST, SILENCE and darkness. A silence so complete I think I've gone deaf. A darkness so black I feel suspended in space. When the whispers start, my relief is only temporary. Whispers intensify to murmuring. And then, panic.

I reach out to touch Dash, to convince myself I'm not alone. "Has this ever happened before?"

He fumbles for my hand. "Never. Father Malachy, what's happening?"

"I, I don't know." His voice shakes.

I strain to hear the noise I've hated since waking in Ironhold. No *thrum, thrum, thrum*. No air circulation. How long can the population of Ironhold survive in stale air? Maybe the power outage affects only this hallway, only the chapel.

Shouts erupt from the crowd.

"I said, make way!"

"Hey! Stop pushing!"

"Ouch! Dammit, get off me!"

"Keep calm, everyone! Please, stay calm!"

Infants cry. Shoes shuffle. Voices argue. Evidently, they've all removed their earplugs.

"Corps of Cadets! Atten—*SHUN!*" Dash's voice booms over the disturbance in a commanding tone I didn't know he possessed. The sound of heels clicking together followed by silence astonishes me. Even the babies stop crying.

He continues. "This is a drill, a test of your training. Carefully seat yourselves. You are to remain in place and in silence until further notice."

"What are you doing?" I whisper to him, stunned again by the sound of soft shuffling and an occasional grunt as the crowd settles themselves on the floor. Whoever tried shoving through the crowd must have decided the time wasn't right to continue their approach because I hear no further complaint.

"It was the only thing I could think of. Do you have a better idea?"

"No. This is brilliant." I try to pretend the air remains fresh and abundant. My heart races.

Dash addresses the priest. "Get us to wherever the system controls are, now. I know you know where they are. Ing, Mette, join hands. Ing, put a hand on my shoulder. Is the baby okay?"

Mette says yes. The baby makes a comforting cooing sound.

"Father Malachy, let's go."

"Let me retrieve a light from my office first. I'll be right back."

"No. We go with you. Don't try to run."

The priest lets out an alarmed "ah," and I sense Dash has grabbed him. We move like a tentative snake in the darkness, bumping into groups of *believers* as we shuffle toward the far side of the chapel. The slightest glimmer from beyond the overhead slicken casts an eerie atmosphere about the place. Straining to see something, anything, I flinch when tiny shining orbs appear to float toward us.

"Watch out!" I say. We slam into one another.

Despite the urgency of our situation, Father Malachy scoffs. "Don't be foolish. It is just our Singers."

"Then, they, they're not—" I stammer.

"They are artificial intelligences. Droids. Machines, if you will. I thought that would have been obvious to you by now." He sounds smug.

Why he thinks I'd know anything about machine people makes no sense at all. Pompous ass. I choose not to respond to him.

"Take us to the control room," he tells the Singers, and the way before us lights up. Six artificial eyes illuminate everything brightly.

They move quickly, noiselessly. I finally understand why. We walk behind them, leaving the chapel through a back door. One stifling hallway leads to another until I'm struggling to breathe.

"Holy hell!" A familiar voice echoes from beyond the open door in front of us.

"Dez!" I push past the Singers into the room. "It's me."

Father Malachy, Dash, Mette, and the Singers follow me, light from their creepy eyes illuminating an exhausted-looking Dez. She runs to me from the far end of an expansive room, nearly knocking me over in a hug. I feel her wild heartbeat as she whispers, "It told me to turn off the shield. You were right. Calyxar is real."

"What have you done, Dez?" Father Malachy's voice cracks.

I nod. "Tell him."

She scans the odd group surrounding her. After a moment's hesitation and a narrowing of her eyes when she glances at the three machines that raised her, excitement animates her face. "Shayla's waiting! They're all waiting. I'm supposed to disable the shield, Calyxar told me so. It told others, too, because it didn't know who could do it."

"Impossible!" the priest shouts. "Why would it speak to anyone but me?"

"Anyway," Dez ignores him, "we didn't know which levers control the shield, so I just said, 'turn them all off.' I kinda messed up, though, and now I don't know which ones to turn back on. Am I the only one feeling dizzy right now?"

"How did you get into this space?" Father Malachy looks furious. "And who is this 'we'? Where are the engineers? You are in a lot of trouble right now, young lady." He gazes around the rows upon rows of shelves holding huge machines with countless knobs and dials, all dark. He takes an unsteady step toward the back of the room. He's dizzy, too.

My head swims.

Someone coughs at the far side of the room. "I think I found it!"

I recognize the voice but can't believe my ears. It's Lou.

Dez hurries toward the sound of his voice, and I follow. A loud metallic clicking precedes a bright light that temporarily blinds me.

"Dude!" Dez yells. "You did it! But what about the shield?"

Lou steps out from behind a shelf. "Hey, Ing." He looks like a child who's been caught in a lie. A big one.

Before he answers Dez, the others gather around.

"How could you?" Father Malachy says, wiping his brow with a shaky hand. "Your father will hear about this, new cadet Lou. I expected more from you, and he—"

"Enough!" Dash places a hand on the priest's shoulder. "I heard the message, too."

Calyxar is communicating with others now. I'm not alone.

I thought I'd never want to hear the thrumming of the circulation system again, but it suddenly sounds like the sweetest song. I take a deep breath and hold it, savoring the fullness in my lungs.

Muffled complaints coming from the end of the long shelf interrupt us.

"They're okay," says Lou. "They didn't put up much of a struggle. Only two scrawny engineers in charge of this place, Padre? Really? As for my father, he was on his way to your chapel to arrest you."

That explains the commotion we left behind.

"Arrest me? For what crime?" He scoffs.

"For interfering with the plans of one more powerful than all of us—Calyxar. The octopus gave us a message, and loudly. My father heard it too, and others in the Academy. You're a heretic, Father, and maybe that's why you haven't heard Calyxar's voice."

Father Malachy's mouth hangs open before he responds. "Have you considered that I may be the only voice of reason here? You call me a heretic? That message you purport to have received—do you have any idea what it means? What possible good can come from disabling our defensive shields, young man?" He questions each of us then, defiance in his eyes. "Dez? Mette? Dash? What possible good?" He ignores me.

"You would question a higher power, Father?" Dash almost smiles.

"My authority comes from One greater than an illusion I witnessed as a child. You fools have been misguided, tricked by a mass hallucination." He tries so hard to convince us. "And this," he points to me, "this interloper will be the death of you all, this alien from above, this—"

"Stop it!" Mette shouts. "If Ing hadn't shown up, we never would have found these children, never would have uncovered the evil things you've been doing all these years."

Wow. I completely underestimated Mette's bravery in the face of uncertainty and probable death.

"Mette's right," I nod at her. "Something more powerful than all of us, the prophesy or whatever, brought me here with a special coin. I'm supposed to do something with it. Soon." As if responding to my words, my chest aches, and the glow blazes. I point at the priest. "And you know about the prophesy, so stop trying to pretend like you're in charge here anymore."

"And Calyxar said we'd be okay," Lou says. He looks at Mette then as if he's just recognized her. He stares at the baby and his jaw drops. "Is that . . . is that Shayla's . . ." He doesn't finish, just stands there staring at the child. I look at the baby, and then at him, and can't deny the resemblance. Same low hairline, same dimpled chin, same full upper lip.

Mette holds the child out to him, and he takes it, gently, his eyes never leaving the tiny girl's face. The baby opens her eyes wide and stares at him.

"So what are we standin' around waiting for?" Dez ruffles Lou's cropped hair. "Shields are down, right?"

Lou nods, studying his child with teary eyes and a goofy smile.

Dez marches to the door. "Let's go get that coin!"

———— ❧ ————

If only it were that easy. We barely take ten steps when Father Malachy yells, "Singers!" and I fall clumsily onto the floor. Their powers evidently aren't restricted to vocal persuasion. It feels like someone shoved me. Dez, Dash, and Mette sprawl near me, but Lou remains standing, holding his baby girl. Guess they have some sense of decency.

"Really, Father Malachy?" Dez struggles unsuccessfully to stand, and I feel like I weigh a thousand pounds. "What now?" she continues. "You can't keep us here. I told the civilians who followed me to come here if we don't return in an hour." She glares at the Singers.

Dash holds one of the priest's robe sleeves, torn off when he fell to the floor. He tosses it to the side. "I wanted to make sure he didn't escape and turn the shield back on," he whispers to me.

"Come on, Padre. It's over," Lou says.

"Oh, but I do not think so. Consider what it means to disable our shield when we know another collision is imminent. How does that make any sense?"

Mette rubs a bump on her forehead from the fall. "How does it make sense that Calyxar is real, and that it spoke to many of us, and that it told us what to do and ensured us we'd be safe? How does is make sense that you, a mere man, could stop it? Now let us up."

Again, wow.

Father Malachy's chin quivers, but I feel no pity for him.

"Lou's right," I say. "It's over. Let me have my coin. Whatever's going to happen will happen. Calyxar knows more than we do. You're the one putting us in danger now."

He gestures limply to the Singers and the invisible weight lifts. "Look at me. I'm an old man, used to the old ways." His exaggerated frailty leaves me cold. "I haven't seen Calyxar since I was but a child, and a child's memories are prone to misinterpretation and exaggeration. The octopus species lives no longer than a few years at best—we have studied them— so how could it be possible that a single one would survive decades?"

"One with three eyes," I say, "who sends the same message to who-knows-how-many unrelated people in an unnatural undersea habitat. *That* kind of single one."

He looks wide-eyed at his Singers as if seeing them for the first time, maybe hoping they'll come to his rescue. They don't.

"GO TO THE COIN NOW," Calyxar's voice warns. **"IT IS COMING."**

"Did you hear that?" Lou asks. Dash, Mette, Dez, and I nod vigorously.

Father Malachy frowns. "Hear what?"

"Another message," I say. "No more tricks, priest." He doesn't deserve the title *Father*. "Take us to my coin now. You must know the fastest way from here."

Dash reaches to grab his arm, but he pulls it away and shuffles past us toward the door. "You are making a horrible mistake," he mumbles. "You will see. But I suppose my time is up anyway."

I turn toward the motionless Singers. "Tell them to come too." I don't trust them alone in the control room.

"Fine, fine. Come along, then." He waves them forward without looking at them, and I let them pass me. I don't trust them behind me, either, after what they did.

As soon as we step into the hallway, I hear the commotion and feel the vibration of countless feet heading our way. Dez's hour is up. She runs ahead of us toward the noise just as the first people appear around the corner. I recognize two people at the front of the group, Doctor Vesper and Shayla. Dez hugs Shayla, takes her hand, and runs with her back to where we stand, back to Lou and their stolen child.

"Look," Lou whispers. "She looks like me, right?"

Shayla's eyes fill when Lou hands her the baby. He puts his arms around them both. I hate to end the moment.

"We have to go—"

"I know," Shayla says. "I heard the message too."

Doctor Vesper stops the crowd at the corner and follows Shayla to us. "It's over, Father."

He looks at her with an expression of hatred. I tremble to control my anger.

"So I've been told." He continues to glare, but she ignores him, approaching Dez instead.

"Dez," the doctor takes her hands, "I have something to tell you."

"What?" Dez pulls away her hands and takes a step back. "And stop being so weird."

"Your mother was a cadet when you were born. I'm sorry to tell you that honestly, she didn't survive—"

"We don't have time for this now," I say, grabbing Dez's hand and pointing to the priest. "We need to hurry." A heavy sense of foreboding grips me. Sweat trickles down my back. Things suddenly seem to move too fast.

They all stare at me with expressions ranging from fear to excitement.

The atmosphere feels drenched with uncertainty.

----- ❧ -----

The crowd parts as we follow the priest to the lab. Strangers touch me as I pass, many weep. I see hands on hearts and hear "bless you" from women and men. I want to run away—I don't deserve their admiration—but there's only one place I have to go.

Someone throws an overripe tomato at the priest. Shouts of "Thief" and "Sinner" spread throughout the crowd. He doesn't stop but stares straight ahead and speeds toward our destination. Ready to meet his maker, maybe. If I could, I'd send him to the lake of fire he threatens us with.

Dez squeezes my hand before letting go. "Gonna get through this together, right?"

"Together," I agree. "Listen, I'm sorry about your moth—"

"Yeah, well, hey, what's that thing you hum when you're stressed?" She scratches the stubble of hair growing back on her head.

The Swimmers' chant. Softly, slowly, I start. "Ahhh-veyyyahhh, ahhhveyyyahhh, ahhhveyyyahhh," and within moments, the chant spreads throughout the crowd, reverently, mournfully, beautifully. Even though it holds memories of past Farewells, the chant still calms me.

But my father's body is still lies here. And Aiden, whose Farewell was denied. My heart skips a beat when I think of our brief moment of passion. Something within me has changed.

Coming to an abrupt stop halfway down an increasingly crowded corridor, we're at the door.

Gasps from the crowd as my chest glows brightly spikes my anxiety again. The mystery of the bizarre coin and my relationship with it is about to be solved.

I'm scared.

Dez opens the door and pulls me inside the lab we passed while creeping through the between walls. Three women and two men in white coats scurry to a far wall away from the coin, which vibrates noisily, hitting against the sides of a thick-walled transparent box.

The priest steps in behind us. "Release it," he tells the huddled group.

"But—"

"No. I said, release it."

"But it's coming," a braver woman challenges him. "It's too late, Father. Look." She runs to a computer, types something, and points to a large display on the wall above her keyboard.

Expressions of fear and awe fill the room.

The vision of a wobbling sphere rapidly approaching our planet stuns, frightens, and thrills me. Though relatively small when the woman first displayed it, it grows larger with each breath I hold. The image must come from the drone birds that have spied on me and my village for countless years.

I run to the box, the ache in my heart unbearable. "Open it!"

The woman looks at her disgraced leader with panic in her eyes, and he nods. She looks at me with a mixture of confusion and . . . hope? She pushes several buttons on the box.

"Dammit!" She blinks hard, shakes her head, and tries again. The coin quiets, seeming to settle in anticipation of its release. The woman's hands shake. "I can't . . . it should open—"

Intense on watching the woman fumble, my heart beating so fast it might explode, I barely notice when Dash whisks past me. He stands by the woman. He puts a hand on her shoulder. "It's going to be okay," he says. "Ing is here. See? When she has the coin, everything will be okay."

The woman nods vigorously, eyes staring at the keypad that thwarted her previous attempts, and slowly pushes a sequence.

The top opens with a *whoosh*, and the coin rises from the box. Aware that every eye is on me, I take one step closer to the box and open my arms. Slowly, gently, my coin floats toward me and settles on my chest, dimming the glow and calming my racing heart. I inhale deeply. It feels like I've just learned how to breathe.

I glance at the anxious faces surrounding me. They're waiting, as I am, for something to happen.

Nothing happens.

The sphere grows larger on the display, undulating as if filled with liquid or goo. I see no aliens yet.

"Whatever you feel called to do, girl," the priest says, "do it now." He stares at the screen, hands clasping his cheeks.

Do what now? Where is Calyxar? It I'd know what to do!

Turmoil by the door interrupts my moment of panic. People push into the room, cadets and officers who've been waiting by the chapel—Lou, his father, Zadak, several from my barracks room—and Doctor Vesper with civilians who followed us from the hallway. Mette forces her way through the gathering toward me and takes my hands.

"I believe in you." Her gray-pink eyes shine.

I look at her like she's crazy—everyone, everything is crazy right now—and try to pull my hands away, but she holds tight.

Mette's glowing face is the only calm one in the room. I hug her. "Thank you." I release her.

"Ing, please!" The priest pleads, still staring at the approaching anomaly. The scientist was right when she said it's too late.

"Dash, come here." I call him as calmly as I can. Dez is already by my side. They've become my closest friends. If we're all going to be crushed by a collision I'm powerless to stop, I want to be near them.

"It's okay," Dez says.

"It's not your fault." Dash places a hand on my shoulder.

Silence fills the room as the sphere fills the viewing screen.

And then everything, *everything*, stops.

22

EVERYONE I SEE appears frozen in time. Everyone but me.

"YOU HAVE CHOSEN YOUR PEERS WELL." Calyxar's image appears on the wall where the approaching blob had been. **"AND NOW YOU MUST DECIDE WHO SHALL SURVIVE."**

"But look behind you! There's no more time!" My voice cracks.

"LOOK AROUND YOU. YOU SEE? ALL IS STOPPED." Its tentacles undulate hypnotically.

My head spins.

"You want me to decide who to save. Who *you* will save. I have no power here!" I'm freaking out.

I look at Dez's face, frozen in an expression of acceptance. And Dash's face, calm and brave in the face of disaster. My coin, a glorious green, throbs on my chest. Waiting.

"YOU MUST CHOOSE."

"Why? Why me? How am I supposed to make this kind of decision?"

"YOU KNOW. PROVE THAT YOU KNOW."

"Is this some kind of test? Because I feel like I've been tested my whole life."

"IT IS WHAT IT IS."

"Why did Aiden have to die? Why wasn't he saved too?" The image of his lifeless body on the table makes me gasp.

"YOUR SORROW IS JUSTIFIED. HIS LOVE FOR YOU WAS TRUE."

Not an answer. He's gone.

I lean against the transparent box and study the statues surrounding me. Without question, Dez and Dash should be saved. Mette, too.

I know only a few of the others, and not well. The priest. I have every reason to hate him. Yes, I hate him for being the mastermind behind attempts to create a new civilization, for torturing innocent babies with knowledge and memories from the dead, for convincing others to carry out his dirty work, for using his mechanical Singers to control those he calls his believers. For so . . . many . . . wrongs.

Doctor Vesper, a pawn, maybe, but she delivered and handed the babies over to be experimented on. What she did was criminal, but she knows it. It weighs on her. She feels sorrow for her part.

Lou became a decent human once he realized he was a father. As for the others in the room, I have no strong feelings.

The horrible, terrible, awful nurse and those who conducted experiments on babies and the dead, well, I hate them, too. Hate them with every fiber of my being. They can all go to Hell, if the place is real. The priest believes in it.

So do I condemn those I hate? How, and why am I in any position to determine humanity's fate?

"That's it, isn't it?" I ask Calyxar. "Some kind of final test. I have to make the *right* decision."

"YOU MUST DECIDE NOW. I CANNOT SAY IF IT WILL BE RIGHT OR WRONG."

"Then, I'm ready. But what happens once I tell you?"

"THE COIN WILL OPEN A PORTAL TO A PLACE WHERE THOSE YOU HAVE SAVED WILL REMAIN UNTIL EARTH HEALS. SHOULD YOU SAVE THEM, THE INFANTS' MINDS WILL BE PURGED OF THE ABUSES THEY HAVE ENDURED."

"A portal? A place? What place? Of course I'll save the children!"

An amorphous blob is about to crash into Earth. Ironhold's protective shields are disabled. In any case, century-old slicken might not be strong enough to withstand a second impact. Calyxar said that anything created can be destroyed.

A prophesy said someone from above would come to Ironhold and—

I swallow hard to keep from getting sick. Calyxar says nothing about the mysterious, safe place. I remember the parallel universe in Mom's creation story, Eyopia, where everything lived together in harmony.

"Everyone!" I scream as if the three-eyed octopus has suddenly gone deaf. "Save them all!" As much as I want to condemn those I hate, I have no right to determine their fate.

"AND SO—" Calyxar says before disappearing from the screen.

A rush of noise shakes me, the circulation thrumming sounds like thunder, and people around me shout and point at the sphere on the display. It's filled with fluid and creatures

I've seen in my dreams. They're beautiful. I feel them! Their peaceful presence fills me with awe.

"What is the meaning of this?" the priest shouts. I turn to see the knuckleheaded lab rats, Doug and Vlad, grabbing him by each arm. "Release me immediately, you simpletons!" He struggles but is no match for his captors.

To my amazement, Doug addresses me. "Forgive us, please." He bows his head. "Calyxar. It, ah, gave us a mission."

"For-forgive me," Vlad says. I didn't know a man could look so broken.

Feeling like I must be in a dream, I nod slowly.

"She's just a stupid girl, a tool!" The priest struggles as they pull him through the gathering.

"To the tubes," Doug announces.

"To the tubes," Vlad repeats, and no one tries to stop them.

"No! You cannot do this! You mustn't! Ing! Stop them! Stop them or bear the consequences of their actions! Release me, you—"

I hear no more from him once they drag him from the room. Confusion grips me. I chose to save them all. Why is he being taken away? But there's no time to question.

I stand between Dez and Dash, face the awe-inspiring screen, and grab their hands.

"I'm scared, Ing." Dez trembles. We all tremble.

"I'm scared too, but we'll be safe." I have no choice now but to believe an alien octopus.

Feeling it's as much a part of me as my breath, I close my eyes and concentrate on the mysterious coin on my chest. My mind pleads, *Save them*. I suddenly realize I'm attached to something more powerful than anyone can predict. The ache in my heart is excruciating. This union could kill me. But if I have to die to save an entire civilization, then I'm ready. "Save them all!" I shout, and glance at my coin.

The three rings spin fast, and then I have to look away when a beam of brilliant light shoots from it, swirling into a vortex of every color imaginable, more beautiful than the most vibrant rainbow I've ever seen above.

The people around us cry out, and many fall to their knees as an enormous, brilliant white tunnel larger than the room we're in swirls open in front of us in a deafening *whoosh* that reminds me of the winds above.

Wide-eyed, Dez and Dash squint at me over the dazzling, swirling beam. Unable to move, my body not my own anymore, I look around at the growing crowd and yell, "Go! Run into the tunnel! Calyxar promises safe passage! Hurry!"

As people surge forward, I release my friends' hands. "Help move them along," I shout above the roar.

The people of Ironhold—civilians, cadets, officers, scientists, old and young, Lou and Shayla and their baby and even the horrible nurse—run through the room and into the light. Mette hums a peaceful tune that somehow breaks through the chaos and makes people smile.

"We know, we know!" Many shout as we encourage them to hurry. "Calyxar told us!" They all point somewhere above.

The octopus has spoken to everyone in Ironhold.

They run into the swirling tunnel, disappearing as soon as they step across the opening. Who or what will be on the other side?

And how much longer do we have before impact?

"Hurry! Don't stop!" Dez rushes people into the vortex, sweat dripping from her frightened face. She looks at me and nods toward the tunnel. "GO! Save yourself!"

When I shake my head, the pained expression on her face tells me she's just realized my predicament.

Doug and Vlad are among the last to run into the void, no Father Malachy between them. I hope it won't be long before they're all somewhere on the other side of this swirling spectacle.

I wave my arms at Dez, Dash, and Mette. "Thank you! I'll be fine! Now go!" I feel my strength draining.

"But . . . come with us!" Standing with Dez and Mette before their final step into the light, Dash calls, reaching a hand toward me. But I'm bound to this metal floor.

The roar from the tunnel—or maybe it's the approaching blob—rattles the room.

"Take them," I whisper to my coin, and they disappear into the light.

———— ❧ ————

I'm standing inside the tunnel's edge surprised to be alive and no longer afraid. My coin, gone, must have pulled me in. I gaze down the length of the swirling tunnel. People appear to tumble into balls—no, eggs?—and float away. Time slows but doesn't stop. An occasional body gets grabbed away from the others by a wispy arm from the portal wall that throws them somewhere outside the safety of the vortex.

"Calyxar! I chose to save everyone!" I yell into the portal, forgetting that even though the creature doesn't always respond, it hears my thoughts. I don't know who was plucked and sent to who-knows-where, but I can guess.

"YES. YOU MADE THE HONORABLE DECISION. THE UNIVERSE ULTIMATELY DECIDES."

"But how is this any different from the priest and scientists creating a new population in Ironhold?" *Why am I arguing with a supernatural creature?*

"THEY WERE MOTIVATED BY GREED AND POWER. THE UNIVERSE CHERISHES GENEROSITY AND HONOR. YOUR CHILDREN WILL LEAD A NEW GENERATION—"

"Children?" Did it just say *children*?

"TWINS," it says, though somehow, I already know. "YOUR CHILDREN WILL LEAD A NEW GENERATION. THEY WILL RETURN TO EARTH WHEN IT HAS HEALED."

Did I flee from the expectations of motherhood in my village for this moment?

My village!

She hears my panicked thought. "YOUR VILLAGE AND THE OTHERS THAT CONTINUE TO STRUGGLE ABOVE WILL BE SAVED. SEE?"

As I continue to look through the portal, another swirling tunnel emerges, heading toward the land I abandoned. There it is, my village. My mother stands outside with still-blind eyes looking skyward. Tulip stands by her side. My family, Javier, Sebastian, and every person the portal lights upon lifts into it and tumbles away toward the other side.

"Thank you! Thank you!" I have no other words.

"NOW, TURN BACK AND WATCH."

I turn toward the empty lab in Ironhold and realize that although I remain at the very opening of the tunnel, I'm suddenly far, far away from the undersea world.

I shake off a brief feeling of vertigo and stand, speech-less, as the creature-filled sphere finally crashes into Earth and bursts, spilling its contents over the entire planet.

Paralyzed, awe-struck, I witness Earth slowly, slowly resume its rotation. I watch as the waters that had surged to the poles during the Halt spread back over the planet in colossal waves, destroying every human-made thing that remained.

Everything but Ironhold.

"NO! Why save that wicked place?" I feel betrayed.

"WATCH."

As the massive bodies of water realign on the increasingly spinning planet, the sea creatures surrounding Ironhold reshape and stretch the bubbles of slicken over different areas.

"YOU SEE? THEY HAVE SAFEGUARDED THE BOOKS, THE FARMS, AND ALL THAT IS NECESSARY FOR CONTINUATION OF YOUR SPECIES."

Time speeds up, or it feels that way. I squeeze my eyes shut to control my dizziness. When I open them, Ironhold stands on dry ground in a huge crater on the planet, the protective slicken gone. The creatures that protected parts of Ironhold lay dead on the land surrounding it. I see no bodies of the dead from the lab. Washed away, probably, into new oceans.

"I'm sorry, Aiden," I whisper. "Farewell, beautiful man."

Hesitant animals raised in Ironhold wander and fly from their previous captivity.

The last thing I hear before my end of the portal closes is the haunting, glitching sound of the Singers as they perform the Ave Maria for the last time.

Now I cry. I cry for the horrors I've witnessed, for the suffering of the innocents, for the years of struggle so many have endured on a harsh, unforgiving planet, for the needless death of my children's father—my burden to bear—for the noble creatures of the sea, and for the promise of a new beginning.

I cry because I've never cried before.

"I'm ready," I whisper through choked sobs. Before I can dry my eyes, I feel myself tumble and roll, and roll, and roll. I should be frightened when a slippery substance attaches itself to me, but it feels like a gentle hug. I continued to roll with it and into it until I must fall into a deep, deep sleep.

A clap of thunder wakes me to a sizzling crack as lightning strikes the shell that formed around me in the portal. I stretch from a fetal position and spill onto thick, cool, green grass. Chunks of pearlescent shell lay around me. With great difficulty, I stand. My abdomen is enormous.

Aiden's children will be born, and soon, in a strange new realm without their father.

For as far as I can see, large, glimmering eggs rest in the grass. I look at my hands, my arms, my naked body still covered in the substance that must have kept me alive for at least eight months.

"I don't understand," I mumble, staring at the eggs as if they'll explain themselves. "Calyxar? Are you here?"

"I AM HERE."

I turn to look above me where the creature floats in an atmosphere that sparkles.

"My coin, these eggs, this place . . ." I'm overwhelmed with wonder. "What are we doing here?"

"HEALING. WHEN IT IS TIME, I WILL RETURN YOUR COIN."

"So . . . you gave it to my ancestor? Why?"

"YES. HE WAS TO SHOW YOUR PEOPLE THAT THEY ARE NOT ALONE IN THIS UNIVERSE. THAT A TIME WOULD COME WHEN THEY WOULD BE CALLED TO SHARE THEIR PLANET WITH MY PEOPLE." Calyxar's voice is somehow muted in this realm.

"But . . . what happened?"

"WHEN HE DID AS HE WAS ASKED, HE WAS SPURNED BY PEOPLE WHO CALLED HIM MAD. IRON-HOLD'S ORIGINAL CREATORS KNEW OF MY PEOPLE'S PLIGHT. OUR REALM IMPLODED EONS AGO AFTER SENDING TWO SPHERES OF OUR POPULATION ON A QUEST FOR A HABITABLE PLANET."

The creature's undulating tentacles make me dizzy. I hold my belly and lower myself to the silky grass.

One sphere from their original quest crashed onto my planet a century ago and stopped its rotation. Yikes. I wonder how many other sea creatures from their realm got abandoned on Earth.

I try to make sense of this new catastrophe. "Did my great, great grandfather start the rumor that there would be another impact? Did you tell him another would come?"

"YES. WE DID NOT ANTICIPATE HALTING YOUR PLANET'S SPIN. YOUR PLANET'S HEALTH REMAINS VI-TAL TO THE BALANCE OF ALL UNIVERSAL SPHERES."

"Then why did it take so long for the second sphere to arrive?" My attention shifts to the sky filled with sparkling stars that—even in the brightness surrounding me—flicker out and reappear.

No clouds emerge, but a deep rumbling shakes the ground. I glance at the egg-strewn expanse all around me.

"TIME IS DIFFERENT IN UNIVERSAL TERMS. WE EXPECTED YOUR PLANET WOULD CORRECT ITSELF. WE ANTICIPATED THE INTELLIGENT PEOPLE OF

IRONHOLD WOULD ALREADY HAVE REPOPULATED THE LAND. THE SECOND SPHERE WOULD RUPTURE BEFORE IMPACT, DEPOSITING OUR BEINGS WITHOUT INCIDENT."

"But the intelligent people of Ironhold had other ideas, right?" So many wonderful things they could have done with their technology.

"SADLY, YES. THE SWIMMERS, THOSE YOU AD-MIRE, BELIEVED THEIR ACTIONS WERE NOBLE. THE PRIEST USED THEM FOR IGNOBLE PURPOSES."

The Swimmers were pawns. My heart breaks for them, for their belief that they sacrificed for a greater purpose. And I almost joined them. The priest used them to play at being a god.

I have to know my purpose in all of this. "Why me?"

Something like alien laughter tickles my ears. **"LIKE YOUR CHOSEN ANCESTOR, YOU ARE INTELLIGENT, STRONG, COMPASSIONATE. YOU WERE WILLING TO MAKE THE ULTIMATE SACRIFICE FOR OTHERS."**

"But how did you know I would? I didn't even know."

"KNOWLEDGE OF ALL IS . . . EVERYWHERE."

Not really an answer. As if to shut me up, a tiny foot presses out from my belly. "How"—I point to my abdomen—"and why did you, or someone, keep us asleep for so long?" My babies roll, and I laugh out loud, startled and delighted by the bizarre sensation. New little people are growing inside me. I feel . . . happy.

"CREATION IS NOT A SIMPLE TASK. YOU AND THE OTHERS REQUIRE STRENGTH FOR WHAT AWAITS YOU. REST, NOURISHMENT, AND TIME PROVIDE THE BEST OUTCOME."

"What awaits us? The best outcome for what?" This creature or alien or who-knows-what is always so vague.

"THERE EXISTS A POWER GREATER THAN ALL. ONE THAT WANTS YOU TO RETURN TO YOUR PLANET TO LIVE LONG, FULFILLING LIVES IN PEACE AND CO-OPERATION WITH ONE ANOTHER. WITHIN EACH EGG HOLDING A HEALTHY INDIVIDUAL, A CHILD WILL ARRIVE WITH THEM, CREATED FROM THEIR DNA AND GENETIC MATERIAL PLUCKED FROM THE UNIVERSE."

"Whoa." What a way to wake up, in a strange place, holding an infant you didn't know was yours to love and nurture. These new children just might understand how to break ancient, destructive habits. "When will they, um, hatch?"

I push myself to my feet and gaze around the eggs at plants so ripe with bizarre fruits and vegetables and trees literally dripping with different liquids—my mouth waters.

"SOON YOU WILL BE REUNITED WITH THOSE WHO HAVE BEEN SAVED."

"You said we'll go back to Earth, but why can't we stay here?" Everything looks so lush, so safe, so perfect.

"THIS REALM EXISTS ONLY FOR A TIME OF TRANSITION. YOU CANNOT STAY."

Still anticipating the flavor of whatever I'll eat first and wondering which eggs hold my family and friends, I turn and ask, "So when can we go back?"

But Calyxar's gone.

Lightning crackles around me striking two eggs and exciting my babies.

I recognize Tulip immediately. Coated in the slick substance, she sits, dazed, a baby in her arms.

As I waddle toward her, our mother spills from another egg. She looks at me with clear eyes. "Ing?" She stands, alone, not strong enough, I guess, to be gifted with an infant.

"Mom!" I run to her awkwardly, my hands supporting my swollen belly.

Two more lightning strikes release Dez and Dash from their shells, each holding an infant, wonder and joy lighting their faces. Able men and women alike will hatch with infants of their own.

We stand together in awe of our lush surroundings, the soft, green grass, the bountiful gardens, the twinkling, swirling atmosphere, the gentle, fragrant breeze.

I will grieve my losses. There will be more tears. But with this new, growing family, I'm finally where I want to be.

When the time is right, we'll return to our healed planet knowing we are not alone in this wild and wonderful universe.

Lightning cracks . . . and cracks . . . and cracks . . .

Acknowledgments

Mike McHargue, my husband of over 42 years, thank you for suggesting my book should be a military romance. This one isn't it, but you were my first, most brutal beta reader, and I love you for your honesty and belief in my work, your patience, and for so, so many other things!

Marilyn Hintsa, my steadfast friend since kindergarten, thank you for believing that all of my novels should be made into movies. Someday? Maybe this one? You are my *goldest* friend.

Mary Wilson, my brilliant cousin, thank you for your deep reading of my story and your intuitive, spot-on suggestions for improving several parts of the narrative. You made me reconsider many passages. I hope my rewrite meets with your approval.

Linda Ditchkus, my author-in-arms friend, thank you for suggesting my military academy be launched in the future as science fiction, and for providing pages and pages (and pages!) of suggestions and insightful questions. You inspired me to answer lots of questions I avoided in my first major draft. Without a doubt, my writing is better because of your involvement in my creation.

David L. Robbins, thank you for teaching me more than anyone else how to write with more clarity (although I'm sure I still used *and* and *was* too many times in this work). Your "Mighty Pen Project" class provided the kick-in-the-butt I needed to tighten my prose. This veteran appreciates you.

Cam Torrens, thank you for reading and critiquing my entire first draft and suggesting I change my first chapter (you were right!); and Central Colorado Writers critique group members, thanks to many of you who offered suggestions as I completed each early chapter. Your thoughtfulness and honesty helped in honing my narrative.

Nadine Collier, co-author of *Peace by Piece: 10 Lessons from a Jigsaw Puzzle*, thank you for planting the seed for a new, "special" garden, and for agreeing that your granddaughter's name, Aveah, would make a great mantra for Ing.

Tristyn Pflanz, your hairstyling made me ready for every literary event, and Diana Moats, your skills as a massage therapist kept my brain, my neck, and fingertips finely tuned.

The United States Military Academy (USMA) at West Point, thanks for four years of cadet education to train me to be an Army Officer. Also, for my very own copy of *Bugle Notes* (which I refer to as the little book with *USMA* stamped on the cover), which I still display on a bookshelf, and which inspired several scenes.

Elize McKelvey, thank you for creating my stunning book cover. Your vision is on point, and your work takes my breath away. OMG, your bio self-portrait!!!

And, of course, thank you, kind readers. If you enjoyed my story, please consider posting a review on Amazon and Good-Reads—and share it with friends!

About the Author

Award-winning multi-genre author **Laurel McHargue**, a West Point grad, was raised near Boston and somehow found her way to the breathtaking elevation of Colorado's Rocky Mountains—where she lives and laughs and publishes and enjoys wild and crazy dreams. She writes about life, real and imagined, and hosts the podcast *Conversations with Laurel.*

www.leadvillelaurel.com

About the Cover Artist

Elize McKelvey is a Marine Corps veteran, illustrator, and nomad who continues her mission to bridge gaps through art. Though no longer in uniform, she uses her creative work to highlight the often unseen aspects of the world. Known for her openness in sharing her process, Elize is passionate about experimenting with different mediums and techniques. She believes everyone has a story worth telling, and through her art, she brings those stories to light.

Inkstickart.com

A Personal Note from Laurel

———— ⅋ ————

I would love to hear from you!

Connect with me here:

YouTube: @LaurelMcHargue

Substack: @laurelmchargue

Website: www.leadvillelaurel.com

Email: laurel.mchargue@gmail.com

Podcast: https://soundcloud.com/laurelmchargue

Instagram: @laurelmchargueauthor

Check out my other books on my Amazon Author page and let me know what you think!

And remember, we struggling authors/musicians/artists love positive feedback, so if you like what we do, **please write a quick review** of our work and share it with friends!